Tea with Milk and Murder

OXFORD TEAROOM MYSTERIES

BOOK TWO

H.Y. HANNA

DEDICATION

For the Blue Boar crowd—thank you for the
wonderful memories during my time at Oxford

CONTENTS

CHAPTER ONE

You know your social life needs work when your first Saturday night out in months ends in murder.

Of course, murder was the last thing on my mind as I peered over the heads in the crowd, trying to see what people were looking at. From their excited murmurs and pointing and whispering, I expected some scene of horrific carnage—or a naked woman at the very least.

It turned out to be just a big grey square with a red blob in the middle. Apparently, from the heated discussion going on between two of the spectators next to me, the red blob could either represent the surrealism of perfect geometric form or the angst of the artist's tormented search for his mother's approval but *certainly* not the pent-up aggression of

1

today's youths.

I sighed and turned away from the crowd. This just confirmed to me that I didn't "get" modern art. You may wonder, then, what I was doing wandering around a contemporary art gallery on a precious Saturday evening off work. Well, I was there to support my best friend, Cassie, who was an artist (and not of the grey-square-with-red-blob variety either)—and she was having her first exhibition, with tonight being the opening night party.

I looked across the room and saw her, face beaming and cheeks flushed—though I wasn't sure how much of it was from the excitement of her first exhibition and how much from the proximity of the tall, attractive man next to her. Jon Kelsey. Owner of the gallery, art dealer extraordinaire, and general smooth operator. As I watched, Cassie flushed even more while Jon slipped a possessive arm around her waist and bent down to say something to her. She giggled, then looked across the room and caught my eye. I hurriedly changed my grimace into a smile.

Yeah, I have to confess, I didn't like Cassie's new boyfriend much and I'm a bit ashamed of my feelings. I know, I know—I should've just been pleased that my friend had found someone she loved and was happy—and believe me, I've tried really hard to like him—but there was something about Jon Kelsey that put me off. He was just a bit too handsome, too smooth, too arrogantly self-assured. It seemed unfair to take against a man just because he was too charming, but something about Jon Kelsey made me bristle.

And to be honest, I wondered why Cassie was with him. Cassie had the typical fiery artist's temperament, but with a warm, down-to-earth approach to life—and Jon Kelsey wasn't her usual type at all. With his posh London accent, flashy car, and loud designer clothes, he was more the type that Cassie would normally only glance at with contempt.

But maybe it was true that "flattery will get you anywhere", because the honour of being chosen as such a high-flying art dealer's latest protégée seemed to have gone straight to Cassie's head. Or in this case, her heart. Their chance meeting at the Tate Modern gallery in London had turned into a whirlwind romance and now, barely four weeks later, Cassie was revelling in her status as the star of his newly opened gallery in Oxford.

Not that her paintings really fit in there. That was another mystery. I knew that art dealers usually specialised in particular styles and, looking around the gallery, I could see that Jon seemed to favour huge empty canvases with random blobs of colour or strange Post-Minimalist pieces which resembled the products of a rubbish compactor. Cassie worked in a more traditional style and her paintings stood out like a paint-splattered sore thumb. I couldn't understand why Jon had taken Cassie on.

Then I glanced over at my friend again and thought maybe I could understand after all. At five foot two, Cassie was a classic "pocket Venus" and had the kind of curves I'd always envied. Rubens would have killed to paint her. And not just for her voluptuous figure. With her flashing dark eyes and generous mouth, she had a warm, sensual appeal that drew men like moths to a flame.

At any rate, her launch party looked to be a raving success. The gallery was crammed with several art critics and wealthy collectors from Oxford, and there were just as many people admiring Cassie's paintings as those looking at works by the more established artists. The gallery, housed in a converted 18th-century Georgian townhouse, provided the perfect elegant setting, and I had to admit that Jon had gone all out in hosting this party for Cassie. He had even set up a bar in the corner of the gallery, with a waitress mixing cocktails on demand for the guests.

I raised my own glass of frozen lime daiquiri to my lips and took a sip. I didn't normally drink much—okay, I admit, I'm a bit of a lightweight when it comes to alcohol—but I had a weakness for cocktails and this was scrumptious. I glanced over at the creator of the drink—the waitress behind the bar, who was now opening the cocktail shaker and pouring out a drink for a man waiting by the counter. She looked like she could be a university student, with wispy blonde hair and a cute upturned nose, although her looks were spoiled by the sulky tilt of her mouth and the air of resentment that surrounded her like a black cloud. I glanced back at my own glass and decided wryly that I had better not annoy her at any point in this evening or heaven knew what she would put in my next cocktail!

I looked at her again. She seemed so young... and then I grinned at my own thoughts. At twenty-nine, it seemed silly to label someone who was probably only six or seven years younger than me as "so young" but in a way, since returning to England, I did feel like I had left my youth behind. Well, I was a grown up now, with my own business to run. After eight years of climbing the corporate ladder Down Under, I had given it all up and come home on a crazy whim to open a tearoom in a quaint little Cotswolds village on the outskirts of Oxford.

In fact, my feet were aching now from all the standing I had done today (Saturdays being one of our busiest days, as we were inundated with tourists keen to have the "English afternoon tea" experience) and I wished now that I hadn't worn such high heels for the party tonight. I looked surreptitiously around for somewhere to sit—why were galleries always so devoid of furniture?—and spotted a couple of velvet upholstered chairs behind a pillar. However, my way there was blocked by a group of people standing around a large frame on the wall next to me.

"Amazing," said one woman, shaking her head admiringly.

"Look at the use of white space, how it hints at the emptiness of our collective souls," said another.

The man next to her nodded. "I love how it just speaks... without speaking."

I leaned over eagerly to see what they were looking at. Maybe I lacked the gene for art appreciation but it looked like they were all admiring a piece of blank A4 paper mounted on a board. Trust Jon Kelsey to stock the sort of pretentious rubbish that attracted all the top prats in Oxfordshire...

"Hey... enjoying yourself?"

I whirled around guiltily to see Cassie beside me. Were my recent thoughts about her boyfriend showing? Quickly, I pinned a bright smile on my face.

"Yeah, fabulous."

Cassie gave me a look. "Gemma. You can't fool me. I can see that you're bored."

I shrugged helplessly. "Well, poncy modern art isn't really my scene—"

"Shhh!" said Cassie quickly, looking hastily around. The group next to us was still contemplating the brilliant talent required to create a blank piece of paper and she drew a breath of relief. She looked at me severely. "Gemma... this is *great art*!"

"Aw, come on, Cass..." I sighed impatiently. "Don't tell me you agree with them and think any of this stuff is good?"

She avoided my eyes. "Well, you know my style is more traditional so I'm not really in a position to judge—"

"Rubbish," I said. "This is like the Emperor's New Clothes where nobody wants to come out and admit that he's naked—or that this so-called art is stupid."

"Hush!" Cassie said, throwing a quick look around again.

I frowned at her. Since when had my friend started to care so much about what other people thought? Cassie had always been unapologetically candid and outspoken—it was one of the things I'd always loved about her and envied her for. Unlike her, I hadn't grown up in a large, rowdy family of creatives, dancers, and artists, all championing honest emotion and self-expression—I was the product of a stiff, middle-class British household where restraint and polite reserve were the ideals. Ever since we were little girls, Cassie had always said and done the things that I wished I dared. And yet recently, my free-spirited friend seemed to be disappearing.

And I knew why. My gaze travelled resentfully across the room to the suave man in the brocade silk blazer. Jon bloody Kelsey.

Still... I felt a twinge of guilt. Maybe *I* was the one being unreasonable. This *was* an important night for Cassie—the first night of the opening of her exhibition—and surely it was understandable that she wanted to make a good impression?

"Sorry, Cass." I gave her a rueful smile. "Maybe it *is* just me and it's my fault that I don't get it."

"N-o-o..." she said, looking uncomfortable. "It's not your fault. Maybe... well, maybe you just need someone to look at the art with you—you know, so

7

you can share opinions and discuss the meanings behind the pieces..."

If I studied that piece of blank paper with a whole library of scholars for ten years, I still wouldn't have a clue how it was supposed to mean anything. But I bit my tongue and kept my thoughts to myself.

"You know you could have brought a date tonight," said Cassie slyly. "Maybe you should have asked Devlin if he had the night off?"

"And why would I have asked *him*?"

Cassie gave an innocent shrug. "Oh, I don't know... Maybe because he used to be the love of your life and you are now both back in Oxford..." She grinned. "Not to mention the fact that he's a dashing CID detective with looks worthy of James Bond?"

"I told you, things between me and Devlin are over. That was eight years ago and we're completely different people now."

"Exactly." Cassie's grin widened. "Maybe that's why you guys might have a chance this time round."

I rolled my eyes. She was like a terrier with a bone on this subject. "You keep your sticky fingers in your own love life and out of mine," I said.

Cassie laughed. "Speaking of love life—has Seth got a girlfriend or something? I was really surprised when he told me he couldn't come tonight and when I asked why, he was very evasive. You know how he never normally misses anything we're involved in— he's usually so supportive..." She sounded slightly wistful. "I wondered if there was a girl or something—

someone he's fallen head over heels for and now he's abandoning his oldest chums?"

I gave Cassie a sideways glance. I could make a good guess as to why Seth hadn't come tonight. It wasn't because of a girl he had—it was because of a girl he *couldn't* have. Seth, Cassie, and I had been a firm trio since university days—ever since that first week in Michaelmas Term when we'd arrived as Freshers together. And I think Seth had been carrying a torch for Cassie ever since that first week too. But Cassie had only ever seen him as a good friend and shy, studious Seth had never got up the courage to try and change her mind.

I had thought that things might be changing at last—I don't know if my return to England had been a trigger or something—but recently, Seth seemed to be making hesitant attempts to get Cassie's attention... a shy invitation to dinner, a sweet gift of flowers... then Jon Kelsey had arrived on the scene and swept Cassie off her feet. I imagined that the last thing Seth wanted to do was come tonight and stand around watching Cassie and Jon act like two lovebirds.

I realised that Cassie was still waiting for my answer. "Um... I don't know. I don't think so. Maybe he's got university society commitments."

After graduation, Seth had chosen to remain in the hallowed cloisters of Oxford University and had steadily climbed the rungs of the academic career ladder, recently taking up an appointment as one of the youngest Senior Research Fellows in Chemistry at Gloucester College.

"Well, I think it's very poor show and I shall tell him when I next see him," Cassie grumbled. "I mean, I went to listen to his three-hour chamber music ensemble and that time when his colleagues decided to do a chemistry-themed pantomime!"

Before I could answer, Jon Kelsey joined us, immediately sliding that possessive arm around Cassie's waist again. I felt my hackles rising slightly, although I didn't know why. It wasn't like I was a rampant feminist or anything, but there was something about the way Jon treated Cassie that made it feel as if she was a trophy. Not that she seemed to mind, I reminded myself—and that was all that mattered.

"What are you girls nattering about?" said Jon with a patronising smile.

"Nothing much," I said quickly, before Cassie could answer. "This is a great party, Jon."

"Yes, my events are always first class," he said. He looked down at Cassie and gave her a squeeze. "Nothing but the best for my artists. Especially my *favourite* artists."

Cassie flushed and giggled. I looked at her incredulously. Cassie didn't giggle. She did big, hearty, belly laughs, or she chuckled evilly in amusement—but she didn't giggle like a vapid schoolgirl. At least, not before she met Jon Kelsey, I thought sourly.

"Oh, you're wearing the new cufflinks I gave you!" said Cassie suddenly, pushing Jon's suit sleeve back to look at his cuffs. "But... I thought you said you were going to wear the Cartier ones?"

"I was but I couldn't find one of them. Anyway, this being such a special night for you, I thought it was more fitting that I should wear yours. Not that I don't think of you all the time..." He gave Cassie a squeeze.

"Oh, you...!" Cassie giggled again and looked up at him adoringly.

I couldn't face the thought of standing there much longer, watching her make goo-goo eyes at Jon.

"Excuse me, I'm just going to pop to the loo," I said, giving them both a bright smile.

They barely noticed my departure and I made my escape with relief. Threading my way through the crowds, I headed for the corridor at the other end of the gallery which led to the rear of the building. But as I approached the swinging doors of the public toilets, I noticed a slightly open door farther down the corridor. From the draught of cold air wafting in, I realised that it led outside, probably to the rear gardens.

On an impulse, I walked down the corridor and out through the door, stepping into a courtyard filled with miniature trees and potted flowers. Slowly, I wandered across the flagstones, breathing in gratefully of the crisp night air. Everyone had told me that I would struggle with the cold winters back in

England after the sunny climes Down Under, but it was actually the central heating that got to me. With the late November weather turning icy recently, everyone and their mother seemed to have put their central heating on full blast—and I spent half my time feeling irritable and muzzy-headed in the hot cloying atmosphere.

There were a bunch of steps at the back of the courtyard, leading up to a second, raised level overlooking the whole garden—a sort of elevated terrace heavily planted with trees and shrubs. I went up and found a stone bench tucked into a corner behind a bush, and sank down on it gratefully. The night air was chilly and I hadn't brought my coat, but I was so overheated that I didn't mind it for the moment.

I leaned back and savoured the panorama around me. The back of the garden must have been built on a natural hill and I was able now, from my raised position, to get a view of not only the whole garden but also the surrounding rooftops—the medieval towers, Gothic arches, elegant cupolas, and high parapets that made up Oxford's "dreaming spires". The gallery was located in the very heart of the historic university city and, once again, I was reminded of the breathtakingly beautiful architecture which made Oxford such a top tourist destination.

I tilted my head back and looked up at the sky, clear and dark except for a sliver of moon and a smattering of a few stars. They looked strange and slightly upside down, now that I'd got used to the way the constellations looked in the Southern Hemisphere. I could see Orion's Belt and, for the first time in eight years, the brilliant North Star shining in the night sky...

The sharp acrid smell of smoke disturbed my thoughts and I glanced around. Although my raised position gave me a view of the whole courtyard garden, much of it was obscured by foliage and shadows. I saw a movement through the tops of the trees right below me, and as I leaned forwards to peer through a gap in the leaves, I saw that it was the waitress from behind the bar. Her pale hair gleamed in the moonlight. She had just come out of the rear door and was standing beside it, her hands cupped around her mouth. I saw the flicker of a flame and then the smell of smoke wafted across to me again. Obviously out for a ciggie break—although as I watched, she took a few furtive puffs, then hastily stubbed the cigarette out and pulled something out of her pocket. There was the sound of ripping plastic and then she slapped a small square patch onto her arm, muttering as she did so.

I felt a twinge of empathy. I'd never tried smoking but I could understand the struggle to break free of an addiction. I sat back again, thinking that I really ought to return to the party—Cassie would probably be wondering where I was—but I was enjoying the peace and solitude out here. A few more minutes, I promised myself.

Then I became aware of the sound of whispering.

At first I thought it was the waitress, but then I realised that the sound was coming from the other side of the courtyard, in the shadows among the trees to the right. I shifted on the bench and peered into the darkness. On the level below me, I thought I could make out two figures, but it was difficult to see properly. I wouldn't really have cared except that there was something in the urgent, furtive quality of the whispering which caught my attention. I leaned forwards, unconsciously straining my ears to discern the words.

"Are we going to do it tonight?"

"Relax... everything in good time."

"I... I can't bear the waiting. The suspense is killing me!"

There was a cold laugh. *"You knew what you were getting into. Don't tell me it doesn't turn you on."*

Was this conversation for real? I felt like I had stepped into some kind of Cold War spy movie. I leaned forwards even more, trying to see through the darkness. Yes, definitely two figures and, from their relative heights, a man and a woman perhaps? It had sounded like a woman who had spoken first. Was it the waitress after all? Perhaps she had crossed the courtyard to meet someone in secret there?

I was just thinking of creeping closer when the sound of footsteps came from the other side of the garden. Someone coming out of the back door, a cough, and then the unmistakable sound of a striking match. That acrid smell of cigarette smoke again. Another smoker coming out to indulge in his habit.

The couple in the shadows went silent, then there was a flurry of movement and, the next moment, the shadows were empty. I stood up hastily and rushed towards the steps, hoping to catch a glimpse of them. I don't know why, but suddenly I needed to know who they were. They had to have come into the garden from the back door so they must have been guests at the party. And one of the voices had sounded vaguely familiar. It was hard to tell with whispers—a voice lost all the tones and timbres you used for recognition—but there had definitely been something in the inflection...

I dived down the steps, trying to take them two at a time, but my haste ended up being my undoing. I'd forgotten about my stupidly high heels and I slipped, toppling backwards.

"Ahh!"

I slid the rest of the way down on my bum and landed in a heap at the bottom of the steps.

"Ow..." I groaned.

"Hey, are you all right?"

I looked up. It was the man who had come out for a cigarette. He was standing over me, eyeing me with concern. I took the hand he offered and let him help me to my feet.

"Yeah, fine, thanks," I said, embarrassed. I

glanced quickly around. "Did you see another couple out here just now?"

"Another couple?" He looked around the empty courtyard in puzzlement. "No, I passed the bar waitress going back in as I was coming out, but then it was just you. I heard you cry out and saw you fall so I came over to help."

Good thing this wasn't a Cold War movie because I was turning out to be a crummy spy, I thought. The other couple must have taken advantage of the distraction from my fall to slip back into the party unnoticed. Well, no point standing out here in the cold pondering it any longer. I was just going to have to accept that this was a mystery which would remain unsolved. Rubbing my sore bottom, I thanked the man and went back in to rejoin the party.

CHAPTER TWO

The warmth of the gallery was actually quite welcoming as I stepped back inside. I hadn't realised how cold I had become sitting on that bench. I noticed instantly that the blonde waitress was back behind the bar. She couldn't have been one of the couple, I reasoned, because the man had said that he had passed her coming in on his way out—and I knew that both figures had still been whispering when he stepped outside and disturbed them.

So who were they? I cast my eyes around the room, scanning the crowd, trying to see if anyone might fit the dark figures I'd seen. Then I did a double take as my eyes fell on four little old ladies on the other side of the gallery. *Oh my God. The Old Biddies. What on earth were they doing here?*

The leader of the group, a stout, formidable woman in her early eighties with a helmet of woolly white hair—tinged slightly blue—and a determined gleam in her eye, marched purposefully towards a canvas suspended by wires from the ceiling and peered at it. Mrs Mabel Cooke. Probably the worst of the Old Biddies and as deadly as the Spanish Inquisition when she was after information. She and her friends, Glenda Bailey, Florence Doyle, and Ethel Webb, ruled the village of Meadowford-on-Smythe, where my tearoom was located (although there were rumours that their influence penetrated to the top reaches of the Oxford City Council).

I felt a hand grab my arm, and turned to see Cassie next to me, her eyes brilliant with excitement.

"Oh, Gemma! Jon's just told me that he's travelling to Italy to attend an auction on Monday. It's in Florence and he asked if I'd like to go with him!" She hesitated. "Do you think you'll be all right without me at the tearoom for a bit? We're closed anyway on Monday so it's just Tuesday really. I'd be back on Wednesday and I know it's never as busy during the week—"

"Go," I said, smiling at my friend. "Don't worry, we'll manage fine. You know you're not a slave to the tearoom, Cassie! I'm really grateful you help out as much as you do, above and beyond your normal hours. Do you think you'll have time to visit the Uffizi Gallery, see Michelangelo's *David* and all that?"

Cassie nodded eagerly. "Yes, we're going to go on

Tuesday before we fly back. I've been there and seen it, of course, but it'll be so different going with Jon!" She sighed dreamily. "He's got such a unique way of viewing things and he's so knowledgeable about art history…"

I squirmed. Hearing Cassie gush about Jon Kelsey was not on my list of favourite activities. Hastily, I changed the subject. Nodding towards the Old Biddies, I said in an undertone, "Why are *they* here?"

"Oh…" Cassie followed my gaze and looked slightly bewildered. "I don't know really. I mean, I invited them but—"

"You invited them?"

She gave a helpless shrug. "Mabel was asking me about my exhibition and I told her about the party tonight and then… I don't know… somehow I found myself giving out invites to them. Jon was a bit annoyed, of course, since they're not likely to become clients of the gallery…"

"No, I should think not," I said dryly, thinking of the exorbitant price tags I'd seen on several of the other paintings so far. You could buy a small mansion for that money! I knew that art was subjective and value was in the eye of the beholder… but I just couldn't understand how two random blobs of paint could be worth so much. Still, if Cassie could get a share of the spoils, then I was happy for her.

I looked back up and suppressed a smile as I saw the Old Biddies accost Jon as he was talking to a group admiring an exhibit. For once, I had no pity for

Mabel Cooke's victim. Cassie made a horrified sound in her throat and hurried over to rescue her boyfriend, and I followed (although I have to admit it was more in gleeful anticipation than sympathetic support).

The crowd around Jon was looking at a small table on which was the "work of art". From where I was standing, it looked like a blob of some soft, blue substance, pressed into the surface of the table. There was even an imprint of the artist's thumb showing on the surface of the blob.

"This is a prime example of abstract expressionism focusing on the juxtaposition of the permanent and impermanent," said Jon. "The blue adhesive draws the eye and suggests an exploration of the transgender politics of the 20th century."

Mabel pushed her spectacles up her nose and leaned over to look at the blob.

"I don't know," she said loudly, her booming voice carrying across the gallery. "Looks like a bit of Blu-Tack stuck on a table, to me."

"Or gum," said Ethel eagerly. "When I used to work at the library, the children used to leave gum stuck on the underside of the tables. Most annoying! And it looked exactly like that."

There were gasps of horror and outrage from the crowd and Jon looked annoyed.

"That, madam, is a priceless piece of contemporary art," he said haughtily.

Mabel looked at him in astonishment. "Are you

sure?"

"Maybe there was something stuck on it and it got knocked off. You know how sometimes you use Blu-Tack to keep things in place," Florence suggested helpfully. She looked at the floor around the table. "Maybe it's fallen down around here?"

Jon's face was getting redder. "I assure you, madam, that there are no pieces missing from this work of art. This *is* the entire piece. Its very simplicity denotes the power of the artist's vision."

Glenda turned aside and said to the other Old Biddies, in a loud whisper, "I think the artist needs to check his vision. Do you think he knows about the two-for-one offer at Specsavers? I got a great deal on my bifocals there."

Jon made a strangled sound in his throat and Cassie hastily stepped in.

"Have you ladies got a drink yet?" she said. "Why don't you go over to the bar? There's a waitress making up cocktails for people."

As the Old Biddies trundled off, I saw Jon unclench his jaw.

Cassie patted his arm soothingly. "They mean well," she said. "Once you get to know them better, you'll see."

"I'm not sure I want to get to know them better," said Jon. Then he took a deep breath and gave Cassie an indulgent smile. "But this is your night, Cassie, and I'm not going to let anything spoil it."

Cassie looked wistfully at the price tag stuck

under the piece of Blu-Tack. "If only my pieces could be worth that much someday."

Jon smiled at her. "Everything in good time."

I stiffened, catching my breath. I stared at Jon Kelsey. Suddenly I was hearing that furtive whisper from the garden again:

"Relax... everything in good time."

Was it Jon I had overheard in the garden? But who had he been talking to? And what had they been talking about? It had sounded like they were plotting something... but what?

The door to the gallery was suddenly flung open by a late arrival to the party. A young woman tottered in, heavily made-up and expensively dressed in a flamboyant pink cocktail dress, jewels sparkling at her neck and ears. She had the kind of arrogant confidence often seen in those born into privilege and used to the best, which gave her a superficial maturity. In fact, she was probably about the same age as the waitress behind the bar, although she looked older with her make-up and sophisticated clothing. There was something vaguely familiar about her—as if I might have met her before—but I couldn't quite place her.

She cast her eyes around the room and her gaze stopped on Jon. A small smile curled the corners of her mouth. Tossing her sleek blonde hair over her shoulder, she sashayed across the gallery towards him. She was unsteady on her feet, stumbling a few times as she came towards us, and several people around her reached out instinctively to catch her. I wondered suddenly if she was slightly drunk. I glanced at Cassie's boyfriend. He had stiffened, his face expressionless and his eyes watchful as she approached us.

"Jon..." She cooed, reaching a hand out to his lapel as she drew near.

"Miss Waltham," he said, neatly side-stepping so that her hand fell short of its target.

She gave a bitter laugh. "Why so formal, Jon? Are you afraid of letting everyone know how close we really are?" Her voice was slurred and heavy.

Jon glanced at the guests around him who were all watching avidly and took a step towards her, saying in a lowered tone, "Miss Waltham... Sarah... Why don't we go into my office? We can have more privacy there..." He tried to put a hand under her elbow.

She shook him off roughly. "Why? I don't want privacy. I'm here for the party. Though I must say, you never invited me..." She pouted at him. "But never mind... I'm here now..." She giggled, then stumbled sideways. Jon caught her just in time.

"You're drunk," he said accusingly.

She tossed her head. "No, I'm not. Not unless you're talking about drunk on love...?" She giggled again.

Jon glanced at Cassie, whose face was beginning

to look stony. Once again, he attempted to move the young woman away. "Look, Sarah, why don't we go into my office and talk there? If you are unhappy about the service you've received..."

"Unhappy?" She gave a shrill laugh. "Oh no, the service was very good. Very good indeed." She leered suddenly at Cassie. "Is he giving you the full service too?" She laughed and wagged her finger in Cassie's face. "I hope you know what you're getting into... the great Jon Kelsey—everyone thinks he's so wonderful, so charming, so brilliant... and nobody realises what a bastard he is!"

There were gasps from the crowd and I saw Jon flush angrily. Cassie looked like she didn't know what to say. I felt terribly sorry for my friend and the sordid scene she was facing.

"Miss Waltham, if you do not behave yourself, I'm afraid I'll be obliged to call the police and have you removed from the premises," said Jon through clenched teeth. "I will not have you threatening and harassing my other clients."

Sarah raised an eyebrow. "Client? Is that what you call her?" She laughed again. Then, as Jon took a threatening step towards her, she raised her hands defensively. "Fine! Fine! I am going to get a cocktail and enjoy myself."

"I don't think you should have any more drinks," said Jon quickly. He looked across the gallery and caught the waitress's eye behind the bar, giving his head a sharp shake. Raising his voice, he called across the room, "Miss Waltham can have a cup of tea, if she likes, but no alcohol."

"Fine!" Sarah snarled. "I knew you'd find some way to spoil it for me!"

Turning, she staggered across the room towards the bar. People parted like the Red Sea around her, their reactions ranging from open curiosity and speculative whispers to a polite blind eye and pretended nonchalance.

Jon turned back to Cassie and said in a low voice, "I'm sorry you had to see that."

"Who is she?" Cassie demanded.

Jon compressed his lips into a thin line. "Sarah Waltham is a customer who came into my London gallery. She told me she wanted to get something for her father's birthday and I tried to assist her in her selection, but I very quickly realised that what she was really interested in was a date with me. She was very pushy and I thought maybe if I was pleasant to her and took her out once for a meal, then she would be satisfied. You know, show her that we could be friends but nothing more. Unfortunately, it backfired on me badly," he said ruefully. "It just made her even more delusional. After that dinner, she seemed to think that we were a couple and she began calling herself my girlfriend. She started showing up at the gallery every day, following me home, even waiting outside my apartment in London to catch me when I came out... and when I made it obvious that I had no interest in her romantically, she became spiteful and vindictive. She came into the gallery and made scenes, scaring the other customers away."

Cassie's eyes flashed. "What a cow."

Jon sighed. "I thought that my coming up to Oxford to set up a new branch of the gallery here might help things—you know, take a break from London and hopefully she might cool off. I didn't realise that she was actually a resident of Oxford and had been going down to London regularly to see me there! Talk about out of the frying pan, into the fire! I'd hoped that maybe she wouldn't find out about me being here but..." Jon glanced across the gallery, then back at Cassie. "I guess she must have found out tonight."

"Can't the police do anything?" I spoke up.

Jon shook his head. "Unless she tries to do me bodily harm, there's no law against her coming into my gallery and hanging around there. I just keep hoping that if I continue ignoring her, eventually she'll give up and go away." He reached out and caught Cassie's hand. "I'm sorry she ruined your evening, Cassie."

Cassie gave his hand a squeeze. "Oh, no, it's not ruined at all! This is the best night of my life!" She reached up and kissed him. He slid his arms around her and they became locked in each other's embrace.

Ugh. Gag.

I turned my eyes uncomfortably away and caught sight of the girl, Sarah, across the room. She was standing by the bar, watching Cassie and Jon with a deep scowl on her face. She turned and snapped something at the waitress behind the bar, who gave her a look filled with so much hatred that even I felt it from across the room.

Sarah leaned over the bar counter and said something that made the waitress flush an angry red. Then Sarah stood back and crossed her arms smugly as the waitress poured hot water from a kettle into a teacup, dunked a teabag in it a few times, poured a dollop of milk into the cup, added a spoon of sugar, and stirred it with bad grace. Finally she shoved the teacup and saucer across the bar.

I wondered if Sarah should have even been allowed a cup of tea—giving her liquid of any kind, especially hot liquid, seemed a bad idea. She was already swaying visibly and seemed to have trouble coordinating her movements as she reached for the tea. I could see several people holding their breaths as she picked up the saucer and began wandering back across the room. Next to me, Jon released Cassie and frowned as he watched Sarah as well—no doubt thinking of the disaster if she stumbled and spilled that hot tea on any of the priceless works of art around her.

She paused halfway down the room and stopped in front of one of Cassie's pieces. "So this is your new protégée, eh?" she said, glancing over her shoulder at Jon and curling her lips back in a sneer. She raised the teacup in a taunting gesture. "I suppose I'd better drink to her!"

She took a big gulp, then turned back to the painting. I saw a waiter hastily approach her and offer a napkin, no doubt hoping to prevent any mishaps. She waved him angrily away, her action causing some of the tea to slosh out of the cup. I heard Cassie take a sharp intake of breath next to me but thankfully none of the liquid landed on her beautiful painting.

Jon's frown deepened. "Excuse me," he said. "I think I'd better have a word with my assistant…"

He left us and made his way across the room to where a young blonde woman in a smart sweater and pencil skirt was standing by the doorway to his office, watching Sarah anxiously. She looked up as Jon joined her and gave a quick nod at something he said, then turned and went into the office. Jon gave Sarah a last worried glance, then followed his assistant. I wondered if he might be calling the police after all.

Slowly, the hubbub of conversation filled the room again but there was an uncomfortable sense of waiting for something to happen.

Cassie turned her back on the girl and hissed to me, "She's unbelievable! What an absolute cow! She's obviously some spoilt rich princess used to getting her own way and now she's having a tantrum, just because she can't get what she wants. Poor Jon!"

I wasn't sure what to say. Yeah, the girl was a major pain in the backside, but I found it hard to feel sorry for Jon. Maybe it was mean of me but I felt that he was well able to look after himself. I started to make some inane reply, when a cry of alarm made us spin around.

The girl—Sarah—was staggering around, flailing her arms. Her teacup smashed on the ground, spilling tea everywhere. She tripped, stumbled, then collapsed on the floor. Her arms and legs jerked spasmodically.

There was a scream from the crowd. "Oh my God! She's having a seizure!"

Cassie and I rushed forwards, along with several others—not sure what to do, but wanting to try and help. I saw Jon come out of his office, his eyes bulging as he took in the scene in the room, whilst all around us, chaos erupted in screams and shouts.

"Someone call 999!"

"Roll her over! That's what you've got to do in a seizure—so she doesn't swallow her tongue—"

"No, no, you've got to restrain her—make sure she can't hurt herself!"

"Maybe she's got one of those pen thingies that you're supposed to jab her with—look in her handbag—"

"Don't be stupid, that's just for an allergic shock—"

"Is she allergic to something?"

"Get her some water!"

"Loosen her clothing!"

I arrived at Sarah's side just as a few others were grabbing hold of her arms and legs, and attempting to restrain her. I bent over her, trying to catch hold of her thrashing head. Then she twitched violently one last time and stiffened. Her tortured breathing faded away, to be replaced by silence.

I jerked back from her. A man next to me hesitated, then leaned over and gently rolled her onto her back. We all saw the truth before he spoke, his voice hoarse with horror.

"She's dead."

CHAPTER THREE

The police and ambulance arrived at the same time. I don't know how many frantic phone calls to Emergency had been made by various guests but the number must have convinced the dispatcher to respond as a top priority. The paramedics marched into the gallery just a few moments before the uniformed police constables arrived at the door.

"Where's the patient?" one of the paramedics demanded.

People stepped back and indicated the still form lying on the floor. One look at the body and the paramedics slowed their steps. Even from where they stood, they could see that there was no need for urgency any more. People turned away discreetly as the paramedics went over to attend to the body, whilst the police came into the room and began taking charge of the situation.

"Oh my God... I can't... I can't believe it..." said Cassie next to me.

I looked at her in surprised concern. Cassie wasn't the fainting type but at this moment, she looked more shocked and distressed than I had ever seen her. I guess coming face to face with death can take you that way. I think I was slightly numb to it because of my own recent experiences—only a few weeks ago, I had walked into my tearoom to find a dead body sitting at one of my tables. The nightmares from that still haunted me, but I suppose in a way, I had been "vaccinated" against the horror. Although Cassie had been involved in that murder investigation, she had never encountered death so directly as this before.

"What... what do you think happened?" asked Cassie hoarsely. "Did she have a seizure or something?"

"I don't know," I said, although a dark suspicion was forming in my mind. I gave my head a sharp shake. I was letting my imagination run away with me; just because I had come across one murder recently didn't mean that every death was suspicious. In any case, it wasn't my problem. The police were here now and they would be taking over things.

And they seemed to be doing a fairly good job, herding all the guests into a corner of the gallery and securing the scene. The roar of engines outside told us that more reinforcements had arrived, and a moment later, a man in a beautifully tailored Savile Row suit strode into the room.

Tall, dark, and handsome... Devlin O'Connor fit the cliché so perfectly, it was almost a joke. I saw several women in the room eye him appreciatively and even the men straightened unconsciously, no doubt responding to that air of cool authority that Devlin exuded so effortlessly. His steely blue eyes seemed to miss nothing as he scanned the gallery. I kept my expression noncommittal and tried to ignore the sudden flip-flop of my heart as his gaze lingered on me for a moment before passing on.

He stepped into the centre of the room and spoke with quiet command. Instantly, the clamour of excited conversation died and everyone turned to listen to him. We were informed that we would all have to be detained until the police could ascertain the cause of death. There were a few grumbles from the crowd, but mostly people seemed delighted to have the opportunity to hang around and watch proceedings. I had had a taste of this sort of ghoulish curiosity with the murder in my tearoom, but it still surprised me. Maybe it was because nobody knew the girl that well, I told myself. So they had no personal emotions invested.

Devlin scanned the crowd. "Who is the owner of the gallery?"

"I am." Jon Kelsey stepped forwards. I noticed that

his urbane manner had slipped a bit and he was looking pale. "My name's Kelsey. Jon Kelsey. I'm the host of the party."

"I'd like to ask you a few questions, sir, if I may," said Devlin. His tone was perfectly courteous but I saw Jon swallow nervously.

"Sure. We can go into my office, if you like," he said, indicating the door at the back of the gallery.

"Do you want me to come with—?" Cassie said, starting to follow Jon.

"No, just Mr Kelsey, please," said Devlin, his eyes drifting downwards and noting the way Cassie clung to Jon's arm and the air of intimacy between them. He flicked his gaze to me and raised his eyebrows slightly, then he turned away and followed Jon to the inner office.

With Devlin gone, it was as if a stabilising force had been sucked from the room and people began to move restlessly, milling around and talking in hushed voices. A sandy-haired young man had followed Devlin into the gallery—I recognised him as Devlin's sergeant—and he went through the crowd now, separating us into those who'd had contact with the girl and those who were background spectators. I found myself in the former group, directed into a corner with Cassie and several other guests, as well as a few of the serving staff.

The sergeant came over to explain that while he and the constables would be taking statements from the other group, Devlin would like to speak to anyone who had had contact with the girl himself. So we would have to wait until he was finished with Jon Kelsey and then see him one by one. I sighed, leaning against the wall and kicking off my high heels. It looked like it was going to be a long night.

My phone beeped suddenly. I pulled it out of my handbag and glanced down at the screen. It was a message from my mother:

Darling, would you like some Christmas pudding?

Huh? My mother's text messages were usually slightly random but this one took things to a new level. I hesitated, then texted back:

Not just now. Why?

She replied promptly:

What about memory foam slippers? They're available in six colours. And different styles. The jester ones are adorable. And delivery is free until next weekend.

Oh God. My mother had recently discovered the world of online shopping and it was scary what she could do with a "Buy Now" button. I hurriedly texted a reply:

No thanks. Don't wear slippers.

My mother wasn't easily deterred. Her reply came a moment later:

They do memory foam neck pillows too. Provides marvellous support. They've got a special deal at the moment where you can get 10 neck pillows for the price of 5! And they deliver them straight to your door.

I was starting to panic now. I texted as fast as I could:

But Mother—I don't want 10 neck pillows! I don't even want one!

I felt a bit guilty and added hastily:

But thanks for the thought. Very sweet of you.

My phone beeped a second later:

I'll just get one then, darling. Would you like it in neon pink or lime green?

AARRRGGHH. I ground my teeth, rueing the day I had got my mother an iPad and helped set her up online. My phone beeped again.

Oh dear. It says they are temporarily out of stock.

Hallelujah. Then I felt a bit sorry for her and texted:

Never mind. I'm sure they'll bring new stock again soon. And there will be big sales for Christmas, don't forget.

I paused, then thought I'd better let her know what was going on, in case I was detained here for ages.

I may be late home, Mother. Accident at the party. The police are here.

There was a pause, then she replied:

Oh wonderful news, darling. I'm so happy.

What? Then I realised that she must have been responding to my previous text. I waited to see what she would say about my second message. Nothing came through. After a few more minutes of silence, I was forced to conclude that my mother obviously thought restocking neck pillows was far more important than her daughter being in an incident involving the police.

I was shoving my phone back into my handbag when a familiar booming voice spoke next to me.

"I saw who did it."

I looked up to see Mabel Cooke standing next to

me, with the other Old Biddies gathered around her. They seemed to be brimming with excitement.

I looked at her in confusion. "Who did what?"

Mabel leaned close to me. "Murdered the girl."

I stared at her. She had given voice to the dark suspicion I had been harbouring in my mind, but still, I didn't want to accept it.

"What are you talking about?" I said. "She had a seizure."

"Seizure, my foot," said Mabel. "She was poisoned."

"Don't be ridiculous," I said quickly. "That's the kind of thing that happens in novels and movies, not in real life. Besides, how could someone have poisoned her in a room full of people?"

"Oh, but it was easy!" said Florence, her eyes wide with excitement. "They put it in her tea!"

Glenda nodded, her cheeks flushed pinker than the rouge she applied so liberally. "We were right beside her when she was at the bar and we saw everything."

"What did you see?" I demanded.

"The other girl—the one behind the bar—must have put poison in her tea."

"The girl behind the bar...?" My voice trailed off as I glanced across to the waitress who was seated on the floor, her back against the wall, several yards away. Thankfully she seemed to be out of earshot. In any case, she didn't seem to be paying much attention to anyone in the room. Her eyes were riveted on the dead body, her face pale.

I swung back to the Old Biddies. "Did you actually see her do it?" I demanded.

"Well, not exactly," admitted Mabel. "But we saw *how* she could have done it."

Ethel nodded eagerly. "Yes, it was in the sugar she added to the tea. Everyone knows how easy it is to hide poisons like arsenic in sugar."

"And they were arguing too," added Florence. "We heard them. They were saying quite nasty things to each other."

"What sort of things?"

"Oh, the dead girl jeering at the waitress, making fun of her job, and the waitress replied that she wouldn't be in that position if it wasn't for the dead girl being such a... er... a female dog."

"Sounds like they knew each other," I mused.

Mabel nodded. "Oh, yes. Definitely. There was bad blood between those girls, mark my words."

She turned suddenly as Devlin came out of the inner office and approached the group. He was followed by Jon Kelsey, looking slightly shell-shocked. Cassie rushed over to her boyfriend, whilst Devlin approached us. He turned to the waiter who had tried to offer Sarah a napkin but, before he could speak, the four Old Biddies marched up to him.

"I've got some information for you, young man," said Mabel, waving a hand at him like she was hailing down a bus.

A look of irritation flashed across Devlin's

handsome face. "If you can wait your turn, Mrs Cooke, I will get to you shortly. I need to speak to some of the other witnesses first, as they may have important information for me."

"Well, we have the most important information of all," said Mabel, crossing her arms. "We know how the girl was murdered and the identity of the killer."

Devlin stopped. "We're not certain yet this is a murder investigation," he said cautiously.

Mabel sniffed. "Then I'm saving you time, Inspector. She was murdered. And we saw how it was done—she was poisoned."

There were gasps from the crowd and I heard several shocked whispers of: "*Poison?*"

Devlin glanced around, then gave a sigh. "I think we'd better speak in private, Mrs Cooke. This way." He indicated the doorway to the inner office.

Mabel gave a regal nod and allowed herself and the other Old Biddies to be escorted into Jon's office. I watched them go, wondering if Devlin would take their accusations seriously. My gaze flicked back to the waitress who had been behind the bar. I remembered the look of pure hatred I had seen on her face and I shivered.

Poison.

It seemed ludicrous. And yet... could it have been true?

CHAPTER FOUR

Devlin leaned back against the desk in Jon's private office and said, "So you believed Kelsey's story about his relationship with the dead girl?"

I shrugged. "It did seem very plausible, the way he told it."

He regarded me shrewdly. "But you didn't *want* to believe it."

Damn. The man was too perceptive for his own good.

"Let's just say that Jon Kelsey isn't my favourite person," I said at last.

Devlin raised his eyebrows. "Any special reason for that? He *is* your best friend's boyfriend, right? And from what little I saw, Cassie seems very happy with him."

41

I winced internally. How could I explain my irrational dislike of Jon? "No, no special reason... just a personality clash, I guess." I leaned forwards. "*You* obviously didn't believe his story if you're grilling me about it."

"I didn't say that. It's good practice to double check everything—get different witness accounts of the same events."

"But you do think it's murder, right?"

"The SOCO team have only just got here and the forensic pathologist is still examining the body. I've only had a quick chat with him so nothing can be confirmed until I speak to him again; in fact, he probably won't be able to tell me anything for certain until he does the post-mortem."

"Aw, come on! He must have given some indication that there was foul play! Otherwise, why are you spending so much time interviewing everybody? Do you think Mabel Cooke and the Old Bi—I mean, her friends—are right? That the girl was poisoned?"

Devlin's expression was guarded. "We're making no assumptions at this point. It's still too early in the investigation."

Grrr.

Devlin's blue eyes twinkled suddenly in amusement at the expression on my face and he relented. "But yes, I do think it's a suspicious death. I understand that she was having some kind of seizure—convulsions—before she died? Unless she has a history of epilepsy or some other medical condition which could bring on seizures, that could very well be a symptom of poisoning." He looked at me keenly. "You were one of the ones who ran over to her—did you touch her?"

I shook my head. "I tried, but she was thrashing around so much and I... I wasn't sure what to do. Some of the others were trying to restrain her but I was afraid to hurt her. To be honest with you..." I said, shamefaced, "I was a bit paralysed."

Devlin's voice softened. "It's perfectly normal, Gemma. Unless you've been specifically trained for it, not many people will know what to do in a medical emergency like that."

I swallowed uncomfortably. "Yeah, but... well, you always wonder if there was something you could have done that might have made a difference..."

"I don't think you have to worry about that. I think whatever caused the girl's death—whatever was introduced into her system—was too powerful for anyone to have prevented the result."

"So you *do* believe what Mabel Cooke said about the poisoning!" I said.

He gave me a dry look. "Mrs Cooke and her friends have an interesting theory, which probably bears more resemblance to an Agatha Christie novel than reality. When I pressed them, they admitted that they didn't actually *see* the girl behind the bar put anything into the teacup. It was just their certainty that the girl *could* have done it and *would* have done

43

it. But they don't have any hard facts or proof. Having said that, we will take everything into account."

"In that case..." I hesitated.

"Yes?"

"Well, I'm not totally sure about this, but... when I bent over her, I thought I could smell something... something sweet... like almonds."

Devlin's gaze sharpened. "Almonds? Like bitter almond?"

I shrugged. "I don't know... What's the difference? It's that sweetish almond smell—you know, the kind you get in cakes and marzipan and creams and shampoos..." I looked at him curiously. "Does it mean something?"

"There is a famous poison that has a characteristic smell of bitter almonds on the victim's breath," said Devlin thoughtfully. "Cyanide."

"Cyanide?" I stared at him. "I thought you said this wasn't like a mystery novel."

Devlin shrugged. "I also said we would consider every possibility. The symptoms Sarah Waltham had would certainly fit with those of cyanide poisoning..."

I suppressed a shudder. *Cyanide?* This was getting more and more unbelievable!

"It may be nothing," said Devlin quickly. "I shouldn't even be speculating like this with a member of the public. Forget I said anything," he said, looking annoyed with himself.

I didn't reply, but a part of me was secretly

pleased that Devlin had slipped up because he didn't consider me like any other member of the public.

"Well, if there's nothing else, Gemma, I have other people to question..." Devlin started to rise.

I started to get up as well, then paused, suddenly remembering the conversation I had overheard in the garden. Could that have any bearing on what had happened to Sarah? But it seemed so ridiculous—like bad dialogue from a B-movie—I blushed to even think of repeating it. In any case, what I had really overheard? Two people plotting to... kill someone? No, this was getting into the realms of total fantasy.

And besides, if I mentioned it, I would have to tell Devlin that I thought one voice was vaguely familiar. Would I have to confess my suspicions that it was Jon? Was I sure it was him? I was aware that my dislike for Jon might bias me against him. Maybe subconsciously, I was looking for a way to discredit him and my overactive imagination did the rest. I didn't like Jon Kelsey but I didn't want to make him the key suspect in a murder enquiry for no good reason, particularly as Cassie would never forgive me.

"Gemma? Is there something else?"

"No, nothing," I stood up hastily. "Sorry, my mind wandered for a moment."

Devlin looked at me intently and I wondered if he could see through my lie. When we had been students together, he had always had an uncanny ability to guess what I was thinking, to almost read my thoughts. If this had been then, he would have known immediately that I was lying. But now... As I'd said to Cassie, we were different people and that special bond between us was gone. The thought made me feel slightly depressed.

I let myself out of the office and rejoined the other guests in the outer gallery. Cassie had been questioned and was free to leave with me now but she insisted on staying with Jon. He would have to wait until the last guest had been interviewed and the police were satisfied with the crime scene before he could shut the gallery. I gave Cassie a quick hug, then left, stepping gratefully out into the crisp night air.

CHAPTER FIVE

The gallery was located in the heart of the city but it wasn't a long walk to North Oxford where my parents lived. Like most local residents, I normally cycled everywhere, but knowing that I would probably be having a few drinks tonight, I had decided to leave my bike at home. Jon picked up Cassie for the party and had given me a lift as well, and I'd decided to walk back myself. Oxford wasn't a big city anyway and it was fairly easy to get around on foot.

It was generally safe in the city centre too—well, except for one's ankles, I thought wryly as my heel sank into another rut in the network of cobblestones lining the street and I wobbled precariously. I remembered now why I had never worn fancy shoes much when I was a student here. Cobblestones were a killer for high heels. I wished I had had the foresight to pack a pair of ballet flats into my handbag. As it was, I had to stumble and trip my way through the streets, past the historic university buildings and college quadrangles, their Gothic spires and bell towers now wreathed in shadows, and up the long stretch of Banbury Road into the northern suburbs.

I finally arrived on my street, footsore and weary, to find a police car parked outside my parents' Victorian townhouse. My heart lurched. Had something happened to them? I quickened my steps and breathed out in relief as I got closer and realised that the constable was at the door of the house next to us. A few curious neighbours had come out of their homes to see what was going on, including my mother—elegantly attired as always in a cashmere twinset and tweed pencil skirt—who was standing at the top of our own front steps.

"What's going on, Mother?" I asked as I joined her.

"I hardly know, darling. I just saw the police arrive..."

As we watched, the front door of the next house opened and a dumpy-looking, middle-aged woman came out. The constable took off his hat and said something to her. I couldn't hear what he said but the woman's eyes widened in horror and she raised her hands to her face. She seemed unable to speak and the constable looked around helplessly. He spied my mother and motioned for her to join him. I found myself following without realising it. We let ourselves into the adjoining garden and the constable came over gratefully to meet us.

"I'm afraid I've had to break some bad news," said the constable in a low voice. "Her daughter was involved in an incident tonight and is dead. Would it be possible for you to stay with her, ma'am? We would normally have a WPC, but we're a bit short-staffed this evening—"

My mother gasped. "Oh, my goodness, how dreadful! Of course I'll stay with her." She went quickly forwards and put a gentle hand under the other woman's elbow

"The CID detectives will be coming to speak to her shortly. The inspector's just tied up in the city at the moment."

I turned to stare at him. Could it be...? Surely it was too much of a coincidence for Oxfordshire CID to be involved in the death of *two* young women on the same night? This must be Sarah's mother, I realised—and I also realised suddenly why Sarah had seemed vaguely familiar. I must have seen her once or twice leaving the neighbours' place when I happened to be coming back myself. She had never been friendly enough to make eye contact or attempt small talk and I had never paid her much attention.

"I'll take her back to our house," my mother said. "She can stay there until the Detective-Inspector comes."

The constable nodded, pleased. "That's very kind

of you, ma'am."

"Come, my dear," my mother said to Mrs Waltham. "A cup of tea is what you need..."

Of course, a cup of tea. Like a typical Englishman—or woman, in her case—a cup of tea was my mother's solution to everything, from a broken heart to global warming. Mrs Waltham nodded numbly and let my mother lead her back to our house.

I followed in silence, trying to recall what my mother had told me about our neighbours. They had only moved next door recently—about six months ago, I recalled her saying. Mr Waltham was in his sixties—he must have had Sarah much later in life, which probably explained why she had been so spoilt—and his wife was a lot younger. In fact, I remembered my mother commenting about the age difference in scandalous tones.

They had one daughter and also a "housekeeper", a daily help who had apparently been with the family for years—a capable, middle-aged woman with a kindly face and a no-nonsense attitude—though in the past few days, I had noticed a younger woman sweeping the garden and taking out the rubbish. I couldn't remember my mother saying much else about them, other than praising Mrs Waltham's beautiful roses.

Now I showed Mrs Waltham into the living room, whilst my mother went to prepare the tea. I was a bit unsure what to say to the grieving woman—what could I say to someone who had just lost their daughter? I glanced at her surreptitiously, noting with surprise that she did seem young. No more than her early forties. She must have had Sarah at a very young age. And her daughter certainly hadn't gained her chic style from her mother. Unlike the glamorous creature who had come to the gallery, Mrs Waltham was plain and frumpy. Oh, she was dressed in expensive enough clothes: her shoes looked Italian and hand-made, and I was sure that I had seen the dress she was wearing in the designer racks at the local department store, whilst her hair had obviously been expertly tinted and cut at a top salon. But somehow, the overall effect felt slightly fake, like a little girl playing dress-up with her mother's clothes and make-up.

She caught me looking at her and I flushed. To cover my embarrassment, I said quickly, "I'm really sorry about your daughter, Mrs Waltham."

"I... I just can't believe it..." said the other woman in dazed disbelief. She stared blankly into space. "I don't know... How can it be...? She was fine earlier this evening... She was going to a party..."

"Yes, I met her there," I said without thinking. Then I bit my tongue. I didn't want Mrs Waltham to start asking me for the gory details. Although I suppose if she found out later that I had been at the party and seen Sarah and hadn't mentioned it, that wouldn't have gone down well either.

Mrs Waltham turned to look at me

uncomprehendingly and I hastened to explain. "I was at a party this evening—at a gallery in Oxford—and Sarah was there."

She shook her head, still with that look of dazed confusion. "The policeman said there was an incident at the gallery and the ambulance didn't get there in time. What kind of incident? Did you see what happened?"

I shifted uncomfortably. "It looked like Sarah had some kind of seizure."

"But that doesn't make sense!" Mrs Waltham burst out. "Sarah didn't have epilepsy."

"And she wasn't a diabetic?"

Mrs Waltham shook her head.

"Did she... did she seem like her normal self when she left for the party this evening?" I asked hesitantly. I really wanted to ask if she had been drunk but I couldn't think of a polite way to broach the topic.

"Yes, I think so," said Mrs. Waltham. "Much happier than she's been lately."

What did she mean by that? Before I could ask, my mother came in carrying a tray laden with a Royal Doulton tea set in rose pink with soft gold accents, a plate of home-made butter shortbread and a stack of linen napkins. She set this on the lounge table, sat down, and gracefully began to serve tea, pouring out the deep red liquid through the silver strainer and handing the teacups around.

I watched her admiringly. Much as I disagreed

with my mother's 1950's housewife approach to life, I did wish I could perform everyday domestic tasks like this with such poise and elegance. It's a bit of a lost art in recent generations of women, I think, with our race to get to the top of the corporate career ladder and our contempt for "ladylike" habits and pursuits.

"Sarah loves... I mean, Sarah loved shortbread," said Mrs Waltham suddenly, eyeing the plate. "Our old housekeeper, Mrs Hicks, used to make some each week." Her lips quivered. "I... I can't believe that Sarah is never going to be helping herself from that tin anymore..."

My mother looked slightly alarmed at so much emotion being displayed. The thought of having to discuss "Feelings" was just too much for her British sensibilities. She was no doubt thinking that Mrs Waltham ought to show more of a proper stiff upper lip in the face of tragedy.

She lifted the milk jug and said brightly, "Milk? Sugar?" as if we were all sitting down to Sunday afternoon tea.

Still, maybe my mother was right about the tea. There was certainly a kind of comfort in the familiar ritual and it gave one something to do, something to focus on. There was a companionable silence for a while as we busied ourselves adding milk and sugar to the cups, tasting the shortbread, handing around napkins—broken only by Mrs Waltham suddenly jerking upright and saying:

"Oh God, I... I'll have to tell David."

"Is that Mr Waltham?" I asked.

She nodded miserably. "He's in hospital at the moment." She saw our expressions and explained, "He went in for a prostate operation, and then unfortunately, developed complications afterwards: he got septicaemia. He was quite bad earlier this week and we were so worried... but thank goodness, he seems to have turned a corner, although he'll be in the ICU ward for a few days." She swallowed. "He's going to be devastated..."

The front doorbell rang and my mother looked immensely relieved. She went quickly to answer it, returning in a moment to say that the police were here to escort Mrs Waltham back to her house where Detective-Inspector O'Connor was waiting to question her. I followed Sarah's mother to the front door and stood thoughtfully on the threshold, watching as the constable led her away.

"What a dreadful business," my mother commented as she shut the door and led the way back to the living room. "That poor woman."

"Do you know much about the Walthams?" I asked as we began to clear up the tea things.

My mother shook her head. "Not really, darling. They're not *unfriendly* but they do keep to themselves. They haven't been here long, of course— only about six months, so I don't know them that well. They used to live in Woodstock, I believe, but Mr Waltham wanted to be closer in to town, especially as Sarah was in her final year and no longer had college accommodation—so she had moved back home and it was easier for her to be closer to the University. And you know the Collinses had been wanting to sell up next door for ages and trade down to a flat in London, so it worked out well all round."

"Have you met Mr Waltham?"

"Only to say hello to," my mother said. "I've seen him a few times, you know, just when we pass each other coming in and out... Oh, I did see him a couple of weeks ago in town, with Mrs Waltham, coming out of our solicitors' office. They must use Sexton, Lovell & Billingsley as well. I was just popping in to drop off a document for your father and we stopped and had a nice chat."

"What were they doing there?"

"I could hardly ask that, Gemma!" My mother looked scandalised. "They didn't look particularly cheerful—but then, legal matters can be so tedious."

"And Sarah wasn't with them?"

"No. In fact, I think I've only spoken to her once. She is—was—a very attractive girl."

"Yes," I agreed, although I thought the attractiveness was only skin-deep, but I didn't voice my thoughts aloud.

"Anyway!" My mother heaved a sigh, then said in a different voice, "How was Cassie's party, darling?"

"Oh, it went very well—until the incident with Sarah, that is. There were lots of people there, especially important people in the art world, and Cassie's paintings seemed to be getting a lot of attention."

"Well, I must say—I'm surprised you didn't ask Lincoln to go with you," My mother pursed her lips. "Such a nice boy, so well brought up—and so handsome..."

I sighed to myself. *Here we go. My mother's favourite subject.*

"... really, any girl would be lucky to have Lincoln as her escort. And he's such an eminent doctor too! And of course, with his mother being my closest friend, he'd be the perfect match! In fact, I was just saying to Helen the other day that if you two decided on an autumn wedding, we could book The Orangery at Blenheim Palace and have—"

"Mother!" I said through clenched teeth. "Don't start jumping to conclusions! I'm not marrying Lincoln Green!"

"Why ever not, dear?"

I felt like banging my head against the wall. "Well, for one thing, I don't even know him that well yet. It's not like we're dating or anything."

"But you've been out with him a few times, haven't you?"

"Only as friends," I stressed. "I've made it very clear to him that those were not romantic dates."

My mother waved this away. "And you're going out again with him tomorrow night," she added with some satisfaction.

I looked at her warily. How had she found out about that?

"It's nothing. Lincoln was given some tickets for a concert at the Sheldonian and asked if I'd like to go along."

My mother beamed. "Well, make sure you look your best, darling. In fact, I saw this wonderful headscarf online—shall I get it for you? They do same-day delivery."

I looked at her in alarm. "No thanks, Mother." Hurriedly, I changed the subject. "Did you give Muesli her dinner?"

My mother's face softened slightly. "Yes, and I must say, that little cat is extremely naughty. She darted past my legs and ran downstairs before I could stop her."

I looked quickly around the living room. "Did you get her back?"

"Yes, yes, I managed to entice her back into your room with some tuna." My mother sighed. "I do feel a bit sorry for her—poor little thing—cooped up in your bedroom all day."

"Yeah, well, you know she's used to having the run of the house in her previous home." I looked at my mother hopefully. "Maybe we could try letting her out...?"

"But wouldn't she scratch the furniture?"

I looked around the living room and sighed. My mother was right. Muesli would make mincemeat of the cream silk damask covers on the sofa suite, not to mention the matching curtains. I wouldn't have cared myself, but living as I was back in my parents' house, I didn't feel that it was fair to them. It had been one of the things I had promised my mother when I told her I was adopting Muesli—that the cat wouldn't cause any trouble.

And it would only be for a little while longer, I told myself. Hopefully, if business continued to go well at the tearoom, I would soon be able to afford a place of my own and then Muesli could shred whatever she pleased...

Five minutes later, the little tabby cat herself came running up to greet me as I entered my bedroom. Her tail was straight up like a flagpole and she vibrated the end of it in greeting as she rubbed herself against my legs. I had to admit, despite never having been a cat person, I was beginning to enjoy the feline welcome I received every time I returned.

"Hiya, Muesli," I said, reaching down to rub her chin.

She purred like a little engine and butted her head against my shins. I scooped her up and cuddled her close, walking over to look out the window. My bedroom overlooked the rear of the house, with a view of our own garden and part of the Walthams' property, which was the last one on the street corner and twice the size of ours. I could see light spilling out of the rear windows next door.

I wondered if Devlin might have finished questioning Mrs Waltham by now, then I thought of the party again. Could it really only have been a few hours ago? And Sarah—so brash and alive then. It seemed incredible to think that she was dead and even more incredible to think that it could have been murder.

CHAPTER SIX

I had a restless night, tossing and turning, plagued by dreams of pink cocktails and strange paintings and then finally a large teapot landing on my chest... its weight suffocating me... and it was rumbling like an engine...

Huh?

I awoke with a start and found myself staring into a pair of green eyes above a little pink nose in a whiskered face.

"Muesli..." I mumbled. "Get off my chest..."

"*Meorrw!*" she said.

For such a small cat, she seemed to weigh a ton. I pushed her off and sat up slowly, rubbing my eyes. From the darkness showing through the gap between my curtains, I knew it must have still been very early.

Early enough that my alarm hadn't sounded yet. I groaned and lay back down, pulling the covers over me and attempting to go back to sleep. Muesli climbed over the blankets until she reached my ankles and draped herself over them. The rumbling started again. I lay there for another ten minutes, listening to her purring. Finally I gave up and sat up.

Muesli looked at me eagerly and said, "*Meorrw?*"

I sighed. I knew what she wanted. Although I provided her with a litter tray in the room, Muesli preferred to go outside and would hold it until she was bursting. I knew she wanted to get on with our usual morning ritual, when I took her down to the gardens for her ablutions. Oh well, I was wide awake now anyway and I might as well take advantage of the extra time. I got up, washed my face, and grabbed Muesli's harness from my desk.

Okay, I confess—when I first got the harness, I thought I would just strap it on and Muesli would trot in front of me like a little dog. Just goes to show you how much I knew about cats. For one thing, they seemed to move backwards instead of forwards. And they didn't really *walk* so much as *bolt* to the end of the leash, then hunch down and sit there for ten minutes, before suddenly bolting to the end of the leash in a different direction. It took about half an hour to travel five feet when you were "walking" a cat. And that was when she wasn't rolling around trying to wriggle out of the harness. Muesli gave me a baleful look now as I slipped the straps on her.

"Sorry, Muesli, but you've got to accept this compromise. It's the only way you're going to get to go outside."

I scooped her up and crept downstairs so as not to wake my parents, letting myself quietly out into the backyard. It was getting light now, the sky fading from indigo to pale grey. The morning air was chilly and I shivered as I set Muesli down. She began prowling along the flagstone path, sniffing the bushes along the way. I followed her absent-mindedly. We reached the large blackthorn tree that grew at the bottom of our garden, its branches spreading in all directions, some of them reaching over the wall into the Walthams' backyard. Muesli paused at the foot of the tree and stretched up, raking her claws down the bark.

I leaned against the trunk and stared into space, my thoughts drifting. I thought of that scene in the gallery last night and grimaced, pushing the memory away and forcing my mind to pleasanter things. My tearoom. Yes. I wanted to speak to my mother about some changes to the menu—maybe cutting back on the finger sandwiches and offering more cakes. People seemed to like their sweet treats. And she had been mentioning something to me recently about a new cake recipe...

When I'd lost my chef at the tearoom recently, I hadn't been too sure about my mother stepping into the breach. She was a wonderful cook, of course, and her baking was divine, and I needed someone full-time in the kitchen while I served the customers outside... so you could say that it was the perfect solution: I was getting a fantastic chef for free, without the hassle and expense of having to hire someone from London. I just wasn't sure my nerves and blood pressure could stand working so closely with my mother every day. Still, so far, it seemed to be working out okay—

Something jerked in my hand, and the next moment, I realised that I was no longer holding Muesli's leash. The little cat had scooted up the tree, yanking the leash out of my limp fingers, and was now sitting on one of the upper branches.

"Hey...!" I stretched up, trying to reach the end of the leash, which dangled just above my head.

Muesli looked down at me innocently. "*Meorrw?*"

"Muesli! Come back down here!"

She cocked her head and regarded me for a moment, then turned and walked very deliberately along the branch, crossing over the wall into the Walthams' garden. She jumped down and disappeared from sight.

"Muesli!" I said in outrage.

A faint, defiant "*Meorrw!*" drifted over the wall.

Grrrr. What should I do now? It was so early, I didn't like to ring the Walthams' front doorbell. But I couldn't just leave Muesli either. Aside from the fact that she would probably dig up Mrs Waltham's prize roses, it was potentially dangerous. The Walthams' house was the last in our street, sitting on the corner of an intersection, and if Muesli went over the wall on the other side of their garden, she would end up on the open road that ran alongside their property.

Then I pricked my ears. Someone was moving on the other side of the wall: footsteps coming down the path, then the creak of a back gate opening and the rustle of plastic. I turned hurriedly towards our own back gate and opened it just in time to see a young woman stepping out of the Walthams' backyard. She was depositing a large black sack into the council rubbish bin in the alley that ran along the back of our houses.

"Hi." I gave her a quick smile. "I'm from next door. I'm looking for my cat—she climbed over the wall and went into your garden—"

"A little grey tabby? With a white chest and paws? I saw her just now—she's over by the rosebushes."

"Do you mind if I come in to grab her?"

"Oh, sure," said the young woman. She gave me a shy smile. "I'm Meg—I'm the Walthams' new maid."

"Nice to meet you," I said absently as I stepped into the beautifully landscaped garden. I spotted Muesli immediately, sitting by a large pink rosebush at the side of the path. She saw me and tried to make a run for it, but I ran over and stepped on the end of the leash, stopping her in her tracks.

"*Meorrw!*" Muesli looked at me sulkily.

"That's the end of your adventures today, you little minx," I muttered, scooping her up.

"She's a cute little thing," said Meg, coming over

to give Muesli a pat.

I hesitated. It seemed rude not to mention Sarah and yet it seemed weird also to suddenly bring up the subject. "Er... I'm sorry about what happened last night."

The girl's eyes widened. "You mean about Miss Sarah? That was such a shock when I saw the papers this mornin'!"

"Did you know her well?"

The other girl shrugged. "Not really. I've only been workin' here a week or so, actually."

"Yes, I thought the Walthams had an older lady as their daily help—did she retire?"

"That's Nell—I mean, Mrs Hicks. Yes, she's worked for them for years but..." Meg looked embarrassed. "She was dismissed. I'm... I'm her replacement."

"Dismissed?"

"Oh, it wasn't anythin' bad she'd done," Meg said hurriedly, misinterpreting my look. "It wasn't really Nell's fault at all. But... well, Miss Sarah wasn't happy with her."

"With her work, you mean?"

"No-o..." Suddenly the girl looked uncomfortable. "I... I shouldn't really be talkin' about it. Sorry, I've got to get on with work now."

She hustled me out the back gate and shut it firmly behind me. I stood staring at the closed gate for a moment, then turned and went back into my own garden. As I walked slowly back into the house,

I mulled over what Meg had just said. Did Nell Hicks's sudden dismissal have anything to do with Sarah's murder? I shook my head, smiling wryly to myself. I was seeing mysteries everywhere.

I set Muesli down in the kitchen while I prepared her breakfast to a barrage of "*Meorrw! Meorrw! Meorrw! Meorrw!*" as she twined herself around my legs and complained about how slow I was being. I don't know why I had bothered to try and stay quiet since she made such a racket; the whole house was probably roused by the time she finally got her breakfast.

In any case, it seemed that my mother had already been up for a while. She breezed into the kitchen just as I was putting Muesli's bowl down. She looked immaculate in a belted wool dress with a bateau collar and with her hair in a perfect French coil, making me feel horribly conscious that I was still sporting my flannel pyjamas and serious bed hair.

Leaving Muesli to her supervision, I hurried upstairs to shower and try to make myself presentable. Half an hour later, we left the house together and headed north-west out of Oxford, towards the little village of Meadowford-on-Smythe. Like many Cotswolds villages, Meadowford was a quaint haven of thatched cottages with arched gables and winding cobbled lanes, all gathered on the banks of a picturesque river. The High Street boasted a collection of antique shops and charming boutiques, with one end overlooked by the Saxon church and the other leading down to the medieval bridge crossing the river. My pride and joy, The Little Stables Tearoom, enjoyed a prime location on the High Street and was housed in what used to be a 15th-century Tudor inn, completed with the original stable courtyard that gave the place its name.

We were slightly late due to an accident on the roads and the village was already crawling with eager tourists by the time we arrived, some already hovering hopefully outside the tearoom entrance. I was surprised to find that it was unopened. Usually Cassie would have got there by now. Perhaps she had been held up by an accident as well? I went around getting the dining room ready, opening up the drapes, checking the tables, and arranging the menus, whilst my mother went into the kitchen to put on her apron and start the day's baking.

My previous chef used to start much earlier, of course, but I didn't feel it fair to ask my mother to come in at the crack of dawn. So I'd figured out a good compromise: I changed the tearoom's opening hours so that we didn't open until 10:30 a.m., giving my mother ample time to get a lot of the fresh baking done. We didn't usually get that much business first thing in the morning anyway—most people only started coming in for "morning tea", which was traditionally around 10:30 to 11 a.m.

This morning, however, there were tourists beating a path to the door and they were outdone only by the Old Biddies who came in first and claimed their usual table by the windows. They gave an order for some toasted crumpets and home-made, thick-cut marmalade, a couple of Chelsea buns, and a pot of English Breakfast tea, but I knew it was all just window dressing. They were really here to gossip about last night with me.

"Have you had any more news, Gemma dear, about that poor girl who was murdered last night?"

"Why would I have had any more news?"

"Well..." Glenda gave me a coy look. "That handsome detective being sweet on you... we thought he might have given you a bit of extra information on the side."

I blushed in spite of myself. "He's not sweet on... I don't have any special relationship with Inspector O'Connor."

Glenda looked at the others and they exchanged a knowing smile.

Irritated, I said, "And besides, the police aren't sure it's murder yet. They're still waiting for the results of the post-mortem and—"

"Oh, fiddlesticks!" said Mabel. "It's murder, all right. I told the Inspector so myself—although why I thought he would listen to me, I don't know... Young people nowadays—always full of their own ideas and never listening to the advice of their elders." She sniffed. "You would have thought that after all the help we gave him on the last case—practically identifying the murderer for him—he would be a bit more appreciative of our contribution."

I suppressed the urge to roll my eyes. The Old Biddies' contribution on the last case had mostly involved skulking around Oxford and getting stuck in college broom cupboards and *I* was the unlucky person who had ended up identifying the murderer.

Mabel leaned forwards and gave an emphatic nod. "There was evil done last night. You mark my words, Gemma—there is much more to that girl's death than meets the eye. And if that Inspector O'Connor knows how to do his job, he should investigate the girl who was the waitress at the party."

I frowned. "You said the girls knew each other... I don't see how. They seemed so different. I can't imagine they would have had much chance to cross paths—"

"They're both students at the University," said Florence excitedly. "They're both doing Fine Art."

"Really? How'd you find that out?"

"Well, I had a little talk with her, dear," said Ethel. "The young waitress at the bar. She served me right after Sarah—made me a lovely hot toddy—and we got chatting. She's having a bit of a tough time with her studies and having to work several part-time jobs as well, to supplement her student funds. To be honest with you, I think she just needed a sympathetic ear. She was quite upset by the way Sarah treated her."

Ethel used to be librarian at our local library and I'd always remembered her gentle, smiling face—she was just the type of kindly soul who you'd want to share your troubles with.

"Her name is Fiona Stanley," added Ethel. "And she's in her third year, just like the dead girl."

"So they were at the Art School together?"

Ethel nodded. "But I don't think you could say they were *friends*."

"Hah! Friends!" Mabel smacked the table scornfully. "Enemies, more like."

"Devlin said you didn't actually *see* anything, though," I reminded them.

Mabel shrugged. Obviously eye-witness evidence was a minor detail. "She was poisoned," she said, nodding ominously. "The question is—by what?"

The bell at the tearoom door jingled, announcing the arrival of a new customer, and regretfully I left the Old Biddies' table. Much as I would have liked to stay and gossip about the murder, I had work to do. In fact, being the only person serving that morning, I soon began to feel overwhelmed. It was wonderful that my tearoom was doing such rip-roaring business but it was also beginning to fall into chaos. Orders were delayed, food got cold before it could be taken to tables, and I could see that customers were starting to look irritated.

"Is Cassie taking the day off today?" Mabel called out to me as I rushed past their table with a tray of cucumber finger sandwiches intended for the family group next to them.

I paused for a moment. "No-o... I'm not sure why she's not come in yet. She's probably held up somewhere..." I tried to conceal my irritation with

Cassie. If she was going to be late, it would have been nice if she could have let me know. I had tried calling her a couple of times but her phone had gone straight to voicemail.

Mabel and the other Old Biddies exchanged a look, then they stood up in unison. Mabel turned to me, pushing her sleeves up to her elbows.

"Come on, dear. We'll give you a hand."

"Oh, no, there's really no need—"

"Nonsense! We can see that you're rushed off your feet," said Glenda, taking the tray out of my hands.

The other three marched to the counter and began helping themselves to various crockery and food items there. I watched in a slight daze as Florence assembled a tray with a Shelley Rosebud bone china teapot and cups, a matching jug of milk, and a bowl of sugar, whilst Ethel whisked a plate of warm scones with jam and clotted cream off to the table of Japanese tourists and Mabel took charge of the menus and order pads. They were bustling off to different corners of the tearoom before I could protest and, to be honest, I was too grateful for the help to object much.

And if I'd been unsure about how the customers would react, I was pleasantly surprised. If anything, they seemed to be delighted to be served by what looked like quintessential sweet old ladies—for the tourists, especially, this fit the image of a traditional English tearoom perfectly. As for the old dears themselves, any guilt I might have felt was mollified by the fact that they seemed to be enjoying themselves immensely. In fact, they seemed to be relishing the opportunity to chat to people at the tables (and meddle in their businesses, no doubt).

In no time at all, peace and contentment were restored to the tearoom and I was able to sit down for a moment for a much-deserved rest behind the counter. It was all going to be fine now, I told myself with a sigh of relief. Still, I couldn't quite shake off the uneasy feeling that this was just the calm before the storm...

CHAPTER SEVEN

It was nearly twelve o'clock when the door swung open and Cassie finally stepped into the tearoom with a sheepish expression on her face. She came rushing up to me.

"Oh, God, Gemma—I'm so sorry! I completely overslept this morning! We stayed at Jon's place last night and didn't get to sleep till the early hours..." She blushed slightly, leaving me in no doubt as to what they were doing up so late. "I thought he'd like a bit of company, you know, after what had happened at the gallery... Anyway, when I woke up this morning and realised the time, I got here as fast as I could."

I swallowed my annoyance. After all, everyone mucked up sometimes and last night's fiasco probably gave her a better excuse than most.

"No worries, as my friends Down Under would say," I said, giving her a smile. "The Old Biddies decided to help out."

"The Old Biddies!" Cassie turned and looked disbelievingly at the white-haired figures bustling around the room. "You're not serious!"

"Uh… Actually, they've been really good," I said. "In fact, the customers seem to love them and the whole place seems to be running a lot smoother."

Cassie looked shamefaced again. "Sorry—I know I must have left you in the lurch, especially with Sunday being one of our busiest days."

"That's okay. So how's Jon?"

"Oh, the poor thing… It was such a horrible shock for him, having someone collapse like that in his gallery."

"And someone he knew too," I said.

Cassie frowned. "Well, not very well. She wasn't much more than a customer, really. It wasn't like Jon knew her personally or anything."

"Did the police believe that?"

"Why shouldn't they?" Cassie flared.

I bit my tongue. "No, no reason. I just thought… you know how police can be so suspicious sometimes…"

Cassie scowled. "Bloody right! I don't know what Devlin's playing at. I used to think that he was a pretty decent guy, but he's acting like a complete plonker in this instance! Anyone can see that Jon's the victim there. That girl was totally barmy and making poor Jon's life a misery—and all he did was try to provide the best service for his clients!"

Cassie's voice had rose shrilly in indignation and customers at several tables turned around to stare. I glanced at them, then caught Cassie's arm and pulled her out of the dining room. We went into the little shop area adjoining the main tearoom, selling Oxford souvenirs and English tea paraphernalia, where we could have some privacy.

"The Old Biddies seem to think that the waitress who was at the bar last night might be involved. Her name's Fiona Stanley, apparently. Did you hear the police mention her?" I asked.

Cassie frowned. "Yeah, I did hear Devlin say something about that to his sergeant. The girl's a student here at the University, isn't she?"

I nodded. "And so was Sarah. In fact, they were both in the same year, doing Fine Art."

Cassie raised her eyebrows. "Fine Art? Really?"

Cassie had read Fine Art at Oxford herself, whilst I had done English. We'd been delighted when we had both been accepted and our close friendship, which had started in primary school, continued strong through our university years. In fact, even my moving to the other side of the world for eight years hadn't threatened our friendship. Nothing had ever come between Cassie and me. *Except Jon Kelsey*, I thought sourly.

Aloud, I asked, "Would Sarah and Fiona have had

much to do with each other?"

Cassie shrugged. "It's a pretty small department—the new intake is no more than thirty students each year—and it's got a very intimate feel; everyone works alongside each other in the studios. In fact, all the teaching is done in the department rather than in the colleges."

"Oh?" I was surprised to hear that.

One of the ways Oxford was so different from most other universities in the world was its collegiate "tutorial system". Basically, this meant that you were taught individually or in small groups of two and three, by the respective dons in their subjects at their colleges. Oh, you might have lectures in the department buildings and some subjects, like the sciences, had practical laboratory sessions, but most of your learning wasn't done in classrooms but in private, one-to-one sessions where you were challenged to analyse, defend, and critique the ideas of your own and others, in in-depth essays and conversations with your tutor and fellow students. There was no hiding at the back of the class or learning things by rote at Oxford—and if there was one thing you graduated with, it was a finely honed skill of independent, critical thinking.

The tutorials—especially in the arts—were usually based in your affiliated college, but it sounded like Fine Art was unusual in having them based at the department. Did that mean that Sarah and Fiona had been in tutorials together? Had there been friction between them? Competition? Jealousy?

"I wouldn't be surprised if that waitress was involved," said Cassie darkly. "Didn't Mabel say at the party that they saw her making tea for Sarah and putting poison in the cup?"

"They didn't actually see Fiona doing anything," I said quickly. "It was just a theory. And we won't know for sure yet if Sarah was poisoned until the post-mortem results come back." I sighed. "I don't know... The thought that Fiona might poison a fellow student seems so far-fetched..."

"A lot less far-fetched than imagining that Jon had anything to do with it!" said Cassie hotly.

"Yes, well... did he explain his connection with Sarah to the police?"

Cassie nodded. "Yeah, he told them the same story he told us. He hadn't seen Sarah since the time they had their last argument in London, when he told her that she had to back off otherwise he was going to report her for harassment. And she made a terrible scene at his gallery in London. His assistant verified that. She was there and witnessed the whole thing..."

She trailed off as she saw my expression. "What?"

"Nothing," I said quickly.

"You don't believe him, do you?" she said.

I gave a helpless shrug. "Cassie—you have to admit, you've only known Jon a few weeks..." I hesitated, then plunged on. "You don't really know anything about his past, do you? There *might* have been more between him and Sarah than he's letting on."

Cassie's eyes flashed. "I don't believe it! Are you telling me that *you* suspect Jon as well?"

"I—"

"You do! You think he might be involved in this murder!"

"Cassie—"

"No, don't deny it! I know you don't like him, Gemma—you try to hide it but I can tell. You've got a thing against Jon and you're ready to believe the worst of him!"

"Cass, no, you've got it all wrong!" I protested. I took a deep breath. I needed to calm her down and if that meant telling a few fibs... "I do like Jon! I think it's wonderful that you're so happy with him. I didn't mean that he might be involved in the girl's murder—but I just thought... well, you know... he is a very attractive man... it would be weird if he hadn't had any girlfriends before you. And maybe he did go out with Sarah but just didn't want to let you know because... because he loves you so much and thinks that might hurt your feelings."

It was cheesy and lame but Cassie was so blind where Jon was concerned, I didn't think she'd notice. I was right. She looked slightly mollified.

"Well, I think he's telling the truth about her just being a customer," she said stubbornly.

I raised my hands in a gesture of surrender. "You're probably right. Sorry, it was a stupid idea..."

We returned to the main dining room but Cassie

remained in an irritable, distracted mood for the rest of the day. In fact, even though she was back, she was much less of a help than she should have been, and if it hadn't been for the Old Biddies, things would have still been a shambles. As it was, we finally weathered the lunchtime rush and all managed to sit down with a sigh of relief as the tearoom emptied out again by three o'clock.

"Mabel, Glenda, Florence, Ethel... I really don't know how to thank you all," I said to them with a warm smile. "You were *wonderful.*"

"Tosh, dear—we enjoyed it!" said Glenda whilst the others nodded.

I had to admit that they looked very well, their cheeks flushed and their eyes bright from the extra activity. And I was amazed at their stamina—for little old ladies, they sure had incredible energy. They seemed far less tired than me after several hours of running around on their feet!

"Any time you need an extra pair of hands, just let us know," said Ethel.

"Yes, we don't do anything much these days since retiring," said Florence. "It's nice for us to feel useful."

"Well, it's not much of a thank you but all your meals this week in the tearoom are on me—and please help yourself to anything you like from the kitchen!" I said.

"Ooh, in that case, I must sample a bit of that new Velvet Cheesecake your mother's made," said

Florence.

"Yes, and the muffins looked fabulous too," said Glenda.

"Pot of tea?" said Ethel, getting up and heading to the kitchen.

The others followed her, already chattering excitedly about what they were going to eat. I glanced at Cassie—she had been very quiet—and I found her looking down at her phone. She seemed to be busy texting something.

"Cassie? Fancy a cup of tea?"

She looked up, an embarrassed expression on her face. "Er... actually, Gemma, if you don't mind... I think I might push off early today? You've got the Old Biddies here anyway and everything seems to be under control. It's just that... well, you know I'm going to Florence with Jon. We're flying tomorrow morning and he said he's taking me out for an early dinner... and then I'd really like to get home and pack..."

I felt that flash of annoyance again, mingled with hurt, but I hurriedly squashed the feelings. I should have been pleased for Cassie and excited for her. Of course she'd want to prepare for her romantic trip away. And if she'd rather spend time with Jon than with me... well, that was pretty natural too.

I swallowed and plastered a smile on my face. "Sure, no problem. Have a great time in Florence!"

"Thanks—I'll see you on Wednesday," she said, giving me a quick hug. Then she took off her apron, grabbed her things, and hurried out the front door.

I watched her go with troubled eyes, unable to shake the feeling that my friend was gradually slipping away from me.

***

The rest of the afternoon passed fairly quietly. We had our usual resurgence at around four o'clock tea time but nothing that we couldn't handle. In fact, the Old Biddies and I were starting to develop a rhythm, working together as a team, and I found myself enjoying their company more than ever before.

Just before we were closing, a black Jaguar XK pulled up at the curb outside the tearoom and a tall, dark-haired man stepped out of the driver's seat. It was Devlin.

"Gemma... Can I have a word?" He said as he stepped in. He glanced around the room, noting the Old Biddies watching him with bright, beady eyes. "In private," he added.

"How about the courtyard outside?" I asked. "It's a bit chilly but we wouldn't be overheard."

Devlin nodded and followed me out to the little courtyard adjoining the tearoom. This used to be the stable yard adjoining the old inn, and it still retained much of its original period charm, with cobblestones and whitewashed walls, and even an ancient horseshoe still nailed to the wall by the stable doors. There were a few wooden picnic tables in the courtyard and I planned to add big tubs of flowers when summer arrived—it would make a very pretty extension to the main tearoom, somewhere to enjoy the sunshine while having your tea and cakes. Right now, though, it was cold and bare—but it would serve our purposes.

"What do you know about Jon Kelsey?" said Devlin without preamble.

"I don't know much about him," I said cautiously. "Cassie's only been dating him for a few weeks."

"You said at the party that you didn't like him."

"I... No, not really," I admitted. "But that doesn't necessarily mean anything," I added quickly.

"No," Devlin agreed. "But I have a lot of respect for your instincts, Gemma."

I flushed with pleasure. "Is Jon a suspect in the murder?"

"Anyone who had any connection with the girl is considered a suspect until proven innocent," said Devlin. "In this case, it's certainly curious that she had a past connection to Jon Kelsey and died in his gallery."

"And the post-mortem? Have you got the results back yet?"

Devlin regarded me silently for a moment, as if trying to make up his mind, then he said, "It's definitely a suspicious death. There's going to be an inquest. And yes, the belief is that she was poisoned."

Poisoned.

That word hung in the air between us. It still

sounded far too surreal and melodramatic and yet each time it was mentioned, it seemed to become a bit more real. And this wasn't just the lurid speculation of a bunch of little old ladies anymore— this was the cold hard conclusion of a forensic pathologist.

"So was it cyanide? That almond smell—"

"They're not sure yet," said Devlin. "The toxicology analysis takes time."

"I don't understand—why can't you just look for the poison?"

Devlin gave an impatient sigh. "It's not that simple... Real life isn't like what you see on TV. You can't just run one test which will give you the exact name of the poison. You've got to do a bunch of tests and that will only tell you the general type of toxin to start with."

I frowned in confusion. "What do you mean, general type?"

"It's like... if the sample tests positive for heavy metals, it could be copper... or mercury... or lead, but you don't know which one. So you have to test for each of those individually and that can take days, even weeks."

"But... don't you just have fancy machines nowadays which you plug the sample into and it tells you the poison in it?"

Devlin rolled his eyes. "You've really watched too many episodes of CSI. It's not just about the machines—anyone can run machines! It's about the interpretation, the skill in reading the results. Samples might be contaminated, or it might be something that already exists in trace amounts in our bodies... like arsenic. We all have a bit of arsenic in our bodies, so the toxicologist has to take that into account.

"But," Devlin conceded, "knowing what to look for does help to speed things up. I've briefed the toxicologist to look for cyanide. So we should hopefully get the results for that soon. In the meantime, we can assume that Sarah Waltham was deliberately poisoned, possibly by someone at the party."

"So who's the prime suspect? That girl, Fiona?"

Devlin hesitated, then said, "I really shouldn't be sharing details of the investigation with you, Gemma... but as you were so helpful on the last case and I know I can trust you to keep things confidential... Yes, Fiona Stanley is one of the key suspects."

"Did you know that she and Sarah were fellow students? They're both doing Fine Art. The Old Biddies said there was bad blood between them."

"The Old Biddies?"

I laughed. "Sorry, I forgot—it's a nickname Cassie and I have for Mabel and her cronies."

"The Old Nosies might be more accurate," said Devlin dryly. "But as usual, their information is spot-on. Yes, I questioned Fiona last night. I gather that she didn't like Sarah much, but that's hardly surprising. From what I've heard so far, Sarah Waltham was not a particularly likeable character. She was also a total snob and liked to lord it over the other students—particularly those like Fiona, who came from a working-class background." He gave an ironic smile. "You and I know that Oxford's elitist image isn't necessarily true, but girls like Sarah really don't help to dispel that stereotype."

"Did Fiona mention a past fight between her and Sarah?"

"She was very cagey but I got the impression that there had been something—something to do with the Art School. I'm going there tomorrow to speak to their tutor."

I wished I could be a fly on the wall at that interview. But Devlin had already told me far more than he should have. Besides, I hadn't exactly returned the favour in kind. There was still something I was keeping from him. I thought back to that conversation I had overhead in the garden and felt a stab of guilt for not telling Devlin about it. But was it really important? What if it was a red herring? Devlin might have been keeping an eye on Jon, but Cassie's boyfriend wasn't a strong suspect yet. If I told Devlin about that conversation, that could all change.

I thought of the earlier scene with Cassie and how upset she had been and I squirmed. She would never forgive me if I turned the focus of the investigation on Jon, especially because of something as flimsy as an overheard conversation where I thought one of the voices *might* be Jon's...

"Gemma?"

I blinked and looked up.

Devlin was looking at me, his blue eyes sharp. "Is there something you're not telling me?"

I evaded his question. "Um... what about Sarah's boyfriends?"

"I asked Mrs Waltham about that last night, but unfortunately she doesn't seem to know much about Sarah's personal life. They weren't close, I gathered. And as far as I can tell, Sarah didn't have any close female friends she confided in."

I got the feeling that Sarah Waltham was quite a lonely character, in spite of the glamourous image and lifestyle.

"So... it's really down to the toxicologist's report now, huh?" I said. "Do you think you might get the results tonight?"

Devlin smiled. "You haven't changed, Gemma— still as impatient as ever. It's Sunday today and this isn't the only case that the toxicologist is working on. I think I'll be lucky to get the results tomorrow, maybe even the day after." He shrugged. "Don't worry—it might take a bit longer, but we'll get there."

I looked at him speculatively. The Devlin O'Connor I used to know would have been even more impatient than me. His impetuosity had been one of the things I had found most attractive about him at nineteen—it had seemed so different and so *exciting*, compared to the constraints of my inhibited upbringing. Now, Devlin was older and... well, maybe not so much "wiser" as more controlled. It wasn't that he had lost that burning energy and drive, rather that he seemed to have learned to channel it into more effective directions.

"By the way, Gemma..." Devlin said casually. "I was wondering... would you be free tonight?"

"Tonight?" I looked at him in surprise.

"Yes, I thought... if you're free... we could go out for a pint, maybe even a bite to eat..."

He said it in an offhand tone, as if he didn't really care what my answer would be, but I saw the flash of disappointment in his blue eyes when I said regretfully, "I'm afraid I can't. I've... I've already got plans for this evening."

"Some other time then," said Devlin lightly.

He gave me a nod, then turned and left before I could say anything else. I stared at his retreating back. What was that about? Had Devlin O'Connor just tried to ask me out on a date?

CHAPTER EIGHT

"Darling, dinner's slightly delayed this evening. I need to pop across to Mrs Waltham first," my mother said.

I paused on my way out of the kitchen. "Are you going next door?"

"Well, I just thought it would be nice to take her something." She indicated the soup tureen on the kitchen counter. "I made extra leek and potato soup this evening."

"Oh, great idea!" I said, coming over quickly and picking up the tureen. "I'll come with you! Help you carry this across."

My mother looked slightly surprised at my enthusiasm for neighbourly relations, but made no comment as she led the way out of the house. She called to my father to let him know where we were going and we heard a vague reply from his study.

"England have lost to Australia in the Ashes," said my mother in an undertone. "Your father hasn't been taking it very well."

My father was a semi-retired Oxford professor who had two passions in life: his textbooks and cricket. My mother and I ranked a poor third. Whilst my mother had been disappointed that I hadn't done anything "worthwhile" with my Oxford education or married and produced grandchildren, I think my father's biggest disappointment was that I hadn't been of the right gender to qualify for the English cricket team.

Mrs Waltham opened the door on our second ring and ushered us into the house. It was an enormous Victorian townhouse, with large bay windows, ornate panelling, and a sweeping staircase that dominated the front hall.

"Thank you so much, Mrs Rose—this is very kind of you," said Mrs Waltham, taking the tureen of hot soup. "Would you like a drink? Or some tea perhaps?"

"Oh, we weren't thinking of staying—" my mother started to say but I interrupted hurriedly.

"Tea would be lovely, Mrs Waltham."

My mother looked at me in astonishment but, to my relief, she didn't object. I followed Mrs Waltham triumphantly into the drawing room. I wanted to pump her for information about her daughter and this was a rare opportunity to speak to her without arousing suspicion.

I settled on a beautiful antique chaise longue and looked around me. The place reeked of the kind of opulent elegance that only a lot of money could buy, although, once again, Mrs Waltham looked slightly incongruous in the sumptuous setting, despite her designer outfit and perfect salon hair.

She brought in a tea service of Earl Grey accompanied by a plate of delicate madeleines and conversation tiptoed around desultory topics. With the typical British distaste for any mention of "unpleasantness", my mother was determinedly avoiding the subject of Sarah's death. I sat impatiently through a discussion of the weather, the best way to plant an herb garden, and the Moscow City Ballet coming to perform at the Oxford Playhouse soon—then at the first lull in the conversation, I jumped in quickly and said:

"I just wanted to say again how sorry I am about Sarah, Mrs Waltham."

"Gemma!" My mother looked at me reproachfully.

"Thank you," said Mrs Waltham in a subdued voice. "I still can't really believe that she's gone."

"Did Sarah have any boyfriends?" I asked, ignoring my mother spluttering in horror next to me. "I was just wondering if anyone might have informed them..."

"Oh... oh, yes, you're right..." Mrs Waltham said vaguely. "To be honest with you, I don't really know.

As I said, Sarah and I weren't close and she rarely discussed her personal life with me. I *have* seen her go out a few times, of course, with various young men..."

"Anyone in particular recently?"

She frowned. "I don't think so. At least not in Oxford."

I looked at her sharply. "You mean she might have been seeing someone somewhere else?"

She hesitated. "Well... I could be wrong but Sarah was going up to London quite a fair bit a couple of months ago. She never came out and said anything, but I got the impression that there might have been a man involved." Mrs Waltham gave an embarrassed laugh. "I almost wondered if she was having some kind of a fling, maybe with a married man or something... She seemed very secretive about the whole thing, which is not normally like her. She's usually very... well... boastful about her conquests." She gave another awkward laugh, shaking her head. "I'm sorry, that sounds terrible. It seems wrong to speak ill of her now that she's dead..."

"Yes, well, we don't have to speak of her at all," my mother said hurriedly. "I'm sure you must find it most upsetting to talk about Sarah—"

"No, that's all right," said Mrs Waltham with a sad smile. "I need to face reality sometime. Can't keep burying my head in the sand forever." She sighed. "I still haven't even gone through her bedroom. The police have searched it but I haven't been able to bring myself to go in. I suppose I really ought to sort through Sarah's things and give some away to charity... She has—had—so much stuff and it's all still in very good condition." She gave that embarrassed laugh again. "Being an only child, and with David having had her so late in life, I'm afraid Sarah was rather spoiled."

I leaned forwards. "Did Sarah mention anything bothering her lately? Anything she was worried about or someone she might have been having trouble with?"

"The police asked me that," Mrs Waltham said. "No, I don't remember anything. But of course... Sarah didn't confide in me much. She wasn't my daughter, you know. She was my stepdaughter. And we didn't really get on." She gave a rueful smile. "It sounds like such a cliché, but I suppose she resented me for taking her mother's place."

"Was Mr Waltham divorced from his first wife then?" asked my mother, her curiosity overcoming her reticence.

"Oh, no... his first wife passed away. She had cancer—leukaemia—and she died earlier this year."

"Oh, dear! I'm very sorry to hear that," my mother murmured.

I could see my mother calculating in her head and wondering at Mr Waltham's quick re-marriage so soon after his first wife's death. Perhaps the present Mrs Waltham picked up on my mother's thoughts, because she added hastily:

"Sarah's mother had been bedridden and required at-home nursing care for several months leading up to her death. I was her nurse actually... It was very hard on David and... and after her death, I suppose, I was able to give him some comfort in his time of grief. We grew close..."

I suppressed a smile at the expression on my mother's face, which was torn between polite interest and horrified disapproval at the speed with which the first wife had been replaced. I realised now why Mrs Waltham had always seemed slightly out of place in her luxurious surroundings. Perhaps there was a kind of natural arrogance which was difficult to acquire if you weren't born into privilege and had grown up taking it for granted.

I also thought I could understand Sarah's contempt and resentment towards this drab little woman who had replaced her mother so quickly. It might not have been so bad if the second Mrs Waltham had come from upper-class circles but her previous position as the family nurse must have really got up Sarah's snobby nose.

Mrs Waltham was speaking again now, saying sadly, "I did really try with Sarah, but I don't think she ever accepted me as family. In fact, she fought me on everything..." She glanced sideways at us and said, "I know you're too polite to mention it but I'm sure you've heard our arguments. I think half the street used to be able to hear Sarah screaming at me."

My mother shifted uncomfortably. "Oh no, one hardly hears anything through the walls, you know," she lied. "And I'm sure one is apt to forget oneself in the heat of the moment."

"Yes, I think back on some of the things I said and I feel terribly guilty..." Mrs Waltham's bottom lip quivered.

"What beautiful roses!" my mother said brightly, indicating the vase of soft pink blooms on the coffee table in front of us. "Are these from your garden? And you seem to have managed to keep the aphids off. How do you manage that, may I ask? All the pesticides I've tried haven't been very effective."

"I don't find any of the store-bought pesticides that good," said Mrs Waltham, allowing herself to be distracted. "I found a special aphid spray that I can only order online—it follows an old-fashioned formulation—but it works a treat."

"Oh! Isn't online shopping marvellous?" my mother cried, delighted to hop on her new favourite topic. "I have found the most wonderful things that I would never have seen in the stores! And so easy to do from the comfort of your home, without having to traipse about the shops... I've even started ordering our weekly grocery shopping online from the Sainsbury's website. Of course, you still have to pick up a few things from M&S but it's really so convenient."

"Well, I can give you the website that I ordered the aphid spray from, if you like," Mrs Waltham offered.

My mother beamed. "That would be lovely, dear. And I must get your advice on the best time to do the winter prune. My friend, Dorothy Clarke, says she does hers in late autumn but I think..."

I sat back in frustration. I could see that I was not going to get much further questioning Mrs Waltham with my mother here. Then a thought occurred to me. If I couldn't ask, maybe I could see for myself.

I sat up again. "Mrs Waltham—may I use your bathroom?"

"Oh, certainly," she said. "I'm afraid you'll have to go upstairs, though—the downstairs loo isn't flushing very well. I've called the plumber but you know what they're like..."

"Oh yes, absolutely dreadful, these tradesmen," my mother agreed.

I left them exchanging war stories about slipshod builders and lazy electricians, and went out to the front hallway. To be honest, I could have kissed the plumber for his slack attitude. It gave me the perfect pretext to snoop around upstairs. I ran lightly up the sweeping staircase, finding myself in a wide hallway at the top. The bathroom was the first door on my right. I stepped inside, turned on the cold tap, and shut the door again. Then, moving as quietly as I could, I crept down the hallway.

I opened every door I passed, peering into each room. I struck gold with the fourth door—it opened onto a bedroom decorated in frothy pink. Remembering Sarah's bright fuchsia dress at the gallery party, I was willing to bet that this was her bedroom, and this was confirmed by the framed photo of the smiling girl on the dresser. She obviously had a penchant for the rosy hue—almost everything in the room was in various shades of pink. I stepped inside, shut the door quietly behind me, and surveyed the room, my heart sinking in dismay.

Clothes were strewn across every surface, across the bed and chairs and spilling out of the drawers and cupboards. The dressing table by the window was cluttered with expensive perfumes, lotions, creams, and make-up, as well as hair accessories, belts, scarves, jewellery, and other trinkets. A door on the other side of the bed led into an en suite bathroom, which housed an even more bewildering array of shampoos, creams, lotions, and fragrances.

My God, the girl could have opened her own luxury cosmetics store! I paused by the bathroom vanity and picked up the bottle closest to me. It was a luxury French brand I recognised: L'Occagnes— they had a store in central Oxford. This was a shower gel and there was an accompanying body butter in a large jar next to it, along with sixteen other bottles and tubes and jars lined up along the vanity counter. Like most of the other bottles, this one looked like it had been opened and used just once, and then discarded—like someone taking the first bite of an apple and tossing it aside.

I felt a wave of distaste. As someone who had recently had a big income cut, I had a belated appreciation for all the luxury cosmetics I used to take for granted when I had been on a high-flying corporate salary in Sydney. I shook my head, disgusted at Sarah's wastefulness. Much as I might have disagreed with Cassie's rose-tinted praise of Jon, I had to admit that her assessment of Sarah Waltham was spot on. The girl really was a spoilt princess.

I put the bottle down and headed back out into the room, looking around in frustration. There was no time to sift through all the clutter in here properly—I had to try and search for something specific. But what? A mention of a boyfriend? *Any connection to Jon Kelsey*, I thought. Maybe a photo of him with a message scrawled across the back? Or a love letter? Okay, so that was wishful thinking. In this day and age, the photo and note were more likely to be in Sarah's phone, which had been confiscated by the police. Still, you never knew if people might prefer the more old-fashioned, romantic way...

I started to move across to her dressing table when I heard a voice calling from downstairs:

"Gemma? Are you all right?"

Oh bugger!

I ran across the bedroom and opened the door a crack, peering out into the hallway. I could hear the tap still running in the bathroom and nobody else was upstairs. It sounded like Mrs Waltham was standing at the bottom of the staircase. Hopefully she might hear the running water and assume I was still occupied.

But I wasn't taking any more chances. Quietly I stepped out into the hallway and shut Sarah's bedroom door soundlessly behind me, then I tiptoed across the plush carpet to the bathroom. I went in, flushed the toilet, washed my hands and turned off the tap, then made my way sedately back downstairs.

"Gemma! We were wondering what had happened to you..." said my mother, rising as I entered the living room. "We must get back. We mustn't keep Mrs Waltham any longer—and your father will be wondering where his dinner is."

"Have you got yourselves a cat, by the way?" said Mrs Waltham as she followed us out into the foyer. "I think I saw you from our upstairs windows, Gemma—you were in your garden with a little cat on a leash? I never realised that you could walk a cat like a dog."

"You can't, really," I said with a wry smile. "But it's a compromise to allow Muesli some fresh air and exercise while keeping her safe. Yes, I adopted her recently; she used to live in one of the Cotswolds villages, so she's not used to traffic. Besides, she's so naughty, I'm a bit nervous about what she might get up to if she was allowed to come and go as she pleased."

"Perhaps you need to get her spayed—I've heard that helps to prevent wandering?"

"She *is* spayed. But now that you mention it, I

haven't taken her to the vet for a check-up since I got her. That might be a good idea. Muesli's my first cat, you see," I explained. "I've always been more of a dog person, really."

"Me too," said Mrs Waltham. "Our previous housekeeper, Mrs Hicks, has a feisty Jack Russell Terrier and I met him a few times when she had him with her out and about in town. He's such a little character." She brightened. "Actually, now that I think about it, Mrs Hicks mentioned that her vet is very good. It's the one just around the corner from here—North Oxford Veterinary Surgery."

"Thanks, I'll remember that," I said with a smile.

"And if you need anything, Mrs Waltham, we're just next door," said my mother as we bade our farewells. "Don't hesitate to pop by!"

CHAPTER NINE

I didn't have much time before Lincoln Green was arriving to pick me up for the concert at the Sheldonian Theatre. I wolfed my dinner, much to my mother's disapproval, then ran upstairs to change. I had a hurried shower to wash off the grime of the day and then dressed quickly in a pretty sweater and jeans, careful to make sure that I didn't look like I was making too much effort.

When the doorbell rang, I managed to get to the door and hustle Lincoln back out before my mother could intervene. We drove into the centre of Oxford in Lincoln's Land Rover and parked in one of the back lanes by the theatre. Ever the properly-brought-up English gent, Lincoln rushed to open the car door for me and hold my coat up as I shrugged my arms into the sleeves.

"You look very lovely tonight, Gemma," he said, his eyes roving over me appreciatively.

I thanked him coolly and hurriedly changed the subject. I'd been out with Lincoln a couple of times before and I had always been cautious about avoiding personal comments, and making a great effort to emphasise that these were simply friendly meet-ups rather than any kind of romantic "date".

I liked Lincoln but I wasn't sure if I could ever see him as more than a friend. At first, I had been rabidly against him and I had spent that first awkward dinner—set up by his mother and mine—in an agony of embarrassment. But funnily enough, our joint humiliation at the hands of our mothers seemed to have forged a bond between us. And in spite of my reservations, I had to admit that Lincoln was a nice guy. Good-looking too, if you liked the clean-cut, English gentleman type.

No, he would never make my heart race like Devlin did—with Lincoln, there were no enigmatic intentions, no agonising dilemmas, no wild joy or fury—but maybe that was a good thing. I was old enough now to realise that love—real love—wasn't just about passionate kisses in the rain. There was something to be said for openness and stability—all those things that you never cared about when you were young and full of romantic ideals. So, I acknowledged that Lincoln was pleasant company and who knew what might happen?

But in the meantime, I didn't want to get his hopes up. So I kept things as light as possible. Lincoln seemed aware of my attempts and took them in good humour, for which I was grateful. If nothing else, it was nice to have a friend in Oxford—especially as, since Cassie had started going out with Jon, she no longer seemed interested in doing anything that didn't involve him. I missed our girlie get-togethers.

I sighed inwardly. Maybe I was being childish. If my best friend loved Jon Kelsey and he was going to become a part of her life, then I had to find a way to like him too or risk losing my friend altogether. But I had to admit that I was still hoping that things with Jon would fizzle out and Cassie and I could return to the way we had been before.

Of course, things with Jon would come to a grinding halt if he was arrested for murder...

I felt a guilty hope at the treacherous thought and hurriedly pushed it away, bringing my attention back to the present. We had just stepped into the main hall of the Sheldonian Theatre and Lincoln was guiding me to our seats. I sat down and looked around appreciatively as the orchestra began tuning up. I hadn't been back here since I left Oxford eight years ago and I found myself flooded with memories of my student days. I had come to the Sheldonian several times during my university years to listen to concerts and recitals (the cheap student seats in the Upper Gallery!) and although I wasn't a huge classical music fan, I'd enjoyed the experience.

There was something special about sitting there under the magnificent painted ceiling of that 17th-century hall and feeling the music swelling around you. Designed by Sir Christopher Wren, the Sheldonian Theatre was built to resemble an ancient Roman amphitheatre—a complete departure from the Gothic architecture which dominated Oxford at the time—and it included a unique octagonal roof cupola, which provided breath-taking 360-degree panoramic views of Oxford's "dreaming spires". It was the University's official ceremonial hall, used for Matriculation and Graduation ceremonies, and the last time I had been there was the day I graduated. I hadn't been able to get away fast enough then and shake the dust of Oxford off my heels, but time and distance away had given me a new appreciation for my university city.

The soft strains of Vivaldi's "Four Seasons" began to fill the hall and I leaned back as the lights dimmed, allowing myself to be carried away by the music. When the lights finally came back on for the interval, I was surprised to find that my mind was pleasantly blank and dreamy.

Lincoln looked at me with a smile. "Enjoying it?"

I nodded. "Yes. Much more than when I was a student, actually. Maybe classical music is one of those things you appreciate more when you get older." I shifted uncomfortably on the hardwood chair and added with a laugh, "The seats haven't changed though—they're as hard as ever!"

Lincoln chuckled. "I think it's to stop you falling asleep if the music isn't that good." He stood up and stretched stiffly. "Fancy a walk to stretch your legs?"

I nodded and allowed him to escort me out of the theatre and into the courtyard of the adjoining Bodleian Library. We strolled through the shadows cast by the Gothic spires and castellated parapets above us. It was chilly but refreshing to be out in the night air.

Lincoln let out a weary sigh and said, "Uncomfortable as the seats are, it's nice to get off my feet after a day at the hospital."

"Do you do a lot of walking then?"

He nodded ruefully. "Between the ward rounds and the on-calls and the Medical Emergency Response calls, you cover a lot of miles. And today was a particularly busy one. We had an unstable patient in ICU who required a lot of monitoring and I was called back to see him a few times."

"What was wrong with him?"

"He developed septicaemia following routine prostate surgery last week. He deteriorated very quickly and required intensive support but seemed to be recovering, and then unfortunately he took a turn for the worse again today. I don't think his state of mind helped—he'd just received some bad news." He glanced at me, his face sober. "It was the father of the murdered girl."

I stopped walking. "Sarah Waltham's father?"

Lincoln nodded. "He took it very hard. I gather

that she was his only child. I was there when his wife came to tell him and I don't think he even took it in at first—kept insisting that there must have been some mistake, that he had only seen Sarah yesterday—"

"*Yesterday?* When did he see her?"

"She came in to visit him yesterday afternoon."

"Did you meet her?"

"Yes, I did, actually," said Lincoln. "I happened to be doing my rounds and there was a real fracas just as I arrived at Waltham's bedside. Sarah was having a huge row with one of the nurses. I almost thought of calling security, but thankfully another visitor arrived at that moment and helped to diffuse the situation. An old family friend, I think. She'd brought some shortbread that she'd baked—I think they used to be Sarah's favourite or something—anyway, she offered some to Sarah, which seemed to distract her, and things calmed down after that."

I was reflecting that Sarah seemed to cause strife wherever she went. "What did you think of her? Sarah Waltham, I mean," I asked Lincoln.

"She seemed to be... uh... a difficult character," he said.

I smiled to myself. Trust Lincoln to be too polite to state the bald truth.

"I don't suppose you'd have any idea of what could have poisoned Sarah?" I looked hopefully at Lincoln. "You know, with your medical knowledge and all that."

He shook his head. "Toxicology is a highly specialised field. I mean, I know how to administer the antidotes for the more common poisons, of course, and to recognise the symptoms, but unless the poison used is pharmacologically based, I wouldn't necessarily have specialist knowledge about it."

"Did Mr Waltham have a heart issue? I've heard that some of those heart drugs are supposed to be really toxic, aren't they?"

Lincoln smiled. "You're thinking of digitalis. Yes, that is a pretty lethal substance but David Waltham wasn't on any heart medication."

I fell silent as we started walking again. It was almost the end of the interval and time to return to the hall. We had circled around the front façade of the Sheldonian Theatre, coming out onto Broad Street. I could hear the faint strains of the orchestra tuning up again. We turned and hurried towards the nearest door and arrived there just as a group of young men were also entering. They were talking and laughing animatedly, clapping each other on the back, and as one of them turned to glance back, I realised with a shock that it was Devlin. I almost didn't recognise him in jeans and a leather jacket, looking dark and dangerous and nothing like his usual debonair detective persona.

The smile faded from his face as he saw me with Lincoln. He gave a curt nod.

"Gemma."

"Uh... hi, Devlin."

His cool blue gaze flicked to Lincoln and I said hurriedly:

"Um... this is Lincoln... Lincoln Green. He's... he's a friend of the family."

I flushed, wondering if I sounded like I was trying to justify my being with Lincoln. It was stupid. Was I worried that Devlin would think that we were on a romantic date? That I had turned down his invitation to go out with Lincoln? And so what if he did?

The two men shook hands, eyeing each other warily.

"Are you a friend of Gemma's?" asked Lincoln.

A ghost of a smile flickered over Devlin's mouth. "Yeah, we were at Oxford together. I'm a detective with Oxfordshire CID." He narrowed his eyes. "Lincoln Green... not *Dr* Lincoln Green?"

"The same."

"I understand that Sarah Waltham's father is your patient?"

Lincoln's manner became very formal. "He is under my care, yes."

"I'm investigating Sarah Waltham's death. I was planning to come to speak to you tomorrow. I believe that Sarah came to the hospital on the day she died?"

"Yes, Gemma and I were just talking about that," said Lincoln. "She was causing a bit of trouble on the ward."

Devlin's gaze sharpened. "What kind of trouble?"

"Just some disagreement with the nurses."

Devlin seemed about to say something else but the lights began dimming in the hall and I realised that we were the last people still standing.

"I'll speak to you tomorrow, Dr Green," said Devlin. He inclined his head at me, his voice cool. "Good night, Gemma."

I followed Lincoln silently back to our seats and sat down in the dark, but this time I found myself unable to concentrate on the music. Instead, my thoughts kept drifting to the man sitting on the other side of the lower gallery, and I couldn't help wondering if he was thinking of me too.

CHAPTER TEN

You know how they say you should step out of your comfort zone sometimes? Well, I didn't just step—I leapt without looking first. Deciding to run a tearoom had been the first impulsive thing I did in my life and, after pouring all my savings into the place, I was desperate for it to succeed. So desperate that, when I first opened it, I spent every waking moment (and some of my sleeping ones too) working like a maniac.

After a while, I began to realise that I needed to give myself at least a day off a week otherwise I would be facing burn-out. So, reluctantly, I decided that I would close the tearoom on Mondays, which was normally the quietest day of the week anyway. As it was, I seemed to find myself spending most of my

Mondays catching up on admin and emails and that's what I was doing the next morning when the doorbell rang.

I looked up, half-expecting to hear my mother's dulcet tones at the door, then I remembered that she and my father had both gone out to the dentist for their check-ups this morning. I heaved myself off my bed, displacing Muesli, who had been curled up happily across my ankles. She gave an indignant "*Meorrw!*", then jumped off the bed and trotted after me as I went downstairs. A middle-aged man in a courier's uniform stood on the threshold when I opened the door.

"Parcel for Gemma Rose?"

"Yeah, that's me," I said, looking in puzzlement at the soft brown package he handed to me. It bore the logo of a nation-wide store which sold various household items. I didn't remember ordering anything from them.

"Sign here..." He handed me a clipboard with a form on it.

"Wait... I think there's been a mistake. I didn't order anything from—"

"You Gemma Rose?"

"Yes, I am," I said. "But—"

"Well, looks like it's yours then, luv. It's your name on the form right here. Online order."

Online? Uh-oh... I suddenly remembered my mother going on about buying something for me online... what was it she had said? I wished I had been paying more attention.

"What's in the package?" I asked warily.

The man tilted his head to read the description on the form. "Says here they're memory foam jester slippers."

"Jester slippers?" I turned the package over. Sure enough, on the underside was a little product information sheet taped to the package. And a picture of a pair of lurid red-and-green jester slippers, complete with a bell at the end of each curled toe. They were hideous.

"I never ordered these!" I exclaimed.

The man looked at me doubtfully. "Well, you can ring Customer Service and take it up with them—get the slippers changed for something else, if you like. Number's there..." He nodded at the information sheet.

"Can't I just get a refund?" I wailed.

The man brightened. "Oh. We've got a special offer at the moment. 'Try Before You Buy'—so yeah, you could get a refund. But it ends today, luv, so there won't be time for you to post it back. You'll have to take the slippers in person to the store in town and get a refund there."

I sighed. "Okay." I signed his form and shut the door behind him, looking down at the package again. What on earth had my mother been thinking?

I hadn't made it halfway up the stairs when the doorbell rang again. Turning, I went back down the stairs and found myself once again facing a courier when I opened the door.

"Delivery for Gemma Rose," he said, holding up a long, slim box.

Oh God. What had my mother ordered me now?

This time I didn't even bother to argue but just signed the form in weary resignation. After he'd gone, I looked at the box nervously. It looked innocent enough, with no picture of ugly weird slippers or other memory foam products on the outside. When I opened it, it revealed six piles of fabric, neatly folded. They were a nice, normal colour—bright, sunny yellow—and when I unfolded one, I saw that it was a frilly apron.

I breathed a small sigh of relief. *Okay, this one might not be so bad. These must be for the tearoom.* I remembered that my mother had been talking about ordering a batch of aprons so that Cassie and I could look coordinated as we served the customers. At the moment, we were using some mismatched options I'd picked up for cheap at a local market. These were in a nice quality cotton, with a pretty yellow gingham check pattern.

I turned them over, then stared in horror at the front. In bright red letters across the apron were the words: "Chefs don't cook—that's what wives are for" together with a print of a 1950's housewife smiling cheerily as she bent over a hot stove. And behind her stood a grinning man raising his hand to smack her bottom.

Oh my God... what was my mother thinking? I

could get arrested wearing these in the tearoom!

I sighed and decided I'd deal with them—together with the jester slippers—later. I had barely sat down in front of my laptop again when the doorbell rang once more. I gritted my teeth. I might as well have just stood by the door at this rate!

"Yes?" I snapped as I opened the door, only to pause in surprise when I saw Cassie and Jon on the doorstep.

"Cassie! I thought you guys would have already left by now!"

"We're on our way to the airport," said Cassie. "But I was wondering if I could borrow your mack? Mine's at the dry-cleaner's and the forecast is for rain in Florence."

"Oh, sure—come in." I showed them into the living room. "I'll just run upstairs and get it."

Before I could move, however, we were surprised by a strange growling sound. I turned to see that Muesli had puffed up to three times her normal size, her fur standing on end and her eyes narrowed to slits as she stared at us.

"Muesli! What's the matter with you?" I looked at her in surprise.

She growled again and I realised that her gaze was directed at Jon Kelsey. She hissed suddenly and spat at him.

"What's wrong with her?" said Cassie in bewilderment.

"Oh, she just needs a bit of correct handling," said

Jon loftily, bending down and reaching his hand out. "Here, kitty-kitty-kitty..."

Muesli spat again and raked a claw at him. He yelped and jumped back.

"My God, she's vicious!" he said.

I hid a smile. "She's not. I've never seen her like this before. She's normally the sweetest, friendliest little cat..." For Cassie's sake, I added, "Maybe she just doesn't like the cologne you're wearing or something. They say cats are really sensitive to fragrances..."

I didn't know why I was making excuses for Muesli's behaviour. After all, I didn't like Jon myself. But maybe that was it. I felt slightly guilty, like maybe it was my own hostility towards Jon that Muesli had picked up on. Didn't they say that animals could pick up on your emotions?

They also said that animals had a sixth sense and could tell good from evil...

I pushed the thought away. *Don't be stupid.* I was turning into one of those crazy cat ladies who went around insisting that their animals talked to them or something.

Leaving Cassie still trying to coax Muesli over, I went upstairs to grab my Mackintosh. I returned to the living room to find Jon standing nervously against the wall whilst Muesli sat and stared at him with unblinking eyes.

"Guess I've finally met a female I can't charm," Jon said with an attempt at a cocky smile.

Cassie laughed and I dredged up a smile from somewhere. I was glad to shut the door behind them. Going to the window, I stood and watched them get into Jon's BMW convertible and drive away. Muesli joined me at the window, her fur now smoothed back to its usual sleek appearance. I glanced down at her. Crazy cat lady or not, I wished she could talk and tell me why she didn't like Jon Kelsey...

This time I managed to answer three emails before I was interrupted again. It was my mother on the phone.

"Darling, I was just ringing to see if they'd delivered my orders," she said brightly. "The website promised delivery first thing Monday morning."

"Mother, why on earth did you order me jester slippers?"

"Aren't they gorgeous, darling? I told you about them the other day. They're made with memory foam, you know. Helen Green tells me that memory foam is all the rage right now. They're supposed to be fantastic for sore feet and swollen ankles, bunions, corns, hammer toes—"

I looked down at my own feet in alarm. They looked reassuringly normal. "But Mother, I don't have hammer toes or bunions or any of those things—"

"All in good time, dear," my mother reassured me. "Besides, I thought—with you being on your feet in the tearoom all day—these would be wonderful for you to wear at home. And the pink ones looked so dull, so I thought—why not the jester ones! And they would match the harlequin dressing gown I bought for you."

"What harlequin dressing gown?" I asked suspiciously.

"Oh, hasn't it arrived yet? I must have forgotten to click on Express Delivery. Dear me, I thought I'd—"

"Mother, I *really* don't want any jester slippers."

"Oh, nonsense, darling, everybody wants a pair of jester slippers."

I ground my teeth, then took a deep breath. "Mother, it was really sweet of you, but honestly, I'm never going to wear them. Do you mind if I take them back for a refund?"

"Oh, very well, dear. But maybe you can swap them for another style instead? They had another in a moccasin style with little tassels in front which looked delightful too."

"Uh… okay, I'll have a look through their range," I said, with no intention of doing anything of the sort.

I hung up, then stood indecisively for a moment. The delivery man had said that the promotion ended today. If I wanted any chance of getting a refund for these slippers, I'd better head into town now.

I coaxed Muesli back into my bedroom with a piece of duck jerky and left her making herself comfortable on my bed as I shut the door firmly and headed out to central Oxford. Before long, I was standing at the Customer Service counter in the store and was surprised to find a familiar face behind the counter. Fiona Stanley—the girl who had been the waitress behind the bar at Cassie's party.

Actually, maybe I shouldn't have been surprised. After all, the city centre was pretty small and it wasn't uncommon to bump into people you knew when out and about in the shops. Six degrees of separation and all that. And I remembered the Old Biddies mentioning that Fiona had to work a few part-time jobs to supplement her student budget; hardly surprising that she would be in one of the biggest stores on the High Street.

She showed no sign of recognition as she took my package and processed the refund.

I hesitated, then said casually, "I hope the police didn't keep you too late on Saturday night."

She looked up in alarm, meeting my eyes properly for the first time.

"I was at the party," I explained. "So horrible what happened to that girl, wasn't it?"

Fiona gave a tight nod.

I leaned across the counter and continued in a chatty tone, "And I heard that you actually knew her? The girl who died? You're both reading Fine Art, aren't you?"

Fiona paled. "Yes," she mumbled. "But I didn't really know her that well..."

"I heard that they think she was poisoned!" I opened my eyes very wide. "It sounds like something out of a novel, doesn't it?"

She didn't reply, but I persisted. "What was she

like? Was she the type to have enemies?"

"What's it to you?" said Fiona suddenly, scowling. "I told you, I didn't know her that well, all right?" She looked beyond my shoulder to the next person in the line. "Next please!"

I walked thoughtfully away from the counter. It was obvious that Fiona wasn't going to talk to me. But there were other ways to get information...

CHAPTER ELEVEN

I stepped out onto the street and paused for a moment, then began walking purposefully towards "The High", one of the main thoroughfares of Oxford. Once described as "one of the world's most beautiful streets", High Street formed a gentle curve from Carfax in the centre to Magdalen Bridge at the eastern edge of the city, and had been the subject of countless prints, photographs, and paintings. Looking down its length, it was still possible to imagine the elegant world of 18th-century England. It was home to many of the iconic landmark buildings of the University: All Souls College, The Queen's College, the University Church of St Mary the Virgin with its famous spires, the Examination Schools... and the Art School.

I stopped outside the quiet, unassuming exterior of the Art School—a modest building compared to many of the other university departments but it seemed appropriate for the intimate, personal nature of the Fine Arts course. I had wondered if I might have trouble getting in but, to my surprise, the front doors were wide open and a stream of people were passing in and out. A sign by the door explained why: it was an Open Day.

I smiled. I remembered coming to an Open Day in my teens. And there were information visits at my school too. You wouldn't think a university as famous as Oxford would need to market themselves but actually, they had a different problem: the stigma of being too exclusive and elitist. It wasn't true anymore but lots of people still believed that you had to be a member of the English aristocracy or have attended one of the snooty public schools to get accepted (I always thought calling posh private schools "public school" was one of the prime examples of the British talent for understatement). Oh, you still had to work bloody hard to get in and Oxford only took the best, but it was based on your own efforts now and not who your great-great-grandparents were.

Anyway, right now, I was grateful for the University's marketing efforts because it meant an easy, unobtrusive way for me to get in the Art School. Luckily, I'd dressed in an old pair of jeans and a faded jumper this morning. With my face scrubbed free of make-up and my hair in a ponytail, I just might pass for a student, as long as nobody looked too closely.

I found a large crowd just inside the entrance and I attached myself to the rear of the group, following them as they were led up the stairs by a guide who was giving a well-rehearsed spiel about the Fine Art department.

"...in addition, there is a world-class library housing over five thousand volumes on the subject of fine art, art history and theory, and human anatomy. Each student is allocated a primary tutor with whom they meet regularly throughout the term, and they are initially encouraged to work across all media before developing their own focus. Alongside the student's individual studio work, they attend workshops designed to introduce a range of techniques, practical classes in drawing, and lectures and tutorials in art history..."

We'd arrived at one of the upper levels and I slipped quietly away into a large airy room that was obviously being used as a communal studio space. There were a few students working at various sculptures and easels around the room and I paused uncertainly. Now that I was here, I wasn't quite sure how to proceed. I guess I had had a hazy idea of speaking to someone about Sarah—or Fiona—and finding out more about the two girls that way... but who should I speak to? The logical choice would have been one of the tutors who had supervised the girls, but I wasn't CID; I couldn't just walk into one of the department offices, flash a badge, and start asking probing questions...

I looked around the studio again and my eye was drawn to a large canvas on an easel in the far corner. No one was working at it. I made my way over and stood looking at the painting speculatively. Even before I saw the flamboyant signature in the bottom right-hand corner, I guessed that it was Sarah Waltham's work. I remembered seeing a painting in a similar style above the fireplace in the Walthams' living room. Whatever I might have thought of her personality, I had to grudgingly admit that Sarah had talent. The strokes were bold and fresh, the colours vivid.

I looked around her workspace. It mirrored the clutter in her bedroom—a jumble of paintbrushes and paints, half-drunk mugs of tea, charcoal pencils, turpentine, open packets of crisps scattered around the easel, rough sketches loosely stacked in piles, oil rags smeared with paint... It was a miracle she managed to produce any work in this mess.

There was a pretty Asian girl hunched over a clay sculpture at the workspace next to Sarah's. I drifted over and, when she looked up at my approach, I gave her my warmest smile and said, "That's such a beautiful piece! Were you inspired by anything in particular?"

She looked surprised but obviously flattered by my interest. "This is just from the idea in my head," she said with a shy smile, in a slightly accented voice.

"Wow, you must have a fantastic imagination!"

She flushed with pleasure. I felt slightly guilty for leading this sweet girl on, but hey, needs must. Like all artists, she loved talking about her work. I nodded and made enthusiastic noises as she began telling me about her childhood in Japan, her favourite artists, her big influences and sources of inspiration.

When I felt that I had lulled her into a false sense of security, I said casually, "By the way, I heard that there was a terrible tragedy recently—one of the art students got killed?"

She gave me a wary look. "Yes," she said.

"Did you know the girl well?"

"No, I don't know well... Why do you ask?"

"Er..." I cast my mind around for a reason. Then I remembered the Open Day and jumped on the first thing that came to mind. "Well, I'm considering applying here to study and I was wondering if it was really 'safe', you know. My mother's a terrible worrier and she saw the news about the girl who died and now she doesn't want me to apply here—"

"Oh no, no," the girl rushed to reassure me. "It is very safe! The school is good. That girl—she was not killed here. She was at a party."

"But wasn't it anything to do with her work? The papers said that the party was in an art gallery so I wondered..."

The girl nodded solemnly. "Yes, the party is inside an art gallery in Oxford. But it is not a University art gallery, not for students. It is private gallery—for tourists only."

I leaned forwards and lowered my voice conspiratorially. "Is it true that she was murdered? I heard something about poison."

The girl nodded, wide-eyed. "I hear the same thing also," she said in hushed tones.

I gave a mock shudder. "How scary! Who would do a thing like that? Did she have any enemies?"

The girl gave an uncomfortable shrug. "I don't know her very well. Only we say hello sometimes." She hesitated, as if debating whether to say it, then she added in a rush, "Sometimes, Sarah is not very nice. She makes other people angry."

I'll bet, I thought dryly. Aloud, I said, "I think I heard that she had a particular problem with one of the other students here?"

"Oh, you mean Fiona." The Japanese girl dropped her gaze. "Yes, she and Sarah—they don't like each other. They have fight sometimes. Big fight."

"*You* didn't have trouble with Sarah?" I said, raising an eyebrow.

She smiled shyly. "I just keep quiet and do my own work. Maybe also, it is because I do the sculpture—this is not the same kind of art as Sarah. She didn't like others to do the same as her. She liked to be special. I think that is why she did not like Fiona—they are both painting the same style and they are always comparing and comparing..."

"You mean they were always competing with each

other?"

"Yes!" said the girl. "Yes, it is exactly like that. They each want to be the better one—but Sarah, especially. And then there was the terrible thing which happened for the Art Scholar's Award."

"The Art Scholar's Award?"

The girl nodded. "It is a very special award, very—how you say—prestigious? They only give it to one person each year—for the best piece of student work. And Fiona—she wants very much to win. She told me the award money is very important to her. Her family is not rich and she has to work many jobs when she is studying and this award will make her life so much easier. But of course, Sarah wants to win also."

"Surely Sarah didn't need the money?" I said.

"No, she doesn't," said the Japanese girl, a dark expression coming over her pretty face. "She just likes to win. Always she wants to win. So she can be better than other people. But she is angry because she can see that actually Fiona's painting is much better. We can all see that. We all know that Fiona is going to win."

I had an inkling of what was coming. "What did Sarah do?"

"She said she did nothing! But we all know it is not true. We know that it must be her who destroyed Fiona's painting."

"Destroyed?"

The Japanese girl nodded. "The night before they do the judging, somebody came to the Art School and cut Fiona's painting. With a knife. On the canvas everywhere. Oh, it is terrible when I see it the next morning! Fiona was crying! Her beautiful painting and it is completely spoiled! The canvas is cut up like many ribbons."

I had been expecting something like this but it was still shocking to hear. "That's awful! Did they find out who did it?"

"No. Of course, we all know it was Sarah but we cannot say. And then when the judge announced the winner and Sarah got the award, she smiled in a funny way and said something rude to Fiona."

"What did she say?"

"I don't know. I did not hear. But Fiona was very angry—like crazy angry. She started to do lots of shouting and she tried to hit Sarah... many people have to hold her to stop her. After that, the tutors asked me if I would change with Fiona. She used to have this position." She indicated the space around her. "But they say it is better for her to work far away from Sarah."

I digested this information. From the sound of things, Fiona had good reason to hate Sarah Waltham... but good enough to want to murder her? Surely people didn't kill someone simply because of a lost award?

But the award wasn't a small thing to Fiona Stanley. Unlike Sarah, who simply wanted it for the accolade and feeling of superiority, the money would have made a big difference to someone in Fiona's situation. Besides, I could just imagine the bitter resentment the latter had felt at the sheer unfairness of Sarah getting away with sabotage.

"But don't worry," said the Japanese girl warmly. "It is not something that happens often. All the other students are very friendly and nobody fights. It is only Sarah and now she is..." She trailed off suddenly, flushing.

"When was the last time you saw Sarah?" I asked gently.

The other girl frowned. "I think it was Saturday. I was here working and she came and worked also."

"Was this in the morning?"

"No, in the afternoon. Just after lunch. Actually, I think I see her have lunch here?" She nodded across at the cluttered mess around Sarah's easel.

"Did she look okay? I mean, was she the same as normal?"

The girl's eyes widened. "Do you mean she had poison already?"

"No, no," I said hastily, not wanting to start any more rumours. "I just wondered if maybe... well, if she was worried about something..."

The Japanese girl shook her head. "No, she looked the same." She was eyeing me curiously now and I realised that my pointed questions were beginning to sound very strange for someone who was just concerned about student safety at the Art School!

"Well, I'd better not disturb you any longer," I said. "Thank you for talking to me. I feel much better now that I know the whole story. I shall tell my mother that the school is really safe."

"Yes." The girl beamed at me. "Yes, it is a great place. Coming to Oxford is the best experience of my whole life!"

"I hope I'll see your work in a gallery someday," I said sincerely. "Good luck with the rest of your course."

I made my way back across the studio, heading for the main staircase that would lead back down to the lower floors. But as I got there, I bumped into someone just coming up. My heart skipped a beat as I realised that it was Devlin.

CHAPTER TWELVE

"Gemma? What are you doing here?" Devlin's brows drew together in a frown.

"I... um..." For a moment, I thought of lying, then I caught the steely glint in Devlin's blue eyes and I knew that he wouldn't take anything but the truth for an answer.

"I was doing a bit of investigating," I confessed. "I... I was curious about Sarah Waltham and I'm not working today and I was in town so I thought—"

"You thought you'd come in here under false pretences and trick your way to getting some information?"

"I didn't trick anyone!" I said hotly. Then I squirmed. "Okay, so maybe a little. But you're the one who used to say that the ends justify the means."

He regarded me silently for a moment. "Yes, I did used to say that. And if I remember rightly, you used to disagree vehemently with me."

"Yes, well... Maybe I've changed my mind after eight years."

"Don't tell me you're actually admitting that I might have been right after all?" A hint of a smile showed at the corners of his lips.

"I'm not admitting anything. I'm just saying that your approach might have some merit sometimes. Anyway, why are we wasting time debating this? I can see that you're busy—I'll let you get on..." I tried to brush past him and continue down the staircase.

"Not so fast." Devlin reached out and caught my wrist.

The touch of his fingers on my skin sent a jolt of awareness through me and I sucked a breath in. Had he felt it too? I hovered on the step, staring up into his eyes, then I jerked my wrist out of his grasp and moved one step farther down the staircase, putting more distance between us. This time, Devlin didn't try to restrain me.

"Look, Gemma..." He sighed and ran a hand through his hair, causing a dark lock to fall rakishly over his eyes.

It reminded me of the way he used to wear his hair during our student days and how often I had reached up and brushed that wayward lock back across his forehead. I clenched my hands into fists at my side and forced my eyes away.

"I know it's natural to be curious but you have to leave well alone," said Devlin. "This is a murder investigation. I can't have you going around asking questions and possibly interfering with witnesses."

"How would I be interfering with them?" I said indignantly.

"You could be asking leading questions. And then when the police do come round to speak to them, they might have ideas put into their heads by you."

"I was simply asking a few innocent questions about Sarah and Fiona. I didn't mention anything that the public couldn't have known through the evening news or other official channels. I was very careful about that."

Devlin made a noise of exasperation. "Since when have you become so interested in being an amateur sleuth? I mean, it's bad enough with Mabel Cooke and her cronies running around thinking they're Miss Marple clones, without you joining the game as well! Why can't you just leave it to the professionals? You know you're never going to have the police's resources and authority so you're never going to have the advantage needed to crack the mystery."

"I didn't do too badly with the last case," I pointed out. "In case you'd forgotten, *I* was the one who made most of the connections and exposed the fake alibis and the real identity of the killer."

Devlin hesitated, then inclined his head, conceding my point. "Fine. You're right, you were very helpful last time and I have to credit you with solving most of the mystery—but a lot of that might have been beginner's luck. It doesn't mean that you're suddenly Sherlock Holmes!"

I gave him a scornful look. "You keep going on about the advantages of official clout and resources but there's something to be said for simple intuition and deduction. I know the University—I've been a part of it—and I have an insider's advantage. And people talk to me."

"People?" Devlin glanced at the studios around us, then back at me. "What have they been saying?"

I raised my chin. "Why should I tell you since you've got so much 'official clout' that you can find out for yourself anyway?"

He considered me for a moment, then sighed and ran his hand through his hair again. "Fine. Tell me what you found out and I won't charge you for obstructing the investigation."

"Oh no," I said, folding my arms. "I'm perfectly happy to share information with you, but only as an exchange. I'll show you mine if you show me yours." I stopped and blushed as I realised how those words sounded.

Devlin quirked an eyebrow, looking amused. "That sounds like an exchange I could enjoy..."

I scowled. "You knew what I meant."

He laughed suddenly, a deep, rich sound. "I see you're as stubborn as ever too..." He blew the breath out between his teeth. "Okay, deal. But let's get out of here. Fancy some lunch?"

I glanced at my watch and saw that it was nearly lunchtime. I also realised that my stomach was growling faintly.

"All right." I preceded him down the stairs.

We stepped back out onto High Street. It was a chilly winter's day, with the weak sunshine trying its best to push through a bank of grey clouds. A sharp wind whipped down the length of High Street. I shivered and pulled the collar of my duffel coat up around my neck. Devlin had no coat, though the fine cashmere wool of his charcoal grey suit probably gave him ample protection. The wind ruffled his dark hair and he narrowed his eyes slightly against the onslaught but he didn't seem bothered by the cold. His Celtic roots probably gave him a hardier disposition, I thought wryly.

"How about the Turf Tavern?" said Devlin, gesturing across the street.

I nodded and followed him across High Street and into Radcliffe Square, past the Radcliffe Camera and other buildings of the Bodleian library, past Hertford College and its iconic "Bridge of Sighs", and then down a narrow, winding alley called St Helen's Passage (although I liked the original name of "Hell's Passage" better) which ended in a tiny courtyard in the very heart of the University.

And here was the hidden gem known as the Turf Tavern. Usually only known by students and locals— and a few lucky tourists who had stumbled upon the secret—this historic pub was nestled inside a low-beamed 13th-century building and tucked away in the shadow of the old city walls. (Rumour had it that the Turf was built just outside the old city walls because of the illegal activities that the original patrons had engaged in.)

We ducked through the narrow doorway into the interior of the pub, with Devlin having to stoop beneath the low-slung roof. Inside, it was full of rustic atmosphere—exposed stone walls and timber framing, mullioned windows and dark wood furniture. An amazing range of beers and other drinks were being served from behind a bar the size of a phone booth. I found an empty table by the windows while Devlin went to get our drinks and food. It was too cold to sit outside today, even though the tourists were braving the courtyard for the sake of the picturesque beer garden setting.

I watched them idly through the window. It was funny to see them eagerly photographing the place. When I had been here as a student, I had taken the Turf for granted. It was just one of the many pubs that I visited with my friends. Now, having spent the past eight years living in a "young" country like Australia with its lack of historic architecture, I had a fresh appreciation for the quaint character and "olde world charm" of these aspects of England.

"Here," said Devlin, setting a steaming mug down in front of me. "I thought you'd fancy a hot drink. And the pub grub is coming."

I cupped my hands gratefully around the mug, feeling the heat seep into my cold fingers. Raising it to my lips, I inhaled the rich scent of cinnamon, citrus, and spices.

"It's mulled wine!" I said in surprised delight.

Devlin took a seat opposite me, grinning. "Yeah, I remembered you used to like the stuff. You never drank anything alcoholic unless it was sickly sweet."

I was touched that he had remembered. I took a sip of the sweet, spicy wine and felt it glide down my throat, warming me to my core.

"Did you enjoy the concert last night?" said Devlin suddenly.

"Yes, thank you," I said primly.

"So Lincoln is a family friend...?" he said it casually but I could see the interest in his eyes.

"Yes, Lincoln's mother, Helen, is my mother's closest friend from childhood. We saw each other a fair bit as children growing up. Lincoln went off to Imperial College in London and did most of his training there. He's just come back to Oxford and my mother thought it would be nice for us to get together..."

"Still doing everything your mother says, like a good little girl?"

I flushed angrily at his tone. "As it so happens, I like Lincoln. He's a nice guy. I wouldn't have accepted his invitation otherwise, no matter how hard my mother had pushed."

"Nice to know that you've grown a bit of backbone in eight years," said Devlin.

I took a deep breath, determined not to let him rile me. I knew that he had a lot to be bitter about. Eight years ago, Devlin had bared his heart and soul to me and asked me to marry him. I had been young and naive and unsure of myself—and I had caved in to pressure from friends and family, especially from my mother, who had viewed Devlin and his working-class background with horrified disapproval.

So I had said "No"—and Devlin had never forgiven me.

Not so much because I had rejected him, but because I hadn't had faith in my own feelings. I think Devlin would have hated me less if I had said no because I genuinely hadn't loved him, but as it was, he was furious with me for letting others decide my destiny and sway my decisions.

I could still remember that terrible day—that look of contempt and betrayal he had shot me before turning his heel and walking away. I had wanted to run after him, to ask him to come back, to give me another chance... but instead, I had stood there, numbly watching him walk out of my life. I had been too weak, too eager to please others, too scared to trust my own feelings. One of the reasons I had jumped at the offer of the graduate training programme in Sydney was to get away from the painful memories here in Oxford.

And now, eight years later, I was back. Devlin was back too. Where did we go from here?

I gave myself an internal shake. Nowhere. I had thought that maybe–especially after that last murder case—there might be a chance for us to try again.

Devlin had seemed to hint that he still had feelings for me and I had to admit, deep down, that I still had feelings for him too. But in the weeks since, he hadn't followed up on that hint, hadn't called me once.

Okay, okay, I know this is the 21st century and I'm a liberated modern woman. Why did I have to wait for the man to call me first? Except that I did. I wanted *him* to make the first move. I suppose it was pride.

And maybe he felt the same way. I could hardly blame him—after what he had gone through eight years ago, it wasn't surprising that Devlin didn't want to be the first one to bare his feelings again.

So that brought us back to where we always seemed to end up: stalemate.

Across the table, Devlin cleared his throat. "I'm sorry, Gemma—that was uncalled for," he said quietly. "I don't know what got into me. You have a perfect right to listen to who you like and do what you like with your life. It's none of my business."

I looked up into those intense blue eyes and wanted to tell him what was in my heart, but something kept me tongue-tied. Instead, I said lightly, "Never mind. It's not important. We should focus on the murder."

The shutters came down over Devlin's eyes and his expression became remote, professional—the cool, resolute detective taking over.

"Why don't you tell me what you've got first," he said.

CHAPTER THIRTEEN

I told Devlin about my visit to the Walthams'
house and my snooping around Sarah's bedroom.
Our food arrived just as I was finishing and my
mouth watered at the aromas arising from the plates
set down in front of us. Devlin had ordered "bangers
and mash" for himself—British pork sausage with
champ mash, beer-and-mustard gravy, and sweet
potato crisps—and a traditional fish and chips for
me: hand-battered cod with minted mushy peas,
chunky tartare sauce, thick-cut chips, and apple
cider vinegar.

We fell into a companionable silence—the case
temporarily forgotten—as we munched the food. For
a moment, it felt almost like the old student days
when we had shared many a plate together at the

various pubs around Oxford.

At last, I leaned back with a contented sigh. "Oh my God, I can't eat another bite."

"What—no pudding?" said Devlin with a smile.

"Oh... well, there's always space for pudding," I said with a chuckle.

I glanced at the Specials board near the bar counter. There seemed to be a choice of pear tart with salted caramel and hazel nuts, sticky toffee pudding with clotted cream ice-cream, or dipping doughnuts with Bramley apple sauce—as well as the eternal favourite: triple chocolate brownie. They all sounded delicious and I didn't know which one to choose.

In the end, I went for the sticky toffee pudding—a traditional British dessert that I hadn't had in a long time. It came warm, with a gorgeous treacle sauce drizzled on top, and the cake rich and moist. It was the ultimate comfort food on a cold winter's day, and when I had licked the last bit of toffee sauce from my spoon, I felt like I could take on the whole world.

Devlin watched me in amusement. "Anyone would think that you'd never had dessert in your life before."

"Not like this," I said, giving the spoon another lick. "People might complain about British food but our desserts are incomparable!"

He laughed as he took a sip of his coffee, then his face sobered as he returned to the subject of the case. As far as Jon Kelsey was concerned, he told me, the story seemed to pan out. Devlin's sergeant had done some checking around and it seemed that what Jon had said was true: Sarah had been a frequent visitor at his London gallery and there had been reports of some "nasty" scenes.

"Kelsey's assistant was very coy," said Devlin. "But of course, she would be. A top-notch gallery like that, they would want to maintain their image and it's not good business PR to admit that a former customer was causing havoc. It's embarrassing and they would want to sweep it under the carpet."

"All this sort of tallies with what Mrs Waltham told me," I said. "You know, about Sarah going down to London a lot. She said that she thought her stepdaughter had been having an affair with a London man and that maybe the man was married—because of the furtive way Sarah had been behaving."

"That might have just been embarrassment and pride on Sarah's part," said Devlin. "After all, if Jon was rejecting her, she wouldn't want to broadcast it around that she was chasing after him."

"So you think the Jon Kelsey angle is a dead end?" I said.

"I'm reserving my judgement for the moment," said Devlin with his customary caution.

I thought again of the conversation I had overheard in the gallery gardens on Saturday night:

"Are we going to do it tonight?"
"Relax... everything in good time."
"I... I can't bear the waiting. The suspense is killing

me!"

"You knew what you were getting into. Don't tell me it doesn't turn you on."

I still hadn't mentioned it to Devlin. Somehow—some remnant of loyalty to Cassie—had kept my mouth shut on the subject. Jon Kelsey was already a suspect and my account of the conversation would only turn the spotlight on him even more. I wasn't sure I wanted to do that—at least, not until I had had a chance to investigate him further myself. And maybe to speak to Cassie first about what I'd found out as well. She'd never forgive me if she thought I'd sicced the police on Jon.

"To be honest, other than the fact that Sarah died in his gallery and had a prior acquaintance with him, there are no strong reasons to suspect Jon of being the murderer. There may be another man involved that we don't know about yet. We're currently checking to see if Sarah might have had other boyfriends. But she didn't seem to confide in many people and no one seems to have seen her with a man recently. In Oxford anyway."

"And what about Fiona? What did the staff tell you at the Art School?"

"Not much. They were apparently both hard-working students... perhaps a bit too hard-working. Their tutor admitted to me that there was some academic rivalry between Sarah and Fiona but he brushed it off as healthy competition."

"It didn't sound that healthy to me," I said and recounted what the Japanese girl had told me about the Art Scholar's Award.

Devlin whistled. "That's a lot more serious than I was led to believe by the staff."

"Well, I imagine they wouldn't want to make a big deal of it—you know, it doesn't look good for the school to have students behaving like that."

"It would certainly give Fiona motive..." Devlin mused.

"Would someone really kill another person just to get revenge for a lost scholarship?"

"I've seen people kill for less," said Devlin grimly. "Bitterness and resentment can eat away inside you..."

"I suppose—of all the people at the party—Fiona had the most opportunity to poison Sarah's tea."

"Actually... there was no poison in the tea."

I stared at him. "What?"

"I've had the preliminary report from the toxicologist. SOCO managed to collect the fragments of the shattered teacup and also some of the spilled tea. Both were tested and neither contained suspicious foreign substances."

"But... but I thought you said Sarah was poisoned—"

"Oh, she was poisoned, all right—just not with the tea."

"So the Old Biddies got it wrong," I said. "They seemed so sure that they saw Fiona putting poison into the teacup."

"Well, remember they didn't actually say that. They simply said that they saw the two girls exchanging words and that Fiona would have had a good opportunity to put something into Sarah's drink. Which is true. But according to the tests, nothing was in the teacup except tea, milk, and sugar."

"So does that mean Fiona is off the hook, then?"

"Not necessarily. She could still have found other ways to introduce the poison..."

I frowned. "But where else could she have put the cyanide?"

"We're not certain yet it's cyanide," Devlin reminded me. "The toxicology analysis hasn't confirmed that yet. I'm hoping to have the full report from the toxicologist by tomorrow. But Fiona could have hidden the cyanide in any number of ways. Maybe she gave Sarah something to eat that the Old Biddies didn't see, or maybe she put something on the rim of the cup... That's been tested, of course, and it's come up negative so far, but if only a thin layer was applied and Sarah drank from that section of the rim, then presumably her saliva might have washed all traces of the poison away... I don't know— this is just me tossing ideas off the top of my head— but it's just an example of how poison could have been administered without being in the tea itself."

I sat back. "But... if you don't know how the poison was delivered, how can you possibly work out who did it?"

"That's one of the toughest things with poison cases. Unlike a normal murder, it isn't just a case of establishing time of death and alibis and finding the murder weapon. With a poisoning, anyone who could have had access to the poison—and who had the opportunity to administer the poison—has to be considered. And then if you add in the possibility of a slow-acting poison, which means that the victim could have been poisoned several hours before their death, then that means that the window of opportunity and the pool of suspects gets even larger."

"I thought cyanide is a fast-acting poison?" I said.

"Yes, one of the fastest. Cyanide can kill within one to fifteen minutes in large doses. But it all depends on the dosage—and also on things such as whether the victim had a full stomach, which may slow absorption."

"So what you're saying is that Sarah could have been poisoned by someone she met *before* she came to party?"

Devlin nodded. "It's a possibility we can't rule out. I'm currently gathering evidence to try and reconstruct her movements last Saturday. We know that she left her house at about 6:45 p.m. to go to the party. Mrs Waltham confirmed that. And before that, she was at the Art School all afternoon... oh, and she popped in to see her father at the hospital before she went home."

"Yes, Lincoln mentioned that last night," I said. "He said he was doing his rounds and he arrived to find Sarah causing a huge scene with one of the nurses. He almost had to call security, but then another visitor arrived and helped to defuse the situation."

"I'm going to the hospital this afternoon to speak to your boyfriend," said Devlin.

"He's not my boyfriend," I said quickly before I realised, then I flushed, angry at myself.

Devlin raised a sardonic eyebrow but didn't say anything.

I cleared my throat. "So you don't have any other suspects at the moment?"

"Not specifically—but we're considering anyone who might have had a reason for wanting to harm Sarah."

"From what I've heard of her so far, that's almost everyone," I said. "She didn't sound like a very nice person." I had a thought. "What about life insurance? Did Sarah have a policy on her life?"

"She was only twenty-three," Devlin said dryly. "No, she didn't have a policy. If anybody wanted money, they would have done better to marry her. She was an only child and the heir to her father's estate. But she had no assets of her own."

I made a noise of frustration. "I feel like we're just going around in circles."

"Well, the good thing about a circle is that it has no beginning and no end—so as long as the killer is going round on the same circle, we'll catch up with him or her at some point," said Devlin. His blue eyes were cold and hard. "It's only a matter of time."

CHAPTER FOURTEEN

Devlin walked me from the pub back out to Broad Street and left me outside the Sheldonian Theatre. I started to make my way up to North Oxford where my parents lived but a sign above a shop on the other side of the road caught my eye. It was Jon Kelsey's gallery. On an impulse, I crossed the road and went into the gallery.

It was strange being back in daylight. The place had been cleaned up, of course, and there was no trace of what had occurred. There were several tourists as well as what looked like a few locals browsing the works on display. I was pleased to see quite a few people in front of Cassie's paintings, pointing and nodding admiringly.

There was a young woman, with the sort of ice-cool blonde looks that went so well with modern art and minimalist chic, standing by one of the canvases, discussing it with a middle-aged couple. I recognised her as Jon's assistant from the party. She looked slightly harassed—I guess with Jon being away in Italy, the whole of the business fell on her shoulders and today looked like a particularly busy day.

I wandered a bit aimlessly around, pretending to look at some of the pieces but really wondering what I was doing there. What had I hoped to achieve? Did I think that by coming back to the "scene of the crime", some clue would magically appear for me to find? *This is stupid*, I told myself impatiently. I was about to leave when I noticed a stairway on the other side of the gallery, half-concealed behind a pillar. I didn't remember seeing it on the night of the party. Curious, I drifted over, wondering where it led.

"Can I help you?"

I jumped and turned around to find myself facing Jon's assistant. "Oh... er... I just thought there might be more galleries upstairs..."

"No, all the exhibits are down here. It's only private quarters upstairs." She smiled at me. "You're Cassie's friend, aren't you? I saw you at the party. I'm Danni."

"Hi." I returned her smile, then added sympathetically, "That must have been a nightmare night for you."

She rolled her eyes. "You can't imagine. We were

here until 1 a.m. and then, of course, the police wanted the whole gallery shut down for the weekend. In fact, we didn't even think that we would be able to re-open today, but thank goodness, they released the crime scene this morning."

"I'm surprised that Jon still wanted to go to Italy— I would have thought that he'd want to stay to help you sort things out."

A flicker of annoyance crossed her face, then was quickly masked. "Oh, Jon had an important meeting in Florence and it couldn't be changed. Anyway, I'm more than capable of holding the fort myself," she said with a smooth smile.

"Oh, I'm sure," I said. "Did you know Sarah Waltham, by the way? I understand that Jon said she used to come into his London gallery..."

"Yeah, I met her a few times in London. She was a pain in the backside," Danni said bluntly. "I know you're not supposed to speak ill of the dead but seriously, that girl had problems. She made poor Jon's life a nightmare."

"I can't believe that she called herself his girlfriend?" I said in a chatty tone.

"I know!" said Danni. "Of course, she isn't the first one. Women love Jon, and even if he doesn't mean to flirt with them, they think he's paying them special attention. They never leave him in peace," she said angrily, with a PA's customary protectiveness towards her boss.

I glanced back up the staircase. "I didn't realise

that Jon lived here?"

"Well, it's really a sort of city pad—he doesn't spend much time here. I think he spends most of his time with Cassie at the moment. He's also got a darkroom up there," she added.

"Jon's into photography?"

She nodded. "Ever since he was a teenager. It's what got him into art in the first place. He still likes doing things the old-fashioned way—you know, developing prints on paper. So he got a darkroom fitted up there with all the solutions and equipment. You should ask him to show you his photographs some time—he's really quite good."

One of the other customers called from across the room and Danni excused herself. I drifted back towards the door. There seemed to be no point hanging around here—I decided that I might as well go home and get on with my chores. I was about to leave the gallery when I glanced back and noticed three small figures skulking by the pillar in the far corner. My eyes widened. It was the Old Biddies. What were they doing here?

I watched in disbelief as they crept to the bottom of the staircase, then—with a furtive glance around—Mabel Cooke waved the others past her up the stairs first. She waited until the rest had gone up, then with one last look over her shoulder, she hurried up after them. For little old women, they could sure move fast!

I glanced quickly over to the other side of the

gallery where Danni was busily wrapping up a small painting whilst talking to a couple at the reception counter. She hadn't seen a thing.

Unbelievable. What were the Old Biddies doing?

I darted back across the gallery to the foot of the staircase and peered upwards. I couldn't hear anything. I glanced back at Danni. Her attention was still focused on the couple. I turned back to the stairs, hovering uncertainly over the bottom step. If Cassie ever found out that I had gone snooping into Jon's private quarters, she would be furious. But the Old Biddies were already up there—what more harm could I do? I was just following them to make sure that they didn't cause mischief, I told myself righteously, and started up the stairs.

The staircase led up to a small landing, from which two doors led off in opposite directions. I tried the door on my left first. It was locked. I turned to the one on my right and found that it opened into a large, spacious loft bedroom with a view onto the street. Quickly, I stepped in and shut the door behind me, then looked around with interest. The room was done up in a Scandinavian interior design style—all white walls and cool greys and neutrals, geometric designs and minimalist furniture. A Bang & Olufsen sound system was mounted on the wall above the bed and a leather zero-gravity recliner took pride of place in the corner by the window. It seemed that Jon Kelsey liked to live in style, even when he was barely there.

The bed was a vast king-sized affair, with a black

leather headboard and shining chrome legs. It dominated the room and was covered with navy silk sheets, a staggering array of pillows, and a faux mink throw. I looked up and realised that it was also placed beneath a mirror mounted on the ceiling. *Eeuuw.* I could just imagine Jon as the kind of man who liked to admire himself in bed...

There was an en suite bathroom with a compact shower and basin. It was bare except for a fluffy grey towel and a black leather bag unzipped to show a complement of men's grooming equipment—the complete opposite of Sarah Waltham's haphazard clutter. I checked the wardrobe next to the bed and rifled through the racks of colour-coordinated suits and shirts. The drawers below must have held his underwear and socks, but I drew the line at going through Jon Kelsey's underthings.

I shut the wardrobe door and turned back to scan the room again in frustration. There was really nothing of interest—it was a spare, bachelor room with hardly any place to hide anything. In any case, I didn't really know what I was looking for—it wasn't as if Jon was going to have a framed photo of himself and Sarah on display!

Feeling slightly foolish, I turned to go, but as I did so my elbow knocked against the Louis Poulsen bedside lamp, sending it crashing to the floor.

I froze. *Oh hell.*

Had Danni heard it downstairs? She knew that no one was supposed to be up here... Faintly, I could hear the echo of footsteps hurrying across the gallery below.

Oh bugger! Danni must be coming up to check on the noise.

I grabbed the lamp and set it back on the bedside table, then looked frantically around. There was nowhere to hide in all this minimalist chic. Even the wardrobe wasn't big enough to squeeze into. Thinking about it now, I wondered suddenly where the Old Biddies had gone. I had forgotten all about them but they must have come in here too. They couldn't have gone into the other locked room and they weren't in here. So where were they?

No time to worry about them now. I could hear the sound of someone coming up the stairs. Danni would be here any second and I didn't fancy having to explain myself...

The bed, I thought. It was the only option. Dropping to my knees, I crawled quickly beneath the bed just as I heard footsteps outside the door. My hip bumped into something soft. I turned my head and stifled a scream. Three pairs of beady old eyes were looking back at me. I stared incredulously at Mabel, Florence, and Glenda wedged side by side beneath the bed slats.

"*What are you—*"

"Shhh!" hissed Mabel, glaring at me. "You're going to spoil everything!"

I clamped my mouth shut as I heard the door open. We all held our breaths. Through the gap beneath the bed, I saw a pair of stilettos walk into the room. They went past us, around the side of bed and into the bathroom, then came back out again.

Please don't look under the bed... Please don't look under the bed... I prayed.

The silence stretched until I thought my nerves would snap. Just when I thought I couldn't bear it any longer, the stilettos turned and headed back towards the door. A minute later, the door shut quietly and I heard footsteps going back down the stairs.

I dropped my forehead down on the floor and released the breath I'd been holding. *Whew.* That had been a close one.

There was a shuffle of movement next to me and I raised my head back up to see Mabel and the other Old Biddies wriggling their way out from under the bed. Hurriedly, I followed their example and stood up to find them dusting themselves off and patting their fluffy white hair.

"What are you doing here?" I demanded in a hushed tone. "Sneaking around in Jon's private bedroom!"

"We could ask you the same thing," Mabel retorted.

"I—" I stopped. She was right. I tried to prevaricate. "Actually, I saw you three going up the stairs and decided to follow you."

"Mabel!" said Florence reproachfully. "You were supposed to act as lookout!"

"What do you suppose the mirror is for, Gemma?" said Glenda, looking up at it curiously.

Oh no. She can't seriously be expecting me to explain that.

"Why were you under the bed, Glenda?" I asked quickly.

"We heard you coming," she explained. "Well, we didn't know it was you, of course. We thought it was that assistant girl. Thank goodness Jon Kelsey has such a large bed!" She turned to Florence with a frown. "I still think you're getting too fat, Flo. There was barely any room when you squeezed in."

"I'm not fat!" said Florence, outraged. "It was your silly cardigan with all those bobbles that was taking up the room!"

"We wouldn't have had to hide under the bed at all if it wasn't for you, Gemma," said Mabel, glowering at me. "If you hadn't been so clumsy with that lamp, the assistant girl would never have even known that anyone was up here."

"That wasn't my fault," I said, annoyed at how defensive I sounded. "Where is Ethel? How come she isn't with you?"

"Aha... she's part of our extraction plan," said Mabel.

"Your... 'extraction plan'?"

As if on cue, there came a wail from downstairs and then a soft thump, followed by several cries and the sound of running feet.

"Diversion," said Mabel smugly. "Everybody

expects little old ladies to be frail so we just play up to the stereotype. Come on, girls, this is our chance. Everyone should be too distracted to watch the staircase now."

Mabel marched out of the bedroom, followed by the others. I ran after them. At the bottom of the staircase, we paused and peered around the pillar. A crowd of people were gathered on the other side of the gallery. I saw a pair of legs in thick compression stockings poking out from between them. Glenda and Florence began hurrying towards the crowd but Mabel whacked a hand on my chest to stop me as I tried to follow them.

"You stay here," she said. "We don't want to be seen with you. You'll totally ruin our operation. Meet us outside in five minutes."

Leaving me gaping after her, Mabel patted her hair, then sailed over to the crowd. She elbowed her way through and people parted. I saw Ethel slumped on the floor with Glenda and Florence hovering over her.

"Some smelling salts is all she needs," declared Mabel, whipping a tiny vial out of her beige handbag and waving it under Ethel's nose.

"Aaaaah!" Ethel jerked upright like a jack-in-the-box, scaring the crowd around her. She sneezed and glared at Mabel, hissing, "Did you have to use quite so much?"

Mabel ignored her and helped her to her feet. "I think we'd better get you home, dear, and to a nice cup of tea," she said loudly as she began propelling Ethel out of the shop. Glenda and Florence scurried after her. The rest of the crowd watched them go in bewilderment. I hesitated a moment, then ran after them, wanting to get out before Danni noticed me.

Out on the street, I looked right and left, and spotted the Old Biddies, who were shuffling down the street as fast as their orthotics could carry them. I jogged after them.

"Why were you snooping around the gallery?" I said, panting, as I finally caught up with them.

Mabel exchanged a look with the others, then said, "We wanted to check out that Kelsey chap—make sure that Cassie's young man is good enough for her."

"And did you find anything?" I asked eagerly.

Mabel put a hand in her handbag and drew something out with flourish. I saw the flash of black satin. "I found this under the bed."

It was a pair of very skimpy black G-string panties, edged with red lace.

"Oooh, that's gorgeous," Glenda gushed. "I wonder if M&S do something similar—"

"Glenda!" Mabel frowned at her, then turned back to me. "Are these Cassie's?"

"How would I know that? I'm not intimately acquainted with Cassie's underwear!"

"Well, can you ask her?"

"What? You want me to ask Cassie if this G-string belongs to her?"

"Well, if they don't, you have to wonder why they were in Jon's bedroom," Mabel said.

I sighed. She was right. Even if you could argue that Jon might have had ex-girlfriends, he shouldn't have had any of them stay at his pad in Oxford, not when he was already with Cassie when he set up here. There was just no reason for another woman's underwear to be under his bed.

Still, I didn't relish confronting Cassie with this...

Mabel thrust the G-string at me, then turned and said to the other Old Biddies, "Come along, girls. Time for a spot of tea in the Covered Market before we head back to Meadow-on-Smythe. Bingo in the village hall tonight!"

I watched them trundle off, then realised I was starting to attract strange looks. I probably looked like some kind of lingerie kleptomaniac, standing there in the middle of Oxford city centre with a black lace thong in my hands. Hastily, I stuffed the G-string into my pocket and started on the way to North Oxford and home.

CHAPTER FIFTEEN

I was surprised to find Seth sitting in the living room when I got home. He was perched on the edge of the sofa with a teacup in his hands, a plate of my mother's coffee and walnut cake in front of him, and a slightly desperate expression on his face. He looked up with relief when I walked in.

"Darling! We were just wondering where you'd got to," said my mother. She gestured to my friend. "I saw Seth walking up St Giles as I was driving home and I offered him a lift. Naturally, I simply had to ask him to come back for some tea!"

From Seth's expression, I guessed the truth was that my mother had probably forcibly bundled him into the car and brought him back like some kind of trophy.

"Where were you off to?" I asked Seth as I dropped down on the sofa next to him and helped myself to a walnut from the coffee icing on top of the cake.

"Gemma!" My mother frowned and slapped my hand. She quickly cut a piece with a silver cake slice and transferred it to a delicate bone china plate, which she handed to me with a dessert fork and a linen napkin.

"I was on my way to Doncaster College to see my old Organic Chemistry tutor," said Seth. "I'm looking for a first edition of *Stereochemistry of Carbon Compounds* and I thought he might have a copy. Thought I might drop in to see him in person, rather than just ring him up."

"You're such a clever boy, Seth," my mother said, beaming. "You must come round for dinner again soon. I'll be sure to make your favourite gooseberry pie. And when are we going to see you with a nice girl?"

Seth went bright red. "I... ah..."

The phone rang out in the hall and my mother sprang up. "Oh, excuse me—I have to take this. It must be Helen with the pumpkin soup recipe..."

She left the room and Seth breathed a sigh of relief. I gave him a sympathetic look.

"Sorry about my mother."

He grinned. "Don't worry, Gemma—I'm well used to it by now. I can still remember that first time I met her when your parents visited you in college; I think that day is forever etched in my memory."

We both laughed, then Seth sobered.

"I heard about what happened at the party on

Saturday night," he said quietly. "Was Cassie all right?"

"Yes, she was fine, just worried for Jon..." I trailed off as I saw Seth compress his lips. "She was a bit upset that you didn't come, though," I added.

Seth looked embarrassed. "Er... something came up that I couldn't get out of. So the police think it's murder?" he said, quickly changing the subject.

"Yes, the girl was poisoned."

Seth raised his eyebrows. "With what?"

"Devlin is still waiting for the toxicology results. It might be cyanide." I told him about the almond scent I had picked up on the victim.

"Do you know, you ought to come and see my old prof with me," said Seth suddenly. "Professor Christophe. He's an expert on poisons—it's always been one of his hobbies and it fits in nicely with his field of organic chemistry, of course." He laughed. "The younger students called him Professor Snape behind his back; he's quite a character, a bit eccentric, and you could really imagine him as a potions master. But seriously, you couldn't find a more knowledgeable person in Oxford about poisons."

"He sounds fascinating," I said eagerly. "But are you sure he'd want to see me?"

"Oh, he'd love it. Any chance for him to talk about his favourite subject. C'mon, come with me and we'll go see him now."

***

Doncaster College was one of the larger colleges on the outskirts of the city centre and one I was not so familiar with. I think I might have only been there once when I was an undergraduate. It had a distinctive red brick exterior, with the white patterned banding and tall lancet windows of the 19th-century Gothic Revival style, and was quite different from most of the other Oxford Colleges. Seth led the way through the main quad and into a building in the south-east corner. We walked down a long corridor and finally arrived at an arched wood door. Seth knocked and waited.

A deep male voice said, "Enter!"

Seth turned the heavy brass handle on the door and we stepped into the gloomy interior. For a moment, I wondered if I had stepped onto the set of a Harry Potter movie. Eccentric was an understatement. The place was like a cross between a Renaissance museum, filled with stuffed animals and plaster cast statues, and Frankenstein's laboratory, with ancient-looking contraptions of test tubes and vials in one corner, and gigantic brass scales in another.

The man in the black scholar's gown coming forwards to greet us looked himself to be someone from the last century. He had a deeply lined face and bushy white eyebrows that seemed to move independently of each other, although the image of

Father Time was belied by the bright blue eyes which regarded us shrewdly from beneath those impressive eyebrows.

"Seth, my dear boy! How nice to see you..." he said heartily, shaking Seth's hand. He turned to me. "And who is this lovely young lady?"

"This is Gemma, Professor," said Seth. "She's got a special interest in poisons and I've been telling her all about you. She was desperate to meet you so I brought her to say hello."

"Delighted! Delighted, of course!" said Professor Christophe, taking my hand and pumping it enthusiastically. "Would you like a sherry, my dear?"

Well, at least he had the traditional Oxford professor's line down pat. I smiled and accepted a glass, wondering if I should be worried about what he might have put in it. His twinkling eyes told me that he had read my thoughts. I blushed slightly.

"Fear not, young lady—I merely study poisons, I do not administer them."

"And even if he did, you couldn't have come to a better person for an antidote," said Seth with a laugh as he took a sip of his sherry.

"Do sit down... if you can find a place to sit," Professor Christophe chuckled, gesturing around the room.

Seth started to pick his way across to the professor's desk and I followed him, marvelling at the things on display. I paused in front of a miniature statue of a woman reclining, propped up on one arm against a cushion. She was dressed in the typical flowing garment that classical statues often wore, with one shoulder and breast exposed and a snake clutched in her other hand. Her head was tilted back, her eyes gazing upwards, and her face contorted in an expression of ecstatic pain.

"That is Cleopatra dying," said Professor Christophe, coming to join me. "The original is in the Louvre, a marble sculpture by Barois—this is a reproduction. Beautiful, isn't it?"

Beautiful wasn't exactly the word I had in mind, although there was a certain riveting sensuousness to the figure, languishing in her last death throes.

"You know, they say that Cleopatra chose an asp because she could not find the perfect poison to kill herself with?" said Professor Christophe. "She experimented with various types, poisoning several of her prisoners and slaves to see what effect each poison had on them. Henbane, belladonna, *Stychos nux-vomica*, a primitive form of strychnine... but she rejected them all. Henbane and belladonna caused too much pain and strychnine caused convulsions, which would have left her facial features distorted." He chuckled. "One gathers that she was quite a vain woman. In the end, she decided on the asp, a kind of small African cobra, which supposedly delivers a quick and serene death."

"I never realised that the story about Cleopatra and the snake was true," I said.

"Ah, well, as to the truth... Who knows? But it

certainly makes for a good story, does it not?" The professor's eyes twinkled at me. "Of course, there have been many queens in history who have used poison—it is perhaps a weapon that is particularly useful for the 'weaker sex'."

He pointed to a framed painting of a woman in Elizabethan garb, with the high ruffled collar and elaborate beadwork in her hair. She was not a particularly beautiful woman—there was something cold and cruel in her expression—but you could sense the power in her, even through the portrait.

"Catherine de Medici," said Professor Christophe, looking at her with something almost like affection. "An Italian princess who married into French royalty. People were terrified of her because from the moment she arrived in France, mysterious illnesses and deaths began to happen everywhere. Her favourite poison was arsenic and, in fact, among the French, the word *Italien* soon became synonymous with 'poisoner'."

"Why didn't people stop her if they knew that she was poisoning them?"

"Ah, but she was clever. She brought her retinue with her to the French court and that included *parfumers* and astrologers, both popular attendants for aristocracy at the time, but of course both occupations which could easily hide the use of poison. Catherine's first victim was her husband's older brother—he was poisoned by a cup of water brought to him after a thirsty game of tennis—and his death cleared the way for her husband's ascension to the throne. She also dispatched various other enemies and rivals, using everything from gloves laced with arsenic to money tainted with poison that penetrated the victim's skin after he'd handled it."

I shuddered. "She sounds horrible."

Professor Christophe laughed. "Yes, you wouldn't have wanted to get on her wrong side! But those were the times that people lived in then—poisonings were a fact of life."

"Is that why the wealthy employed tasters for their food?" asked Seth.

"Oh, certainly," said Professor Christophe. "After all, the food during that era was so heavily spiced, it was often impossible to taste a bitter flavour."

I frowned. "If there were so many poisons being used, wouldn't they have found antidotes for them?"

"Yes, indeed—there was a great belief in a universal antidote: something that could cure all poisons. Of course, that's a myth. There is no such thing; poisons are highly specialised and each requires its own specific antidote. But that didn't stop people searching for it for centuries. For example, they used to think that milk could be a universal antidote and a lot of the royals drank it in the gallons. Probably all that did was give them lactose intolerance!" He laughed heartily.

It was slightly disturbing how much humour he seemed to find in the grisly subject. Seth caught my eye and grinned, then he said:

"We were particularly interested in picking your brains, Professor, because of the recent murder—"

"Ah, the girl at the art gallery last Saturday?" Professor Christophe said. "Yes, I heard about that on the news. They reckon it was a poisoning, do they? The news didn't say which kind."

"They're still waiting for the results of the toxicology analysis," I explained. "But there's a strong suspicion it might be cyanide."

"Ah, cyanide..." The old professor smiled. "One of the great classic poisons—you know it was one of Agatha Christie's favourites. She used it in ten of her novels, in all sorts of inventive ways, such as by injection, in drinks, smelling salts, and even in a cigarette."

I raised my eyebrows. "I thought those kinds of things in Christie novels were all made up. They seem too fantastical to be real."

"Oh no, my dear!" said Professor Christophe. "Christie based many of her stories on real-life cases. It *is* true that life can sometimes be much stranger than art, and it is amazing how ingenious people can be. There was a famous case in France in 1977 when a man plotted to kill a woman whom he thought was responsible for his mother's death. He used atropine—that's the toxin found in belladonna, which is now used in small beneficial quantities in eye drops. Well, he put some into a bottle of wine which he left for the woman to find. And there was another case in the 1940s of a woman here in England who mixed nicotine into her husband's aftershave lotion. And with cyanide itself, there was a terrible case of multiple poisonings in 1983—it was known as the Chicago Tylenol Murders—when capsules of the painkillers were tampered with and laced with potassium cyanide. The poor victims just bought the Tylenol bottles from various supermarkets and chemists. It was after that incident that manufacturers stopped making capsules, you know."

Ugh. This stuff is going to give me nightmares.

I frowned. "But how would anyone get hold of something as dangerous as cyanide?"

"Ah, my dear, you do not necessarily need to find cyanide in its pure form," said the professor. "In fact, it is more commonly found as potassium cyanide and sodium cyanide, which are both white solids that can be ground into a powder. Cyanide compounds have several industrial uses, and of course, it is also found in the compound ferric ferricyanide, also known as Prussian Blue, which is where it gets its name."

"I remember you mentioning this in one of your lectures," said Seth suddenly. "It always stuck in my head as being ironic—that everyone thinks cyanide is blue because of its name and yet, actually, it's not blue at all."

Professor Christophe chuckled. "Yes, that's a common misunderstanding. Cyanide was actually named in reverse—because it was originally isolated from Prussian Blue, an intense blue pigment often used by artists. So they named it cyanide, after the Greek word '*kyanos*', which means 'dark blue'." He looked at me. "Ferric ferricyanide is also used by photography enthusiasts as well. They use it to alter the tones of a print and to produce cyanotypes or 'blueprints'. Of course, these compounds in themselves are not particularly toxic, but you can extract cyanide from them—anyone with some knowledge of chemistry could do it easily."

And in a place like Oxford, I thought, it wouldn't be hard to find someone with that kind of knowledge. A fellow student in the University, a helpful tutor, an academic colleague... I found myself wondering if Fiona Stanley had any friends who were chemistry students. As an artist, she would certainly have easy access to Prussian Blue... And what about Jon Kelsey? I thought suddenly of his darkroom above his gallery—a quiet, private place where he would have access to cyanide compounds and peace and privacy to extract the poison at will...

I roused myself as I realised that the professor was talking again, answering Seth's question about a book. I remembered the original reason my friend had wanted to come see his old tutor and decided to leave them to their discussion.

I smiled at the professor. "Thank you so much, Professor Christophe, for a really fascinating talk."

"Oh, any time, my dear, any time. My door is always open." He took my hand again and patted it in an avuncular manner. "And I hope they solve this case quickly. Of course, with modern forensic science, it is usually much easier to determine the toxins used and to identify them—it is one reason why poisoning has fallen so out of favour as a choice of murder weapon. Plus, with the medical advances and improved care these days, it is difficult to guarantee death even with the most lethal of poisons. But still, it can take time for the toxicology results to confirm things and by then..."

His blue eyes turned serious. "It takes a particularly cold-blooded murderer to choose poison. I do hope the police catch him soon because he could be very dangerous indeed..."

CHAPTER SIXTEEN

The talk with Professor Christophe left me vaguely disturbed and preoccupied all through the evening. I hardly took in anything my mother said at dinner as she rattled on about some "marvellous addition" to the tearoom and a pair of wellingtons for my father that she had ordered online.

After supper, I helped myself to some chocolate mints from the pantry and went up to my bedroom, intending to curl up in bed with a mindless thriller novel for a few hours. Muesli greeted me with a happy *chirrup* and hopped eagerly onto the bed with me. She climbed into my lap, padded about in a circle, and settled herself in such a way so that her furry bum blocked my view of the page.

I sighed. *Great. Remind me again why I adopted a*

cat?

When I first brought Muesli home, I had optimistically thought that I could keep her off my bed and in her own section of the bedroom—I guess that showed how little I knew about felines. Muesli had taken one look at the expensive, luxurious cat bed I had bought from the pet store and turned her little pink nose up in disdain. Then she had jumped on my bed with alacrity and claimed her spot next to my pillow.

To be honest, I didn't mind her sleeping with me that much—my bed was wide enough to accommodate both of us—but the problem was that Muesli liked to snooze at the bottom of the bed, with her body draped across my ankles. It was like sleeping pinned down by a hot, furry leg shackle and I found myself struggling to turn over in the night. It drove me crazy. Did all cat owners live in this kind of perpetual helpless frustration?

I shifted now so that I could see the book around the side of Muesli's furry bum and tried to focus my mind on the story. But I found it hard to concentrate. Bits of the conversation with Professor Christophe kept drifting through my mind. Finally, I yawned and gave up. I closed the book and got ready for bed. My tearoom would be re-opening for the new week tomorrow and I had to be there bright and early, ready to tackle the new day.

***

I was in a maze, trying to find Cassie. I could hear her screaming for help but I didn't know how to reach her. Everywhere I turned there were dead ends and blind alleys, and the floor of the maze was littered with bottles marked "Poison". I rounded a corner and came across my mother having afternoon tea with Jon Kelsey.

"Where's Cassie? Have you seen Cassie?" I demanded.

They shook their heads and smiled at me. My mother cut a slice of cake and put it on a plate in front of Jon, who offered me a cup of tea.

"Don't drink that—it's poisonous!" cried Fiona Stanley, springing out of nowhere.

I turned and ran on, passing the Old Biddies, who were pruning roses growing out of the hedge.

"Have you seen Cassie?" I asked desperately.

"No, dear, but smell these roses—aren't they lovely? They don't smell of roses at all—they smell of almonds..."

"Gemma!"

I turned at the sound of Devlin's voice. Where was he? I couldn't see him. I ran blindly, my hands outstretched. There was a figure ahead—was it Devlin? I tripped and stumbled, and then I was falling down—down—down—

RRRRRRRING!

I gasped and sat up in bed, clutching my chest, my heart pounding.

It was a dream, I realised shakily. A nightmare. It had been so vivid. I shivered as I reached across and shut off my alarm, then glanced towards my windows. Pale sunlight was seeping between the crack in the curtains, and the clock showed that it was time to get up and get ready for work. I staggered to the bathroom and after a brisk, hot shower, came back to my room feeling a lot more human.

As I was drying my hair, I glanced down at my bedside table and paused. I seemed to remember that there had been two chocolates left over last night. There was only one now. I frowned, then my heart skipped a beat. Had Muesli eaten it? I knew that chocolates were poisonous to dogs and I supposed it was the same for cats. Muesli had never seemed to show any interest in chocolate, but what if she had decided to sample some this time? I wanted to kick myself for leaving the chocolates there for her to find—I had been so preoccupied last night that I hadn't been thinking...

I looked frantically around the room. Where was Muesli? Wouldn't she normally be winding herself around my legs by now, loudly demanding her breakfast? I found her curled up in the folds of my blanket, her eyes squeezed shut. Was she just extra sleepy this morning or was there something wrong with her? I felt a lurch of fear. The thought of losing the little cat was terrifying. I put a gentle hand on her head.

"Muesli? Are you okay, sweetie?"

She opened her eyes and looked at me, but didn't talk back as she would have normally done. I threw on some clothes, then dashed downstairs.

"Mother!" I burst into the kitchen, where my mother was pouring out some cereal. "I need to rush Muesli to the vet! I think she's eaten some chocolate and that's really poisonous to cats—"

"Oh my goodness," my mother cried, her face creasing in concern. "Yes, you must take her instantly!"

She sounded far more alarmed than I had expected. I hadn't thought she liked Muesli that much, but it seemed that my little cat had wormed her way into my mother's heart too.

"Where are you going to take her, darling?" asked my mother.

I hesitated, then remembered Mrs Waltham's recommendation. "There's a vet around the corner. Remember—Mrs Waltham said her housekeeper took her dog there? The North Oxford Veterinary Surgery." I glanced at the clock on the kitchen wall. "I hope they'll be open."

I started to turn away, then I paused in horror. "Oh no—what about the tearoom? Cassie's still away in Italy. Who's going to serve the customers?"

"Now, don't you worry, darling," my mother said. "I'm sure Mabel Cooke and her friends would be delighted to help out again. They enjoyed it so much last Sunday. I'll give them a ring." She patted my hand. "You run along and take Muesli to the vet.

That's the most important thing now."

I started to argue, then changed my mind. She was right. Ten minutes later, I was running up the front steps of the veterinary clinic. Thank goodness they opened early.

"Oh... chocolate poisoning, do you say?" said the vet nurse. She looked at the cat carrier a bit sceptically.

I followed her gaze and had to admit that I was feeling slightly sceptical myself. Muesli looked perfectly fine, peering through the bars of her carrier, her eyes wide and curious.

"Has she shown any symptoms?"

"I don't know—what are the symptoms?"

"Vomiting, diarrhoea, rapid breathing, rigid muscles, increased heart rate and body temperature—and then seizures, weakness, and coma, in the advanced stages..."

She looked again at Muesli who was demonstrating a perfect lack of all those symptoms. "Er... she doesn't seem to be in too much distress."

"No," I agreed, feeling stupid now. "She seems perfectly fine but—"

"Well, chocolate isn't something you want to take a chance with," said the vet nurse. "In case there's a delayed onset reaction or something." She indicated the waiting area. "Dr Baxter is just seeing his first patient now, but if you take a seat, I'll see if he can squeeze you in before his next consult."

I nodded and went to the waiting area. There was

only one other person there: a middle-aged woman with a small Jack Russell Terrier. The dog stiffened as we approached. He growled, then launched himself at the cat carrier with a volley of barking. I flinched backwards, shocked at how such a tiny dog could be so aggressive, but to my even greater shock, Muesli puffed up to three times her normal size and launched herself, hissing and spitting, at the dog in return.

"Whoa!" I shouted as the cat carrier jerked in my hands.

The Jack Russell lunged again, dragging his hapless owner out of her chair towards us.

"Aaaarrgghh!" the woman cried, lurching across the room after him.

The dog rushed up to the carrier and shoved his snout against the bars, snarling and yelling at the top of his lungs. Muesli hissed and spat and yelled right back.

I stumbled backwards. I didn't know which to be more scared of: the dog or the demon in my cat carrier. Who would have known that such a sweet little cat could turn into such a ferocious feline? I would have thought that Muesli was the type to run screaming from dogs. Instead, she stuck a paw out through the bars of her carrier and swiped the Jack Russell across the face, causing him to yelp and jerk back, pawing his nose.

"Bambi!" cried the woman.

Bambi? She'd named her psycho rat terrier

"Bambi"?

Okay, to be fair, Muesli wasn't exactly living up to her name of a healthy Swiss cereal either. And I thought the Swiss were supposed to be neutral? The terrier retreated rapidly behind his owner's ankles and peered out at Muesli. He gave a half-hearted growl, but didn't dare come closer again.

"I'm so sorry," I said to the other woman. "I had no idea that she could be so... I think she might have had some chocolate and maybe she's not feeling quite herself... She's normally a really sweet, affectionate cat..."

My really sweet affectionate cat narrowed her eyes and gave another hiss for good measure, then she turned her back on the dog and began to wash her face.

The other woman chuckled suddenly. "I've not seen Bambi bested by a cat before, and by such a wee thing too." She peered at Muesli in the carrier. "Did you say she had been poisoned?"

I looked at Muesli doubtfully. I was really beginning to wonder if I had overreacted this morning. "I thought so—I thought she might have eaten some chocolate mints I left on my bedside table."

"Ah well, you can't be too careful with chocolate. Can be fatal, you know. Better safe than sorry." She sat down companionably next to me, the Jack Russell keeping carefully to her other side, a safe distance from Muesli.

"Yeah, I was really glad to have the vet so near so I could bring her straight in," I said.

The other woman looked at me thoughtfully. "I know you."

I looked at her in surprise. "You do?"

"Yes, seen you come and go—your parents have the house next to my old employer."

"Oh..." I looked at her as understanding dawned. "Are you...?"

She smiled. "I'm Nell. Nell Hicks, the Walthams' old housekeeper."

CHAPTER SEVENTEEN

"Oh! I'm here because of you!" I saw the look of puzzlement on Nell Hicks's face and quickly amended, "Well, not because of you directly; what I mean is—it was your recommendation that helped me find this vet. I only adopted Muesli recently, you see. Mrs Waltham gave me this clinic's name. She said you brought your dog here."

Nell's face softened. "How is Mrs Waltham doing? Nice lady. I heard about what happened to Sarah," she added with a grim look. "Rang Mrs Waltham up to give her my condolences yesterday."

"Yes, I think it's all been a bit of a shock to her. Although... Sarah isn't actually her daughter, I understand? And I don't think they were close?"

Nell guffawed. "Not close at all. Not that poor Mrs

Waltham didn't try, I tell you. But that Sarah... well, she never gave her step-mum a chance. Was right nasty to her at times. That woman was a saint to put up with it. I know you shouldn't speak ill of the dead but it's God's honest truth. I've known Sarah for years, since her teens, and she's always been— excuse my language—an absolute cow."

"Er, yes... I've spoken to a few people who knew Sarah and it seems that she could be a bit... um... difficult," I said diplomatically.

"Difficult?" Nell Hicks slapped her thigh and laughed, but it was not a nice laugh. "A real bit—oh, I beg your pardon, a real madam, that's what she was! Always wanting everything her own way. And she could be real vindictive if she didn't get what she wanted or she thought that you'd crossed her." Her face darkened and her mouth twisted. "That's what happened to me."

I looked at her curiously. I wasn't sure if I should pry but Nell seemed very keen to talk. "You mean, you made her angry?" I said.

Nell nodded. "I found a stash of marijuana hidden in her room and I went and told her father about it."

"Sarah was doing drugs?"

"Well, not serious drugs, mind you. Not cocaine or heroin or anything like that. Just marijuana. And just occasional, like, I think. But I knew her father wouldn't be happy about it and I thought he ought to know. It's his house, isn't it? And she was still living under his roof. Well! Threw a fit, she did, when she found out—called me an interfering old witch. And me almost a member of the family! Or at least, I thought I was," she said bitterly.

"What do you mean?"

"Well, when Mr Waltham went into hospital for his operation, Sarah turned around and dismissed me. Just like that. Told me to pack my things and get out. Ten years of service I gave that family!" Nell said angrily.

"But... didn't Mrs Waltham stop her? I mean, she's the mistress of the house—"

Nell gave a cynical laugh. "Mistress in name only. Sarah's the real mistress there. And, of course, her father indulges her in everything." She shook her head. "I couldn't believe that I found myself out of the job, just like that! And they were such good employers. Mr Waltham always gave me a generous bonus each Christmas—we're going to have to do without this year," she said forlornly, reaching down to rub the Jack Russell's ears.

"I'm sorry to hear that," I murmured, thinking to myself that here again was someone who had good reason to want to harm Sarah. The girl seemed to make enemies wherever she went!

I glanced sideways at Nell Hicks. I couldn't quite see this friendly, homely woman resorting to murder, though. Especially cold-blooded murder through poisoning. But then, what did I know? People could do all sorts of things when they were really angry...

The vet came out of his consult room and into the

waiting area—a kindly-looking, middle-aged man with a receding hairline and ruddy cheeks. He smiled at Nell and gave Bambi a pat, then asked if she wouldn't mind if he took a look at Muesli first.

Nell waved her hands. "Sure, sure—we're in no hurry, are we, Bambi?" She nodded at me. "Nice chatting with you, miss."

I smiled and returned the sentiment while Muesli gave Bambi a parting hiss before I lugged her cat carrier away. I followed the vet down the hallway into the consult room and set the carrier on the examination table. He opened the carrier door and Muesli strutted out, looking around with great interest.

"So what seems to be the matter with Muesli?"

Feeling even more sheepish now, I recounted the story of the missing chocolates from my bedside table. "But maybe I was wrong," I said as I finished my story. "I mean, she looks so well now—maybe I was just panicking for nothing."

"No, you did the right thing," said the vet. He picked Muesli up and placed her in front of him, and gently began giving her the once-over.

"Hmm... heart rate is slightly elevated," he commented as he listened to her chest with the stethoscope. "But that might be simply due to the excitement of coming in here."

"And she had a bit of a... er... tiff with Bambi."

"Ah." The vet smiled. "Well, just to be on the safe side, I think we'll keep her in for observation overnight, if you're happy with that? That way, if she does start to deteriorate, the vet nurses will be on hand to give her emergency treatment."

"Thanks, that sounds like a good idea," I said. "I wouldn't be able to pick her up until tomorrow evening though—would that be a problem?

"No, not at all. We'll make sure that she's comfortable—and we'll keep her well away from any dogs," he said with a grin.

***

I raced to Meadowford-on-Smythe as fast as my legs could pedal, worried about what was happening at the tearoom with neither me nor Cassie there to oversee things. As it turned out, I needn't have worried. I rushed in the door to find the place a cosy haven of happy conversation and contented munching, accompanied by the soft clink of china and the delicious smell of fresh baking.

The four Old Biddies were shuffling from table to table, smiling and chatting and serving tea and cakes with a practised ease. You would have thought that they'd run a tearoom their whole life! They were wearing the matching new aprons my mother had ordered—I winced again at the message and image on the front—and they looked quite adorable with their fluffy white hair and spectacles perched on the ends of their noses, almost like the stereotype image of a sweet Mrs Claus.

If only people realised how deceiving looks could be...

"Gemma, dear! How nice to see you..." Glenda hurried towards me, her pretty face wrinkled in a welcoming smile.

"I can't believe it... Everything looks wonderful..." I said.

Glenda gave a tinkling laugh. "Did you think that we wouldn't be able to handle things just because we're in our eighties? We were running households when you were still in nappies, you know."

I gave her a sheepish smile. "I know, Glenda. I guess it's the arrogance of youth—always thinking that no one else has done it before us."

Florence came over and hustled me into a chair behind the reception counter, and placed a hot cup of tea and a plate with a wedge of cake in front of me. Florence loved her food, as evidenced by her rotund shape, and when she wasn't eating, her next greatest enjoyment was getting other people to eat. She pointed eagerly to the cake now.

"You must try some—it's that new recipe of your mother's. Velvet Cheesecake. It is absolutely divine. Everybody is ordering it."

I vaguely remembered my mother telling me about this addition to the menu and Florence also mentioning it the other day. She said we had sold out of it, hadn't she? I really should have been paying more attention, I thought guiltily. Some tearoom owner I was turning out to be! I should have noticed as soon as something was good for business and been quick to turn it into an opportunity.

Now I looked down at the plate in front of me with interest. It wasn't an elaborate cheesecake—the top was covered with a smooth layer of cream cheese and sour cream, decorated only with a cluster of raspberries and blueberries, their rich pinks and deep purples showing vividly against the snowy white. I picked up the fork and carefully cut off a section, feeling the fork bite down through the crunchy biscuit base, and then put it in my mouth. It was heavenly—creamy and sweet, with just a touch of tangy zest, and the juicy flavours of the berries mingling with the buttery sweetness of the base.

"This is delicious!" I said.

Florence beamed. "It's our bestseller. Everyone has been ordering it and asking for more. Your mother says it was an old recipe of your grandmother's and it's incredibly simple to make."

"Maybe we should make it a permanent addition to the menu," I said.

"Oh, your mother would love that! It would make her very happy," Florence said.

I felt a stab of guilt, remembering my previous offhand attitude towards my mother's suggestions for the menu. Maybe I had been resistant and stubborn for no good reason, other than the fact that I was so paranoid about my mother "interfering with my life", and had been unwilling to listen properly to anything she had to say. It couldn't have been easy for her to have all her helpful suggestions constantly met with antagonism. In fact—although she had been initially dismissive of my tearoom—since she came on board, she had embraced my business whole-heartedly, worked tirelessly in the kitchen, and had been nothing but supportive. Yes, she could be (incredibly!) frustrating but she did mean well. I felt suddenly ashamed that I hadn't been nicer to her.

I'll pop into the kitchen later and tell her how much I loved her cheesecake and that I would make it a special on the menu, I decided.

"How is little Muesli? Your mother was telling us that she was poisoned?" said Ethel, coming to join us at the counter.

I sighed. "I think it was probably just a false alarm. I thought she might have eaten some chocolate but she seems far too well for that. In fact, she nearly took a chunk out of a dog she met in the waiting room."

Ethel chuckled. "Never underestimate cats, especially the little ones," she said. "But it was good that you took her to the vet. Better safe than sorry. You'd never forgive yourself if she had got ill and you hadn't reacted in time."

"Yeah, I guess. And as it turned out, it was a lucky coincidence: I met the Walthams' old housekeeper, Nell Hicks. It was due to her recommendation that I went to that vet, actually. Mrs Waltham told me about Nell taking her own dog there."

"The Walthams' housekeeper?" Florence frowned.

I looked at her. "Yes, why? Do you know her?"

"No... but do you know... I have a feeling I heard of her recently. Now, where had I heard her mentioned...?" Florence gazed off into space.

"So is Muesli all right then?" Ethel said.

"They're keeping her overnight for observation," I said. "But I have a feeling that the only thing that will need emergency treatment when I pick her up tomorrow will be my wallet." I made a grimace.

"I know! I just remembered!" Florence burst out suddenly. "My niece, Delia, who's a nurse up at the hospital... she mentioned seeing the Walthams' housekeeper... She was chattering about it because she'd read about the murder in the papers and she was really excited. She said she'd seen Sarah on Saturday just before the party, only a few hours before she was murdered!"

"What do you mean?" I asked.

"Well, Delia works in the ICU and she was on duty when Sarah came in to visit her father. Caused a bit of a scene, apparently. Tried to throw her weight around, but the Ward Sister would have none of it. Anyway, they were about to come to blows and the doctor was there and it was ever so embarrassing... and then the Walthams' housekeeper arrived and poured oil on troubled waters."

"Really?" I said in surprise. From the conversation I had had with Nell Hicks, I wouldn't have expected her to want to help placate Sarah—in fact, I would have expected her to join the lynch mob against the girl!

"Are you sure it *was* the Walthams' old housekeeper that Delia saw?"

Florence nodded. "Yes, Delia said she'd made some of Sarah's favourite shortbread biscuits. That was what had helped to distract Sarah and calm her down. Nell gave her a whole tin, which she said was especially baked for her."

I was even more astonished. Nell Hicks had sounded more like she would poison Sarah than bake the girl some of her favourite shortbread bisc—

I drew a sharp breath.

Nell Hicks had sounded more like she would poison Sarah...

Maybe that was exactly what the Walthams' old housekeeper had done? Made Sarah Waltham a gift of some poisonous shortbread?

CHAPTER EIGHTEEN

The tinkling of the bells on the front door made us look up. A young man in a courier's uniform came into the tearoom.

"Delivery for Gemma Rose?" he said, looking around and holding up a clipboard.

My heart sank. *Oh no. Not again.* I stepped forwards with some trepidation. "That's me."

He held the clipboard out to me. "Sign here please."

I looked him over and felt slightly reassured that he wasn't carrying a huge box or anything equally alarming. "What is it?"

He jerked a thumb outside. "I'll bring it in. Just need you to sign here first."

I scrawled my name on the form and watched

anxiously as he went out, then returned a few moments later wheeling an enormous padded object on a trolley. It was about the size of a fridge and barely fit through the door. All the customers stopped what they were doing and turned to watch curiously.

"Where shall I put it?" the young man said.

I gestured helplessly to the empty spot at the side of the counter. "Er... Over there, I guess."

He wheeled the trolley over, carefully deposited the enormous package, then doffed his cap. "Cheers." And he was gone.

"What is it, Gemma, dear?" Ethel asked, peering through her spectacles.

"I don't know," I said. *And I'm not sure I want to find out*, I thought, eyeing the object nervously.

Several of the customers had risen from their tables and come forwards to inspect the giant package. There was an atmosphere of hushed expectancy.

"Well? Aren't you going to open it?" Mabel demanded.

"Yes, Gemma—let's have a look," said Glenda eagerly.

I started tearing off the brown padding around the object and many of the customers sprang forwards to help me. Everyone seemed to be enjoying themselves immensely, like children on Christmas morning, talking and laughing as they ripped and tore at the padded cardboard. I pulled off the final section of wrapping and stood back, gaping.

I must be hallucinating.

It was an elephant. An enormous elephant in hideous purple fibreglass, with its trunk curled up above its head and its mouth open in a maniacal grin. It was sitting on its ample behind, with its front legs raised, in the middle of an empty fibreglass pool with a rim of fake rocks and artificial flowers.

The kitchen door swung open and my mother sailed out, resplendent in a chef's hat and snowy white apron.

"Oh, darling, how marvellous—it's arrived!" she said.

I turned glassy eyes on her. "Mother. *What* on earth is this?"

"Don't you remember, darling? This is that water feature I was telling you about!"

I stared at her. "Water feature? What water feature?"

"For the tearoom, silly! You see, Helen Green's been doing this Feng Shui course and she told me that the Chinese believe that running water symbolises money flowing in—and especially if it runs into a pool, then it signifies wealth and a pile-up of assets. The pool must be at least eighteen inches deep, mind you. Anyway, so I thought—what could be more perfect than a water feature for your tearoom?" She beamed at me. "And luckily, I saw this one online—it was marked down hugely..."

I wonder why, I thought sourly.

"... and I thought it would be *perfect.*" She tilted her head and inspected the monstrosity in front of us. "Well, it *is* a little larger than it looked online..."

I turned an incredulous gaze on her. A little larger? The thing was absolutely bloody enormous! It dominated the whole room—it was the only thing you could see as soon as you walked in—this monstrous purple elephant with a creepy smile.

"I can't have this in here," I cried.

"Why ever not?" said my mother. "It would go very nicely in this corner. Or by the front door..." She turned to look, then added, "But not on the right-hand side, darling. Helen says it may cause your husband to have a second family and become unfaithful."

Oh God. I feel like I'm having an out-of-body experience. My earlier charitable thoughts towards my mother vanished. I wanted to throttle her.

Conscious of the entire tearoom watching and listening, I stretched my lips into a sickly smile and said, "Mother, why don't we discuss this later?"

"Well, all right, darling, but don't you think we ought to plug it in and see how the water—oh!" My mother whirled suddenly as we all became conscious of a smell of burning coming from the kitchen. "My scones!"

She dashed into the kitchen and the door swung shut behind her. The customers returned to their tables, and gradually the tearoom regained its previous state of calm, albeit with a new purple addition in the corner. Several of the children couldn't resist coming over to look at the elephant and one particularly brave little boy climbed into the empty pool and reached up to touch the elephant's trunk. I sat behind the counter and tried not to think evil thoughts about my mother.

At least the rest of the day passed relatively uneventfully (and without any more deliveries of online purchases). At five-thirty, I locked the tearoom door with relief and climbed wearily onto my bike for the ride back into North Oxford. My mother had left earlier in her car; she had a bridge party to go to with my father that evening and I was glad. I was still fuming about the wealth-accumulating water feature and wasn't sure I could sit through dinner with my parents without blowing a blood vessel.

Instead, I enjoyed a solitary ready-meal from M&S on a tray in front of the TV, followed by a steaming cup of hot cocoa—made with rich Belgian milk chocolate and creamy, full-fat milk—and felt mellow enough afterwards to consider a truce with my mother the next morning.

The BBC was showing a documentary about sexual fetishes, in particular those who were addicted to the thrill of cheating and the danger of "getting caught" by their spouse or partner. There was even a pompous psychologist quoting an article published in the *Journal of Personality and Social Psychology* about "the cheater's high" and how people were aroused by the smug satisfaction of being able to "get away with it".

Yeah, a nice neat academic explanation for someone who's simply being a weasel, I thought. It was amazing how there was always some syndrome or psychological illness to excuse basic lousy behaviour these days. I made a face and switched channels, settling at last on a repeat of an *Inspector Lewis* episode. This was one of my favourite crime dramas on TV, not least because I enjoyed the Oxford setting and loved trying to guess the locations that each scene was filmed in. Although I had already seen the whole series, I eagerly watched the episodes again, marvelling at the interesting characters and clever mysteries. I would normally have been absorbed, but tonight, I found it difficult to keep my mind on the screen.

Instead, my thoughts kept returning to the real-life mystery I was embroiled in. Who had poisoned Sarah Waltham? Was it Fiona Stanley? The girl certainly had ample motive and the means—as an artist, she had easy access to Prussian Blue, a source of cyanide—but I wasn't sure that she had opportunity. There had been no cyanide in the tea at the party, so where and how had she managed to poison Sarah?

What about Jon Kelsey? Again, he had the means—his darkroom must have contained sources of ferric ferricyanide—but would he have had the opportunity? He certainly wouldn't have had a chance to doctor Sarah's tea at the party... but what about earlier? Devlin had said that the poison could have been administered a few hours before Sarah came to the party. What had Jon Kelsey been doing last Saturday? I assumed that Devlin must have checked the man's movements and it had all been kosher. Still, alibis have been known to be faked before... But he didn't have any motive for killing Sarah, did he? I mean, yeah, she had been a nuisance and an embarrassment to him but surely that wasn't enough to make you want to *murder* someone?

And then there was Nell Hicks. I frowned as I remembered my conversation with the Walthams' old housekeeper at the veterinary clinic that morning. I hadn't imagined the bitterness and anger she had felt towards Sarah. Nell definitely had motive. But would she have had the means? I couldn't see how she could have got hold of cyanide... On the other hand, she would definitely have had the opportunity when she met Sarah at the hospital on Saturday afternoon and offered the girl some of her favourite shortbread...

I wondered suddenly if Devlin knew about Nell Hicks's dismissal and the animosity between her and Sarah. He probably did—I was sure he would have been thorough in his questioning—but perhaps it would've been good if I told him what I'd learnt, anyway. It was just to help with the case, of course. Not because I'd longed to hear his voice or anything...

He answered on the second ring. "Hello, Gemma."

"How did you know it was me?" I said in surprise.

"Your name came up on my screen."

I felt a silly rush of pleasure that he had programmed me into his phone. "Have I... have I caught you at a bad time?"

"No, just finishing up dinner." I heard the sound of crockery in the background and wondered if Devlin was moving around his kitchen. I had visited his place once, during the investigation for the last murder, and been pleasantly surprised by his tastefully furnished converted barn in the Cotswolds countryside. Very much a bachelor pad as well, but nothing like Jon Kelsey's pretentious lodgings.

"Is something the matter?" he asked.

"N-no... I was just... Did you speak to Lincoln this afternoon?"

"Yes."

"And did he tell you about Nell Hicks—the Walthams' old housekeeper—being there when Sarah went to visit her father on Saturday?"

"Yes, he mentioned it. Mrs Hicks arrived at an opportune time, apparently—helped to calm things down between Sarah and the charge nurse."

"Especially because she had brought some of Sarah's favourite shortbread biscuits, right?"

Devlin's voice showed a trace of impatience. "That's right. What are you getting at, Gemma?"

"Have you spoken to Nell Hicks herself?"

"Not yet—I was planning to follow up with her tomorrow."

"Well, I have. This morning. She happened to be at the vet when I took Muesli in and she told me something rather interesting: she was dismissed recently from the Walthams and it was Sarah's doing."

"Was she?" I could hear the interest in Devlin's voice.

Quickly, I recounted my conversation with the Walthams' old housekeeper. "But it doesn't make sense," I said as I finished. "Nell was really bitter about her dismissal and quite hostile towards Sarah. So why on earth would she suddenly bake a batch of Sarah's favourite shortbread biscuits and take them to give to her?"

"You're thinking that she may have put something in them..." mused Devlin. "It's a hell of a risk to take, though. Anyone else could have helped themselves at the hospital and been poisoned too. Nell Hicks doesn't strike me as the kind of woman who would be a serial killer. Even if she had a grudge against Sarah, she wouldn't want to harm other people. Still... it bears following up."

"The only thing is I don't know how she could have got hold of cyanide," I said with a frustrated sigh.

"Well, that's actually irrelevant now because, as it turns out, the poison was *not* cyanide."

"What? Not cyanide?"

"I've had a report back from the toxicologist," said Devlin. "Just a preliminary one but it very definitely rules out cyanide as the cause of death. There just weren't high enough levels in Sarah's body to account for her death."

"Well, then, what *was* it that killed her?"

"It's still not confirmed—he needs to run a few more tests—but the toxicologist thinks it may have been a compound called Beta-Pyridyl-Alpha-N-Methylpyrrolidine, better known to you and I as nicotine."

"Nicotine? You mean... like the stuff in cigarettes?"

"Yes. Apparently nicotine is a highly toxic plant alkaloid—in high enough doses, it depresses the brain and spinal cord and paralyses skeletal muscles, including those in your diaphragm."

"So is that what Sarah...?"

"She showed several of the symptoms of nicotine poisoning, such as unsteadiness, confusion, convulsions, difficulty breathing... and ultimately respiratory failure."

I shuddered. Even though Sarah hadn't sounded like a nice person, no one deserved to die like that.

"So does that mean we're back at Square One?" I asked, dismayed.

"Not exactly—but it does mean we have to reassess. For one thing, nicotine can be a slower-acting poison than cyanide. Death often occurs a few hours after ingestion, depending on the rate of absorption. Several of the witnesses I spoke to at the party mentioned that they thought Sarah was drunk, because of the way she was slurring her words and having trouble coordinating her movements... but the pathologist actually found normal levels of blood alcohol in her body, meaning that she was *not* drunk. So that may indicate that the poison had already started to work when she arrived at the party, but she hadn't realised."

"That girl, Fiona—I saw her using nicotine patches," I said suddenly.

"When was this?"

"At the party. I went out to get some fresh air and I saw Fiona come out and start smoking a cigarette, then she changed her mind and applied a nicotine patch instead."

"Hmm...Very interesting. Nicotine patches have one of the highest concentrations of nicotine," said Devlin. "I think I'm going to have another little talk with Miss Stanley tomorrow."

"There was something else..." I said hesitantly. "When I was in the garden that night... I overheard something."

"You didn't mention this before." Devlin said, a tinge of reproof in his voice.

"I... I wasn't sure it meant anything and I didn't want to upset Cassie..."

"It's something to do with Kelsey?"

"Well, I'm not sure it was him. They were whispering so it was hard to recognise voices. But I thought it sounded like him..."

I repeated what I had heard to him, then added with a sheepish laugh, "It sounds so cheesy, doesn't it? Like some kind of bad B-movie dialogue. That was one reason I didn't mention it before now. It sounded so ridiculous, I didn't think it could really mean anything serious... And besides... Well, I know I don't like Jon and I wondered if my own bias against him was colouring my interpretation. You know, sometimes you hear what you *want* to hear."

"You should still have come to me with the information," said Devlin sternly. "You should have trusted me to be sensible and discreet."

"I know... I'm sorry. I just... you don't know how sensitive Cassie is about Jon. I didn't want to throw suspicion on him unnecessarily. If I'm wrong, Cassie will never forgive me..."

"Better that she gets mad now than find out later that she's with a potential murderer," said Devlin.

"Are you seriously considering Jon a strong suspect?"

"I had my suspicions about him from the start. Oh, he's got a very good story, but... call it sixth sense if you like. I don't trust Jon Kelsey. And in my experience, when it comes to murder, the killer is often someone who knew the victim. Whatever Jon might say, I think there was more to his relationship with Sarah Waltham than he let on."

I thought suddenly of the lace thong that the Old Biddies had found under Jon's bed. *Should I tell Devlin about that?* But if I did, Devlin would probably want to claim it as evidence. *No, I'll check with Cassie first*, I decided. It was only one more day. She'd be back from Italy tomorrow. It would be terribly embarrassing if it turned out to be just part of her lingerie wardrobe.

"And what about any other boyfriends? Last time you mentioned that you were checking that out."

"We haven't turned up anything so far—but I've sent off Sarah's laptop and phone to our IT department to see if they can find anything of interest in her emails and other files. They have a bit of a backlog at the moment, but I'm hoping to hear back from them soon."

There seemed to be nothing more to say and I expected Devlin to ring off but he surprised me by asking suddenly, "Are you free tomorrow night, Gemma?"

"Tomorrow night? Me?"

He sounded amused. "Well, there's no one else on the phone. Yes, you. Would you like to go out to dinner with me?"

My heart gave a leap. I could feel a silly grin come over my face and was glad that he couldn't see me. "You mean... to discuss the case?"

"No, I mean to have dinner." I could hear him smiling. Then his voice changed. "Unless you're busy again with Lincoln or something."

I grinned to myself. Was that jealousy I heard in Devlin's voice?

"No, I've got no plans tomorrow night. I'm all yours." I realised what I'd said and flushed, stammering, "I... I mean..."

Devlin laughed. "I'll remember that the next time I see you with the eminent doctor," he said lightly. "So... that's a yes?"

"Yes... Yes, I'd love to."

"Great. Fancy Thai? We could go back to the Chiang Mai Kitchen," said Devlin, naming one of our favourite haunts from student days. Chiang Mai was a sophisticated Thai restaurant that was always saved for special occasions. "I'll come and pick you up at 7:30."

As soon as he had hung up, I grabbed a cushion and hugged it hard, twirling in a circle. I couldn't get that silly grin off my face. Then I skipped up the stairs, my mind already busily dissecting my wardrobe, wondering what I should wear. A date with Devlin O'Connor! I felt like I was eighteen again, my head dizzy with anticipation and excitement.

I didn't want to admit it—even to myself—but I couldn't help thinking that this might be a second chance, a new beginning for Devlin and me...

CHAPTER NINETEEN

My spirits were still soaring the next morning and I hummed a happy tune as I opened up the tearoom. Even the sight of the huge purple elephant in the corner couldn't vex me—in fact, I fancied that the elephant's grin was matching mine at the moment. Every time I thought of the date with Devlin that evening, my heart skipped a beat. I couldn't remember the last time I had looked forward so much to something.

Then Cassie arrived and my spirits plummeted as I remembered that I had to speak to her about Jon and that lace thong. She was looking wonderful after her trip: her eyes were shining, her cheeks flushed, and she looked the epitome of a girl happily in love. I shrank from the thought of being the one to dampen her happiness. She had brought back presents for everyone—a pretty terracotta Florentine bowl for my mother, little gift bars of soap for each of the Old Biddies, and a beautiful set of Chiaverini jams for me. Her thoughtfulness made me feel even worse.

"Oh, Gemma! It was amazing—we did the Uffizi and then Jon took me to the Belmond Villa San Michele and the restaurant there had the most incredible views of Florence... and then we walked along the Arno River and it was *so* romantic! And then we had dinner in this gorgeous little *trattoria* down this side street where they served the most delicious little *bruschettas*..." She laughed. "I told Jon that I was really jealous he got to stay there and sample more delicious Italian food..."

"Didn't Jon come back with you?" I said, surprised.

"No—he was supposed to, but there was a change of plan. He had the chance to set up a meeting with a fellow art dealer and he said it was too good an opportunity to miss. So he's delayed his return 'till tomorrow. But he organised a car to pick me up at Heathrow and bring me back to Oxford. He's just so thoughtful!" She fished a bottle of lotion out of her handbag. "Look, he'd even got me something from that new range at L'Occagnes before we left Heathrow, because I'd mentioned that I love their stuff... and then when we were in Florence, he bought me the most beautiful gold filigree brooch from a local artisan shop. Ohhh..." She sighed dreamily. "It was just absolutely wonderful..."

I stared at her bright happy face and cringed again. For a moment, I thought about putting off asking her about the lace thong—but it wasn't going to get any easier later.

Taking a deep breath, I said, "Uh... Cassie? Can I have a word with you?"

"Sure," she said, giving me a quizzical look as she reached for her apron.

"Why don't we go outside? There's more privacy there."

"Okay, Gemma, you're starting to scare me," Cassie joked, as she dropped the apron back on the counter and picked up her coat instead. She put this back on and followed me out into the tearoom courtyard.

I leaned against one of the wooden trestle tables and licked dry lips, not sure how to start.

"For heaven's sake, Gemma—what is it?" Cassie said.

I stuck my hand in my pocket, pulling out the flimsy piece of black satin and red lace. I held it up. "Um... Is this yours?"

Cassie furrowed her brow. "No, it looks like something a prostitute would wear! I wouldn't be seen dead in something like that. Why? Where did you get it?"

I swallowed uncomfortably. "In Jon's bedroom. Above the gallery."

Cassie stared at me, then she demanded, "What

were you doing in Jon's bedroom?"

"We... we were just checking it out, you know..."

"We?"

"The Old Biddies and me," I said sheepishly.

Cassie's face started going red. "Are you telling me that you were snooping in Jon's private quarters with the Old Biddies?

I shifted uncomfortably. "Well, it wasn't exactly like that—"

"What was it like then?" Cassie's voice rose with anger. "What the hell did you think you were doing, Gemma? Going behind Jon's back and sneaking into his bedroom! That's bloody despicable!"

"We were worried about you, Cassie! I mean, what do you really know about Jon?"

"I know he's the most wonderful man I've ever met," Cassie snapped.

"But you don't really *know* anything about him!" I put a hand on her arm as she began to turn away. "Cass—please—you've got to listen to me! I mean, what if..." I trailed off, unable to say it.

"What if what?" Cassie demanded.

"What if he's not telling the truth about his relationship with Sarah Waltham? What if he *is* somehow connected to her murder?"

She stared incredulously at me. "I can't believe you just said that, Gemma! It's bad enough that the police would even consider Jon a suspect, but I never expected you to be so dirty-minded too!"

"But, Cassie, you have to admit—it does look very

suspicious—"

"It doesn't look suspicious at all," she said fiercely.

I could feel my own temper rising. "Oh, come on, Cassie! Why are you being so blind about this? If this was anyone else, you would have been hounding me to report him to the police by now! I never thought that you'd be the type to lose your brains over some stupid infatuation!"

"How dare you!" shouted Cassie. "It's not a stupid infatuation!"

"Well, you haven't offered any explanation for that lace thong! Why was it in Jon's bedroom? If it's not yours, then whose is it?"

Cassie threw her hands up. "I don't know whose it is and I don't care! I'm sure there's a perfectly good explanation and I'm not going to let your sordid imagination ruin my feelings for Jon!"

"You're just scared!" I said angrily. "You don't want to face the truth: that the man you're going out with might actually be a womaniser, if not a murderer! It's not like you Cassie; you've never been afraid of facing up to anything. Why are you being so pathetic this time?"

"I don't have to listen to this," said Cassie icily. She leaned towards me, her eyes cold and furious. "I know we've been friends a long time, Gemma, but you've really overstepped the mark this time. You had no right to go and check up on Jon behind my back and you've got no right to suspect him either! If I'm happy with him, then that's all that matters!" She jabbed a finger in my chest. "I know you never liked him—yes, I know you try to hide it, but I could tell. You're completely biased against him and just want to think the worst of him. You might think that being my friend gives you the right to interfere with my love life. Well, let me tell you—it's none of your sodding business!"

She whirled and stormed back into the tearoom. A moment later, I heard the front door slam, footsteps hurrying out onto the street, and then the creak of a bicycle rolling away.

I sat down slowly on one of the outdoor benches. I was shaking. Cassie and I had never had such a bad fight before. Sure, we had our little differences and arguments—what friendship doesn't?—but never anything like this. I felt a mixture of anger, hurt, and frustration. Why was she so quick to believe Jon but so reluctant to see my side of things? Did our years of friendship mean nothing to her? Why couldn't she give my doubts and suspicions some credit too?

I went back into the tearoom and dropped dejectedly down into the seat by the counter. The Old Biddies drifted over to me. They had come in early to help out again and had obviously seen Cassie's stormy departure.

"Never mind, dear, I'm sure she'll come round," Ethel said, patting my shoulder.

Mabel nodded emphatically. "Yes, she'll be grateful to you later—you'll see."

I nodded miserably, not convinced that Cassie would ever forgive me. I wondered if I might have just lost my best friend forever.

CHAPTER TWENTY

The rest of the day was quiet and subdued. I tried not to think about Cassie and threw myself into the work. We were inundated with customers and it was a great sign for the business, but it did little to lift my spirits. My mother's new Velvet Cheesecake was once again the top seller and she was rushed off her feet, baking more to replace the ones that were rapidly being depleted. The Old Biddies were very kind and I was grateful for their presence—their bustling around and gentle gossiping stopped me from brooding too much and they were a huge help in relieving the workload. Otherwise, without Cassie there, I would have been swamped.

The vet nurse rang around lunchtime to let me know that Muesli was fine and ready to go home. I

211

could collect her any time it suited me. The little cat had shown no symptoms of chocolate poisoning, but she had kept herself busy trying to dismember every dog who came into the veterinary clinic, including a Great Dane who had been traumatised for life.

As the afternoon tea rush was dying down, my phone rang again and I pulled it hurriedly out of my pocket, hoping that it might be Cassie. It wasn't. It was Devlin.

"Hi," I said.

"Hey Gemma... something the matter?"

"What do you mean? Why should anything be the matter?"

"Your voice. I can tell. Something's upset you."

I was touched by his perceptiveness, but I didn't want to go into it now on the phone. "It's nothing. I mean, it's not nothing, but it's not something I can explain right now."

"Maybe you can tell me tonight, then. Actually, that was the reason I was ringing... can we make it eight instead of seven-thirty? I have a feeling I might be held up at the station."

"Yes, sure... Has something come up in relation to the case?"

He hesitated, then said, "It's not official or anything but we're bringing Fiona Stanley in for questioning, with a view to arresting her."

"Fiona!" I saw the Old Biddies prick their ears across the room. I turned my back on them and walked into the little shop area adjoining the dining room, where I could have some privacy. "Why? Have you found new evidence against her?" I asked.

"IT found something on Sarah's computer. A bunch of hostile emails between Sarah and several people. Most of it is tame stuff—you know, the kind of sniping and petty nastiness that you see on Facebook and online forums sometimes, but there was one set of emails between Sarah and Fiona which stood out. Fiona's in particular. She wrote a long, ranting message blaming Sarah for ruining her life and vowing to get revenge. In her own words, she said, 'You'll be sorry!' Now, that might just be a melodramatic cliché, but given the other factors it would be enough to bring her in for questioning— even if we didn't have the information from the pharmacy."

"What information?"

"Well, following your tip last night about Fiona's nicotine patches, I had my sergeant go out and check all the chemists around Oxford this morning. He found a place in Cowley where the clerk remembered Fiona, because she had bought a bulk pack of nicotine patches last week and then came back a few hours later and asked for another. She claimed that the first box got nicked with the rest of her shopping from the basket of her bicycle and that's why she had to replace it so quickly. The clerk remembered it because they rarely sell such big packs and so many in one day."

"You think she was trying to extract nicotine?"

"It wouldn't be the easiest method—but nicotine patches do contain the highest amount of nicotine per mg and you could do it with a solvent extraction. Fiona might have college friends who are chemistry students who could help her. At any rate, it's worth questioning her about it." He paused. "Of course, that still leaves the question of *how* she administered the poison to Sarah. If she didn't do it at the party, then she must have done it earlier in the day..."

I thought back to the day I had gone to the Art School and the way Sarah's workspace had been cluttered with art equipment, half-filled mugs, and food packets.

"Sarah was at the Art School on Saturday afternoon, before she went to the hospital and the party," I said. "Do you know if Fiona was there on that day too?"

"Yes, she said she had popped in briefly earlier in the day. Why?"

"Well, it wouldn't have been that hard to slip something into Sarah's drink or food unnoticed. That girl was a total slob and the area around her workspace was littered with stuff. And the Japanese girl I spoke to told me that she saw Sarah eating her lunch at the school that day. There's a communal room where students make hot drinks and stuff. Maybe if Fiona was at the school too, she could have put something into Sarah's drink or sandwich filling or whatever."

"Yes... it sounds possible. Something else to

question her about," Devlin agreed. "I might speak to her tutor and some of the students again too—see if they remember seeing the two girls interacting on Saturday afternoon."

"Sounds like you've got a lot to do. Are you sure you're still okay for tonight?"

"You're not getting out of the date that easily," Devlin teased. "I'll be done here and on your doorstep at eight o'clock."

I put my phone down and stared into the distance, feeling both better and worse. Better because just talking to Devlin had lifted my spirits a bit. Worse because it seemed that Jon Kelsey might not have been involved in the murder after all, which meant that I may have had the fight with Cassie and possibly ruined our friendship for nothing.

Suddenly I wanted to talk to my friend again, to apologise and try to make up. I could barely wait for the day to be over and, as soon as the tearoom was closed, I hopped on my bike and cycled to Jericho, the trendy, bohemian Oxford suburb where Cassie lived. She rented a studio flat in one of the converted Victorian work houses near the canal, but as I pulled up outside, I could see that the windows were dark. It looked like nobody was home. I rang the bell for good measure. Nothing.

I heaved a sigh of frustration. Where could she have been? Jon wasn't back from Italy yet so she couldn't have been at his place. I had tried calling but she wasn't answering my calls. I thought for a moment, then turned my bike around. I had an idea where Cassie might have gone: to her parents' place, just around the corner. She always used to retreat into the warm, rowdy bosom of her family whenever she was upset about something.

I made my way to the 19th-century Victorian terrace where Cassie's parents lived and ran up the path to the front door. The old-fashioned doorbell echoed hollowly, and a moment later the door opened to reveal Cassie's mother in a woolly smock.

"Gemma! How nice to see you," she said, stepping forwards and enveloping me in a hug. She smelled of incense and turpentine, and made me think of my schoolgirl days when I used to come over to play.

"Mrs Jenkins—is Cassie home?"

"Yes, she is, but... well... I'm not sure it's a good time at the moment."

"I really need to speak to her."

Mrs Jenkins looked uncomfortable. "Well... Actually... She said that if you were to call, she didn't want to see you."

I drew back, hurt. It felt like a slap in the face. Cassie had never refused to see me before. Even in our worst fights, she had always agreed to see me, if only to scream at me some more.

"Can you please talk to her and try to get her to change her mind?"

Mrs Jenkins sighed. "I'll try. Would you like to come in?"

I shook my head. "I'll just wait here."

She gave me a troubled look, then turned and went back into the house. The wait wasn't long. Mrs Jenkins was back in less than five minutes, looking even more uncomfortable than before. I could see from the expression on her face even before she said anything that the answer was no.

"I'm really sorry, Gemma," she said, reaching out to squeeze my hand. "I don't know what's happened between you girls but it's not like Cassie to be so stubborn." She gave a sudden laugh and rolled her eyes. "What am I saying? Being stubborn is Cassie's specialty! But I've never seen her like this before. Was it something very serious?" She looked at me anxiously.

I gave her a wan smile. "It was a... a bit of misunderstanding between us. I said something that upset Cassie. I just wanted to see her to apologise."

She patted me on the shoulder. "You know Cassie's temper. It's that artistic temperament of hers." She gave a weak chuckle. "Maybe you'd better let her cool down a bit, eh? Give it a few days. Once she's calmed down, she might be more amenable to reason."

I sighed and stepped back. "Okay, thanks, Mrs Jenkins. But can you please tell her that I'd really like to make amends and if she... if she feels like talking to me, to give me a ring? Anytime."

"I will, Gemma. Take care of yourself."

I walked back to my bicycle, feeling even more dejected than before. As I was about to get on again, however, I suddenly remembered something. I glanced at my watch and gasped. Oh heavens— Muesli! I was supposed to pick her up from the vet! I jumped on my bike and pedalled as fast as I could to North Oxford, hoping that the vet clinic wouldn't close before I got there. As it turned out, the waiting room still held a few dogs and their owners when I ran into the reception.

"I'm here to pick up Muesli," I said, panting slightly.

The girl behind the reception grinned. "Oh, Muesli! She's such a little personality! Everyone's in love with your cat." She rose from her chair. "I'll just go and grab her for you."

She returned a few moments later with Muesli in her cat carrier. I saw the little cat's tail go up when she saw me and she let out a loud "*Meorrw*!" in greeting.

"Hello, Muesli," I said dryly. "Enjoyed your stay?"

Muesli kept up a running commentary as I paid the bill, then I carried her out of the clinic. Twilight had fallen and the streets were in darkness, the activated street lamps still not at their full strength yet. I had originally intended to cycle home with Muesli's carrier balanced on my basket, but now, in the fading light, I changed my mind. Safer just to wheel the bicycle.

I placed the carrier as securely as I could in the basket—it didn't quite fit but I managed to squeeze it in tilted at an angle—and then grasped the handlebars and began wheeling the bicycle down the pavement. It was only a short distance to my parents' house anyway. We were almost there—just passing the corner with the Walthams' residence—when Muesli surprised me by suddenly letting out a hiss and a menacing growl.

I stopped and looked at her in astonishment. She was staring into the darkness of the lane leading down the side of the Walthams' house and all her fur was standing on end. Another growl erupted from her, accompanied by angry spitting. I followed the direction of her gaze, straining my eyes to see in the darkness. I couldn't see a thing.

Muesli growled again and hissed, narrowing her eyes. She could obviously see with no problems at all in the dark and whatever she saw was not making her happy. I wondered if there was a dog down there setting her off. Then, as my eyes began to acclimatise to the dim light, I suddenly made out the shape of a man. He was skulking down the narrow lane, keeping his head down, but I recognised the set of his shoulders and that long, handsome profile.

It was Jon Kelsey.

CHAPTER TWENTY-ONE

What was Cassie's boyfriend doing here in North Oxford? Wasn't he supposed to be in Italy? Before I could react, he had hurried down to the end of the lane and disappeared around the corner, out of sight. A minute later, I heard the sound of an engine and then a car came around the corner and shot past. I caught a glimpse of the passengers—Jon was in the passenger seat and, next to him, I saw someone with long blonde hair in the driver's seat. A woman.

I stood gaping after the car as its rear lights faded away into the distance, until a plaintive "*Meorrw!*" from Muesli reminded me where I was. Slowly, I resumed wheeling the bike, my mind in a turmoil. Could that really have been Jon? It had been dark and I couldn't be a hundred percent certain. I was so sure I had recognised him but what if I had been wrong? And besides, what was he doing here? According to Cassie, he wasn't coming back from Italy until tomorrow. Had he lied to Cassie? But why should he lie? And who was that woman?

My head was still spinning with questions as I finally let myself into the house. I paused in the hallway, wondering what I should do. I didn't dare call Cassie to check about Jon—and in any case, she wasn't speaking to me. I sighed. I would worry about it tomorrow morning, I decided. I didn't want to let Jon Kelsey ruin my evening with Devlin.

My parents had gone out to dinner at some friends' so I had the place to myself. I was relieved— it would be nice to prepare for my date without my mother breathing down my neck. I hadn't been looking forward to facing her questions about my date with Devlin. I didn't know if his makeover as a debonair CID detective had convinced her to rethink her opinion of him, but I knew that there was no way he could ever win in a comparison with Lincoln Green: eminent doctor, son of my mother's closest friend, and "one of us". Yeah, my mother was a bit of a snob.

I fed Muesli her dinner, then scooped her up and retreated upstairs. I had a quick shower, then had a girly discussion with my cat about what to wear.

"What do you think?" I said to Muesli, holding a red Lyra figure-hugging dress against my body.

"*Meorrw*!" said Muesli from where she was sitting

in the midst of the pile of discarded clothes on the bed. She licked a paw and swiped it over her face, covering her eyes.

"Too blatant, huh?" I said, tossing the dress onto the pile to join the others.

I turned back to the wardrobe and pulled out a demure navy dress with a white peter pan collar. "How about this then?"

Muesli considered it, her green eyes serious, then she gave a big yawn, showing her sharp little white teeth.

"Yeah, you're right—a bit boring," I said, throwing the dress onto the pile too. I put my hands on my hips and sighed. There seemed to be nothing that was right for the image I wanted to achieve. The thing was—what image *did* I want to achieve? Did I have to worry about making a specific impression? Surely we were past the age now of being coy and playing games?

I turned back to my wardrobe and rifled through the racks again. Finally, after several more changes and feline fashion advice from Muesli, I settled on an elegant Karen Millen dress in midnight blue with long, sheer sleeves, a fitted bodice, and a short A-line skirt that showed off my legs without being too risqué.

I glanced at the clock worriedly. A quarter to eight. I had taken so long over deciding what to wear, I had barely left myself any time for hair and make-up. I rushed through the rest of my primping, going for smoky eyes in soft shades of charcoal and violet and a sheer plum lipstick for my lips. At least my hair didn't need much work. After years of sporting long wavy tresses, I had chopped it all off just before I returned to England and my dark hair was now styled in an Audrey Hepburn-esque pixie bob. My mother hated it and complained about it constantly, but I thought it suited me much better. I wasn't a big, tall person and all that hair just seemed to weigh me down. With my new haircut, my eyes seemed larger, my cheekbones more prominent. I was just running a quick comb through my hair when I heard the doorbell ring downstairs.

"Wish me luck," I said to Muesli, giving her a last pat on the head.

She purred sleepily, still curled up in the heap of clothing on the bed. I thought fleetingly of the hairs she would leave on my clothes, then I gave a resigned smile and turned away. I didn't have the heart to move her. She looked too comfortable.

I'm turning into a typical cat owner—a complete slave to kitty's whims, I thought to myself wryly as I descended the stairs and went to answer the front door.

"Hi," I said softly, as I opened the door to see Devlin standing on the threshold.

His eyes darkened slightly as he looked at me and I felt a surge of pleasure at the admiration I saw in them. Suddenly I flashed back to ten years ago, when Devlin used to come pick me up from my parents' sometimes for a university event or student party. He had looked very different then, of course. His hair had been long and swept back in a slightly leonine style that highlighted his high cheekbones and aquiline profile. But his steely blue eyes were the same.

"Hi," he said. "These are for you."

I took the bouquet of long-stemmed roses he handed me. "They're gorgeous!"

And they were. Not the common garish red roses that you see everywhere—no, these were like the roses from the old fairy tales, growing in enchanted forests and guarded by magic spells. Their colour was a deep blood red, their petals velvety soft and just unfurling.

"I remembered how much you love these," said Devlin.

I buried my nose in the fragrant blooms, not wanting to show him how touched I was that he had remembered. In our student days, Devlin had barely been able to afford one single long-stemmed rose, but it was something he had done each year for my birthday. I used to press them carefully between the pages of my textbooks, turning them into precious faded keepsakes. But when things had gone wrong and I was packing for Australia, I had tossed them all out in a fit of anger. Now I regretted it and wished I had saved them.

"Thank you. Do you want to come in for a moment? I'll just put them in water."

Devlin stepped into the foyer, instantly dominating the place with his tall frame. I moved back, suddenly conscious of how close he was to me.

"You look beautiful," he said.

"Thank you," I said again, blushing. I wanted to say something witty in reply but my mind was blank. I seemed to have turned into a stupid, tongue-tied schoolgirl.

"You had a dress similar to this in college," said Devlin suddenly. "You used to wear it to Formal Hall."

He was right. Again, I was incredibly touched that he remembered all these little details.

He smiled, his blue eyes whimsical. "In fact, for a moment there when you opened the door, it was almost like seeing you back in college again."

I laughed self-consciously, putting a hand up to my head. "Except for the hair. I had long hair then."

His gaze followed my hand. "Yes, you're right—but I like your new hair. It suits you, brings out your gamine charm."

I felt my face flushing even redder. I tried to gather my scattered thoughts. "Um... Would you like to sit down while I put these in water?"

"No, I'll wait here. We'd better get going. I've booked the table at the restaurant for eight-fifteen."

I nodded and was about to turn away when Devlin's phone rang. He frowned and slipped a hand into his pocket. Pulling out the phone, he glanced at the screen and his frown deepened.

He answered the call. "O'Connor."

He listened for a moment and I saw his face change: my old college love being replaced by the cold, hard investigator. Even before he ended the call, I knew what was coming.

"Gemma... I'm really sorry..." His eyes were full of chagrin. "I'm going to have to cancel our date this evening."

"What's happened?" I asked.

Devlin's face was grim. "That was my sergeant. There's been another victim: Meg Fraser, the Walthams' new maid, has just been rushed to hospital with suspected fatal poisoning."

CHAPTER TWENTY-TWO

I slept very badly that night, tossing and turning and plagued by more nightmares. I woke up, bleary eyed, and felt like a zombie as I went through the motions of showering and getting dressed, feeding Muesli and taking her into the garden for her morning ablutions. For once, I decided to leave my bicycle at home and get a lift with my mother to Meadowford-on-Smythe, and we arrived at the tearoom slightly earlier than usual, which wasn't a great idea as it gave me plenty of time to agonise over whether Cassie might come in after all.

She didn't. The hands of the clock moved slowly around, and by the time they reached eleven-thirty, I had to accept that it was very unlikely that Cassie was going to turn up. I felt another wave of despair.

I had been hoping that, after a good night's sleep, she might have calmed down and been willing to mend fences. She had never stayed angry at me for long before—she was always the first to phone in the morning, wanting to make up. This time, however, there was an ominous silence.

I thought of my possible sighting of Jon Kelsey last night and wondered if I should ring Devlin to tell him. But what if I had got it wrong? Things were already so bad with Cassie now, I didn't want to do anything to make them worse. And the more I thought about it, the more I was convinced that perhaps I had made a mistake; that it hadn't been Jon after all. Maybe I had seen what I *wanted* to see.

The Old Biddies had turned up bright and early again, ready to don their aprons. I felt bad letting them work without reimbursement, but when I mentioned the subject of payment, I was met with a dismissive wave and gruff refusal. I had to admit, I would have felt much guiltier if it hadn't been obvious that they were enjoying themselves immensely. Suddenly, instead of having to go around the village, all the gossip was coming to them. I could see the Old Biddies starting to consider the tearoom their own little HQ in Meadowford, and to be honest, I didn't mind. Their busybody manners seemed only to add to the charm of the tearoom—after all, nosy, chatty old ladies serving tea and giving (unasked for) advice was almost exactly what the tourists expected!

My phone rang just after lunch and I had a

sudden hope that it might be Cassie, but it was Devlin.

"Gemma—I was just calling to say sorry again about last night."

"That's all right," I said quickly. "It wasn't your fault. How's Meg Fraser?"

"She seems to be stable. Your friend, Lincoln Green, is the doctor looking after her, actually, and he says there's a good chance she'll pull through."

"Was it nicotine?"

"Looks like it," said Devlin grimly. "She had the right symptoms, and in fact, after I briefed Green on the case, he decided to take a punt and give her some atropine, the antidote for nicotine poisoning. It worked beautifully, which seems to confirm that we were right."

I frowned. "Why do you think Meg was targeted? What's her connection to Sarah?"

"That's what I need to find out. But Green won't let me question her at the moment." Devlin made a sound of frustration. "Says she's not up for it and won't let me in the ICU."

"What about Fiona?"

"She was released late last night. We didn't have enough to hold her." Devlin sounded even more frustrated.

I could understand his feelings. I asked, "So do you think that Fiona was also responsible for...?"

"Actually, no. I told her about the latest poisoning before releasing her and she seemed genuinely shocked. Of course, she could just be a very good actress, but I got the distinct impression that she didn't even know of the Walthams' maid until I mentioned Meg to her."

"And if she was detained at the station most of yesterday, she wouldn't have had a chance to see Meg and administer the poison, would she?"

"You're right. But of course, she *could* have put something in the mail or left it somewhere the day before, for Meg to find later, and it wasn't opened until yesterday... Anything's possible... But I think that's getting too convoluted. The simplest explanation is usually the right one." Devlin paused. "Which means that perhaps Fiona isn't the killer after all. It seems very unlikely that there would be two people responsible for two separate poisonings using the same kind of toxin—so it seems to suggest that the murderer is not Fiona and that he is still at large."

My thoughts flew back to Jon Kelsey and that possible sighting of him next to the Walthams' house. *Should I tell Devlin about it?* But I was feeling less and less sure now about recognising him and, although I knew it was stupid, I was still holding out in the vain hope that Cassie might call me any minute for a reconciliation. If I sent Devlin after Jon, I knew I'd be scuppering any chances of that. I felt torn. I desperately wanted to make up with my best friend— I was terrified that I had lost her forever—but what if I was holding back information that could be crucial to solving the murder?

"Gemma? Are you still there?"

I gave a start. "Yeah, sorry. Um... so, what are you going to do now?"

"Well, until I can speak to Meg, I'll have to try and gather evidence from other avenues. I've spoken to Meg's mother and Mrs Waltham and they both confirmed that she went straight home from work. The only thing she had to eat and drink all day were a sandwich she had made herself at home and some biscuits and a cup of tea at the Walthams'. The biscuits were from a supermarket packet that was freshly opened and the mug Meg had used was still in the dishwasher. It was unwashed, so we were able to test it and it came up clean: no traces of nicotine— or anything else unorthodox for that matter."

"So it's unlikely that she was poisoned at the Walthams' place. What about after work?"

"Well, as I said, she went straight home. Had an early supper with her parents and they all had the same thing: fish fingers, mushy peas, and potatoes. Her mother prepared the meal herself and swore that no one else had been near the ingredients. In any case, both her parents were fine."

"Maybe she went out somewhere after dinner?"

"No, according to her mother, Meg went straight to her room after supper and was there all evening. Her mother went up to ask Meg if she wanted a cup of tea and found her daughter in distress. Lucky she did. If they hadn't found her until later, it might have been too late."

I shuddered. It was frightening to think how easily there could have been another murder.

"It looks like she was at her computer, posting on Facebook, that sort of thing, until she started to feel unwell... We checked the times of her comments online this morning and they matched," said Devlin. "What we really need to find out now is *how* Meg Fraser was poisoned. Same as with Sarah. We know both girls were poisoned with nicotine—but how? Once we know that, we'd be in a better position to work backwards and find the murderer. If only Green would let me speak to Meg...." He cursed beneath his breath. "Anyway, I'll keep you updated."

Devlin's phone call left me feeling worried and agitated. I found it impossible to concentrate on the tearoom. All I could think about was Cassie and Jon and the mystery. I served scones with jam and mustard instead of clotted cream, forgot to add tea leaves to a teapot, delivered a plate of Yorkshire roast ham sandwiches to a table of vegetarians, and left a plate of apple crumble and vanilla ice-cream forgotten on the sideboard until the ice cream had turned into a puddle. Thankfully the customers were all very understanding but I could see the Old Biddies eyeing me in exasperation.

Finally, they sent me into the little adjoining shop to look after the customers there, in the hope that I might do less damage if I wasn't handling edibles. I had just finished serving a group of Japanese tourists (who bought copious amounts of traditional English Breakfast and Earl Grey tea, jars of local Cotswolds preserves, an assortment of little bone china teacups, several umbrellas decorated with the Union Jack, and a range of T-shirts with the iconic Oxford skyline in different colours) when my friend, Seth, walked into the tearoom.

"Hey Gemma..." He stood aside and waited until the Japanese tourists had filed out, beaming and comparing their purchases, then he looked at me, a frown on his usually cheerful face. "What's going on with Cassie? I rang her this morning and she sounded very odd. When I mentioned you, she changed the subject and was very frosty. Have you guys fallen out or something?"

I gave him a sheepish look. "Yeah, we've sort of had a fight."

Seth raised his eyebrows. "You've had fights before. I've never known her to behave like this."

I shifted uncomfortably. "Yeah, well, it's different this time. It's about Jon..."

Seth's expression changed, his brown eyes hardening. "What about him?"

Quickly, I brought him up to speed on the case, including my suspicions about Jon Kelsey.

"Cassie could be in danger if Jon is really the murderer!" said Seth in alarm. "What if he decides that she knows too much and he needs to get rid of her as well? You've got to speak to Cassie!"

"I've tried, Seth! She just won't listen—she won't

even talk to me now!" I shook my head miserably.

"You've got to find a way to make her listen," Seth insisted. "I'll call her now myself and tell her to speak to you—"

"I don't think that's a good idea," I said hastily. "She's so angry at me right now—if you tackle her too, she'll just think that we're ganging up against her."

Seth clenched his fists in frustration. "I just can't believe what a fool she is over that man!"

I sighed. I couldn't believe it either. Cassie had always been so sensible, so down to earth—if anything, she was the one who used to laugh at others for behaving like infatuated idiots. Maybe it was because she had never really been in love before—I guess it was true that when you finally fell, you fell hard. Oh, Cassie had had her fill of boyfriends—with her looks, she'd never had a shortage of offers—but she always seemed to view them as nothing more than a bit of fun flirtation. They had never competed with her real love: Art. Until now...

"I've got to get back to college," said Seth. "I only popped in because I was worried and I wanted to see you in person." He looked at me, his brown eyes dark with concern. "You'll let me know what happens, won't you, Gemma? With Cassie, I mean."

I gave his shoulder a pat. "Yes, but don't worry, I'm sure Cassie will be fine. I mean, even if Jon *is* the murderer, why would he want to harm her? She doesn't know anything. In fact, she won't believe a single bad word against him!"

"If he's the murderer, he doesn't need a good reason," said Seth darkly. "They don't think like the rest of us. And besides, you know what Cassie is like: even if she denies it in front of you, she might start asking Jon questions and he might decide that the best thing is to silence her before she digs up stuff he doesn't want revealed."

I watched Seth go worriedly. I didn't want to admit it but his words had frightened me. Could Cassie have been in danger? But until we found out how Meg—and Sarah—were poisoned, there was so little to go on...

On a sudden impulse, I dashed back into the dining room and asked the Old Biddies if they would mind if I popped out for a bit. They practically ushered me out the door. I think I was being so little help that they were pleased to see me go. I jogged across to the bus stop in front of the village school and got there just in time. With a last look at my tearoom, I hopped aboard a bus that was heading south, towards Oxford and the hospital.

CHAPTER TWENTY-THREE

I had never been in the ICU ward at the hospital—probably a good thing—and I hovered just outside the doorway, unsure how to proceed. To be honest, I hadn't really thought this through and, now that I was here, I was beginning to wonder if I was mad to think that it could work.

Then I saw what I had been looking for through the doorway: the familiar tall figure of Lincoln Green, looking very different in scrubs, with a stethoscope around his neck. He was standing at the nurse's station, flipping through some charts. I waved as he glanced up and his face broke into a smile of delight.

"Gemma! What are you doing here?" he asked as he came over to greet me.

"I'm sorry to disturb you," I said breathlessly. "But

I heard about Meg Fraser and the poisoning."

Lincoln's face became grim. "Yes, it was touch and go for a while. But I think she's going to be all right. Most patients who survive the first four hours with nicotine poisoning will usually recover fully. She's out of Intensive Care and has been moved to the High Dependency Unit."

"Can she have visitors? I mean, to ask her a few questions?"

"No. O'Connor has already been hounding me about that." Lincoln's lips thinned in annoyance. "As I told him, Meg is still much too ill to be questioned."

"You mean, she's still unconscious?"

"No, she's awake. But I don't want her to be stressed; it could affect her recovery. Being questioned could be very traumatic." Lincoln paused, then added savagely, "Especially by that O'Connor."

I glanced at him and wondered how much of Lincoln's resistance was due to genuine professional concern for Meg and how much of it was personal antagonism towards Devlin.

"If I spoke to her, it wouldn't be like the police questioning her," I said quickly. "I've chatted with Meg a few times when we met out in the garden; we're... we're sort of friends." (Okay, that was a bit of a white lie. One meeting next to the rubbish bins in the rear alley didn't quite make me and Meg bosom buddies but what Lincoln didn't know wouldn't hurt him) "In fact, it might do her good to see a friendly face," I added blithely.

237

"Her parents have been with her so she hasn't been alone," said Lincoln.

"Are they with her now?"

"No, they went down to the hospital café for a bite to eat."

"Well, then I could pop in—just a really quick visit." I looked at him pleadingly.

Lincoln sighed impatiently. "Gemma, I'm sorry. I can't—"

"Please, Lincoln, I wouldn't ask if it wasn't really important." I took a step closer and put my hand persuasively on his arm. "Please?"

He hesitated, looking down the ward corridor, then back at me. Finally he blew out a breath of resignation. "Fine. But only five minutes. She's the second cubicle on the right."

"Thank you!" I stretched up on tiptoe and gave him a peck on the cheek, which left him slightly pink, then I hurried down the corridor to Meg's bed. I slipped through the curtains around her cubicle and was relieved to find the Walthams' young maid propped up against her pillows. She looked pale and weak, but otherwise better than I had expected.

"Hi," I said softly.

Her eyes widened in surprise. "Hullo..." Then recognition dawned. "You're the girl from next door. Gemma, right?"

I smiled at her. "Yes. I heard about what happened to you. I thought I'd pop in to see how you were."

"Oh... thanks." She looked at me quizzically, no

doubt wondering what had prompted this sudden excess of neighbourly concern.

I sat down in the chair by her bed and wracked my brain for a way to broach the subject. "Er... Dr Green told me that it was nicotine poisoning. That sounds really scary!"

Meg nodded, a perplexed expression on her face. "That's what he told me too, but I don't understand— how can I be poisoned by nicotine when I don't smoke and nobody in my family does either?"

"Did you eat anything strange yesterday?" I knew Devlin had already asked Meg's mother and Mrs Waltham about this but I wanted to hear it from the girl herself.

She shook her head. "No, I had elevenses as usual at the Walthams' place—"

"What did you have?"

"Just tea, with milk and sugar, and some bickkies. The ones I always have. It was a new pack."

"And then?"

"And then at lunch I had a sandwich I'd brought from home. Cheese and tomato. And an apple."

"What about tea?"

"Didn't have time for tea yesterday—I was a bit behind with the ironing and I wanted to get it done before I finished. So I skipped my tea, but I was starvin' when I got home!"

"And you just had dinner with your parents?"

Meg nodded again. "Yeah, fish fingers and peas. Oh, and some potatoes. And I had a cuppa afterwards with some chocolate cake that Mum had baked. But Mum and Dad both had the same as me and they weren't sick."

I frowned. It did seem a complete mystery how Meg could have been poisoned. "Okay—what about anything else you might have done? Like... maybe you inhaled something by mistake?"

"Inhaled?" She looked bewildered.

"You know, like sniffed something. Like..." I was grasping at straws here. "Like... I don't know... like, did you sniff any strange perfumes or something like that? Something which didn't belong to you?"

"No," she said quickly, but something in her expression alerted me.

"Meg," I said gently. "You won't get in trouble—but it's important that you tell the truth. It could help to catch the person who did this to you."

She flushed, then said, "Well, you know Miss Sarah used to have all these nice things in her bathroom and she'd open one and use a bit and then open the next one. And sometimes she'd just chuck out the old stuff, even though they were still perfectly good—real posh lotions and creams and such... So pricey... Such a waste..."

"Yes?" I prompted.

She ducked her head, looking embarrassed. "Well, I... I could never afford anythin' like that, of course. So when I heard Mrs Waltham sayin' the other day that she was throwin' out some of the stuff in Sarah's room, I thought I'd try to get some to take home. I mean, it's not like it's food, is it? Creams don't go off."

I leaned forwards. "Meg, are you saying that you took something from Sarah's bedroom and used it last night?"

Meg nodded. "Well, not her bedroom, exactly. I mean, I did pick up some things from her room. But that wasn't the one that I tried. You see, I was takin' out the rubbish before I left yesterday and I saw this bottle of lotion in the bin outside. Almost new, it was, too! So I fished it out and took it home. It was from that posh French store in town—Loccany or somethin' like that."

"L'Occagnes?" I said.

"Yeah, that's the one. Lovely smell it was—like almonds. My hands were so dry and scaly from all the washin' and cleanin', so I thought I'd put some on. And I put some on my arms and legs too."

My mind was racing. I remembered suddenly the story that Professor Christophe had told me and Seth the other day, about the man whose wife had poisoned him by putting some nicotine into his aftershave lotion. The man had been particularly susceptible because his freshly shaven skin had absorbed the lotion—and poison—more easily.

I thought back to Sarah's movements on Saturday: she had probably showered just before coming to the party and maybe even shaved her legs. That's the kind of thing a girl would do, particularly if she was going to a party where a love interest was going to be and she wanted to look her best. And if she applied some lotion to her skin, fresh from the shower...

Absorption into her bloodstream could have been slow, which would have explained why her death was delayed until she reached the party, although she was already showing symptoms of poisoning when she arrived...

Another thought occurred to me. Maybe the Walthams' maid hadn't been poisoned intentionally—maybe it was all just coincidence, a rare case of bad luck because she had picked up the same lotion which had been intended for the original victim.

I thought suddenly of Jon Kelsey. Maybe I *hadn't* been wrong when I thought I saw him in that lane by the Walthams' place last night! If someone had poisoned Sarah by adding nicotine to a bottle of lotion, then that someone would be keen to get rid of the evidence... Was that why Jon had come back from Italy early? Had he been trying to get into the Walthams' place to remove the tainted lotion?

I looked at Meg, my pulse quickening. "Listen, Meg—where's the bottle? The lotion that you used last night? Have you still got it?"

"Yeah." She pointed to a large leather tote slung across the back of my chair. "It's in my handbag, I think."

"Do you mind if I take it and show it to the police?"

Her eyes widened as she grasped my implication. "Do you mean... Was the poison in *that*?"

I didn't answer. Instead, I opened the handbag and looked inside. There, at the bottom, amidst a pile of tissues, chewing gum, keys, loose change, hair ties, lip balm, pens, old receipts, and a miniature deodorant, I saw a slender plastic bottle with the distinctive silver top and label of the L'Occagnes store. In fact, it looked very familiar. Using one of the tissues to cover my fingers, I lifted the bottle out carefully. I grabbed a small plastic waste disposal bag from the table next to the bed and dropped the bottle in, then knotted the top securely.

"I'm going to take this to the police right away," I said excitedly. "This could be a really important piece of evidence."

Lincoln stuck his head through the cubicle curtains. His stern expression relaxed when he saw Meg propped up against the pillows.

"I'm just leaving," I assured him, stepping around him. I gave Meg a warm smile. "Thanks for speaking to me and I hope you feel better soon."

I added to Lincoln as we stepped out of the cubicle, "Thank you so much again for letting me speak to her."

"Did you find out anything useful?"

"Yes." I held up the bottle of lotion wrapped in the plastic bag. "This could be key evidence in tracking down the murderer. I just need—" I broke off as I stared suddenly at the bottle in the bag.

I remembered now why it had looked so familiar: I had seen a similar bottle recently. Yesterday morning, when Cassie had come into the tearoom and was telling everyone about her trip, she'd mentioned Jon buying her some lotion in Heathrow. In fact, I remembered her brandishing the bottle in front of me. It was a bottle of L'Occagnes body lotion, just like this one...

Seth's words came back to me:

"...she might start asking Jon questions and he might decide that the best thing is to silence her before she digs up stuff he doesn't want revealed."

I froze, my heart thumping in sudden fear. The poisoned lotion had been a brilliant idea... No one would have thought of looking in Sarah's numerous bottles of creams and lotions and it would never have been found out, except for the unlucky coincidence of Meg finding the tainted bottle. What if Jon had thought it the perfect method of murder... perfect enough to use again?

"Oh my God!" I gasped. *"Cassie!"*

CHAPTER TWENTY-FOUR

"Gemma? What is it?" Lincoln looked at me quizzically.

I didn't answer. I was frantically dialling Cassie's number on my phone. It rang and rang but no one answered.

"Pick up... pick up... please pick up!" I muttered, listening to the hollow ringing. I didn't know if she couldn't hear the ringing or was just still ignoring me.

Or was unable to get to her phone.

I hung up and rang the gallery. Jon's assistant, Danni, answered and told me that neither he nor Cassie was there.

"I think they might have gone to Cassie's place," she said.

I thanked her and hung up. *I'll go to Cassie's flat straight away,* I decided. *But I'm sure nothing's happened to her—it's just my over-active imagination.* She'd had the lotion since yesterday and Seth had spoken to her this morning, right? She was fine then. There was no reason to think that she would suddenly use the lotion now...

"Gemma? What's going on?"

I refocused on Lincoln's worried face. "Oh God, Lincoln—I'm sorry but I can't explain now. I've got to go. I need to see if Cassie's okay. I'll give you a ring and explain everything later!"

Before he had a chance to reply, I turned and ran out of the ward. I didn't bother with the lifts, flying down the hospital staircase like a maniac and nearly colliding with an orderly carrying some boxes. In the lobby, I dodged frantically through the stream of people crossing the room.

"Sorry... excuse me... excuse me... pardon me, sorry..." I gasped, pushing my way through the crowd.

Just as I reached the main entrance, I collided with a tall, male body.

"Gemma!" Devlin caught me by the shoulders. "Steady—where are you going in such a hurry?"

"Oh, my God, Devlin..." I panted. "I must... I must... find Cassie... I must warn her... the lotion—"

"The lotion?" Devlin's gaze fell on the plastic bag clutched in my hands. I thrust it at him and quickly explained what I had just learned from Meg.

"The cunning devil," said Devlin, whistling under

his breath. "I did suspect something like this—it's why I wanted to question Meg so urgently but Green was being particularly obstructive." He looked at me dourly. "I was just coming back to try again. I suppose I should be glad he's got a soft spot for *you*."

"Jon gave a bottle of that lotion to Cassie as well!" I said breathlessly. "I tried to ring her but she's not picking up. I've got to find her to make sure she doesn't use any of the lotion! I've got to—"

"We'll go in my car. It'll be a lot faster." Devlin caught hold of my elbow and swung me around, herding me out of the hospital and towards the carpark.

A few moments later, we were shooting out of the hospital grounds in his black Jaguar XK. Devlin handled the powerful car with expert precision, cutting skilfully between the lanes and driving at a speed which took my breath away. In less than fifteen minutes, we were pulling up with a screech of the brakes in front of Cassie's flat in Jericho.

I was out of the car before Devlin had even brought it to a complete stop and banging on the front door.

"Cassie! Cassie! Open the door!" I yelled. "Cassie! Can you hear me?"

Suddenly, the door was yanked open and Cassie stood there, a scowl on her face.

"What do you want?"

"That lotion that Jon gave you—have you used it?" I demanded.

She looked at me like I was crazy. "What?"

"Just answer me!" I begged her. "Have you used any of that lotion, Cassie? Do you feel okay?"

Something in my urgency must have got through to her and her expression softened. "Yes, I feel fine, Gemma. Why?"

I took a deep breath and tried to speak a bit more calmly. "Have you used any of that lotion?"

"No, I haven't opened it yet. I was finishing up my old bottle first." She looked at me in bewilderment. "Gemma, what *is* this about?"

"Do you have the lotion here? Can we see it?" Devlin spoke from behind me.

Cassie's expression grew suspicious. "Is this some stupid attempt to incriminate Jon? Because if it is—"

"Cassie, please!" I said. "This isn't us being spiteful or anything. A girl's been murdered and another is in hospital. This is serious!"

Cassie looked undecided for a moment, then stood aside to let us in. She shut the door, then led the way into her tiny living room.

"Cassie? What's going on, darling—?" Jon sprang up from the sofa as he saw Devlin. "Inspector O'Connor!" I thought I saw a flash of fear in his eyes but he said smoothly, "How nice to see you again. What can I do for you?"

"You can answer some questions concerning your relationship with Sarah Waltham," said Devlin bluntly. "And this time, I want the truth."

I saw Jon pale slightly. "What do you mean, Inspector? I told you the truth. Sarah was a customer and she was trying to get me to have a relationship with her, and when I refused, she became unreasonable and started causing scenes at my gallery in London..."

Devlin raised the bottle of lotion encased in the plastic bag in front of Jon's face. "Did you purchase a similar bottle of L'Occagnes body lotion to give to Sarah Waltham?"

Jon stared at the bottle. "I..." He hesitated, then admitted, "Yes, I did. But it didn't mean anything! I was just trying to placate her."

"Placate her?" Devlin raised an eyebrow. "Mr Kelsey, do you smoke?"

"Well, no, I don't smoke cigarettes. But I do have a cigar after dinner sometimes," Jon said.

Typical, I thought. Of course Jon Kelsey would be the type of man to have a pretentious cigar habit. And with cigars containing up to twenty times the amount of tobacco found in cigarettes, they would also be a highly concentrated source of nicotine.

Devlin regarded Jon for a moment, then said, "I think you'd better come down to the station with me, Mr Kelsey, to answer some questions. You can come voluntarily or I can arrest you and formally charge you with the murder of Sarah Waltham and the attempted murder of Meg—"

"WHAT!" cried Jon. "No, no! I didn't murder anyone! This is crazy! You have to believe me!

Look..." He looked desperately at Cassie, then turned back to Devlin. Raising his hands up, palms forwards, he said, "Okay, okay—I admit it—Sarah was more than just a customer. We... we did have a relationship."

I felt Cassie stiffen next to me.

"But it was just a brief fling, nothing serious," said Jon quickly.

Devlin held up a hand. "I must caution you, sir, that you do not have to say anything, but anything you *do* say may be given in evidence, and it may harm your defence if you fail to mention something now which you later wish to rely on in court."

Jon nodded, then took a deep breath and said, "Sarah came into my London gallery, as I said, and was very flirtatious. I took her out to dinner—and then we started seeing each other for a while—that is, until I realised that she seemed to be taking it very seriously. I saw it as a fling, nothing more, whereas she saw a ring on her finger. So I tried to break it off and that's when she got nasty. The part about her stalking me and causing scenes in my London gallery is true." Jon gave a helpless shrug. "I tried to reason with her—explained that I wasn't interested in a long-term commitment—but she just wouldn't take no for an answer. Then I hoped that things might fizzle out when I was away from London for a while, setting up the gallery here in Oxford—so imagine my dismay when I realised that she lived in Oxford! I had a nasty shock when she walked into the gallery on the first day we opened."

"So you lied to me that night at the party," said Devlin. "You told me that you hadn't had any contact with Sarah after leaving London—that the party was the first time you'd seen her again—when in fact, you had seen her since coming to Oxford."

"Only twice," said Jon. "The first time was the day she came in and the second was when she bullied me into taking her out for a drink. I agreed on the condition that it would be the last time. Sarah seemed to agree and I thought maybe she was finally coming round. That's when I gave her the lotion—as a sort of a parting gift, I guess. Anyway, I thought it was all fine after that... until she turned up at the party."

He gave Cassie a pleading look. "I didn't say anything because I was worried that I would lose you, Cassie! I wasn't sure you would believe that Sarah was just a fling and that it was all in the past anyway. I was trying to figure out a way to tell you, and then she came to the gallery that night and spoiled everything."

Cassie's face softened. She started to move towards Jon but I jumped forwards, barring her way.

"Where were you yesterday evening?" I asked him.

He looked at me warily. "Yesterday? I was in Italy. I flew back this morning."

I narrowed my eyes. "You're a liar. I saw you myself in North Oxford yesterday evening. In the lane beside the Walthams' residence, in fact. You were probably trying to sneak into the Walthams' house to get hold of this bottle of lotion from Sarah's room and remove it."

"What? That's a ludicrous idea!" cried Jon. "Why on earth would I want to do that?"

"Because the lotion is poisoned. It contains a lethal amount of nicotine and is what was used to kill Sarah."

Jon stared at me, his jaw dropping. I had to admit that if he was faking surprise, he was doing a really good job. "That's... that's crazy! Ridiculous! I never put poison in anything!"

"You just admitted to giving Sarah a similar bottle of lotion," Devlin reminded him.

"Yeah, I did, but I didn't put poison in it! I had nothing to do with Sarah's murder and I can prove it."

"How?" said Devlin.

"That's not the same fragrance as the one I gave her," said Jon, pointing to the bottle in the plastic bag. "That one says it's Sweet Almond. The bottle I bought Sarah was Lavender—same as the one I gave Cassie. And in fact..." He dug into his pocket and pulled out his wallet. "I think I've still got the receipts here. And you can check on my credit card account too—it's got the product number with the purchases. I'm sure if you check with the L'Occagnes store, they'll confirm that my purchases were all Lavender."

I fell back and looked at Devlin in confusion. Could Jon have been telling the truth? Did that mean that he wasn't the killer after all?

"You still haven't explained what you were doing in North Oxford when you should have been in Italy," Devlin said evenly. "I can confirm that easily enough with a call to the airport authorities."

"I—" Jon hesitated, his eyes going to Cassie again.

She frowned. "You told me you weren't coming back from Italy until this morning."

"I lied," he admitted. "I came back yesterday. But it wasn't to break into the Walthams' property or anything," he added quickly.

"So why did you return early?" asked Devlin. "And why did you lie about it?"

Jon squirmed slightly. "I... well, I had a sort of... assignation, I guess you could call it."

"An assignation?" said Devlin sharply.

"Oh, not a criminal one!" said Jon. "A... a romantic one."

Cassie took a sharp intake of breath.

Jon looked down, unable to meet Cassie's eyes. "I... I'm sort of having an affair on the side... with my assistant, Danni."

"So why were you by the Walthams' property then? You haven't explained that," said Devlin.

"That day I came to pick up Sarah for that last drink, she told me to come to the side gate because she didn't want anyone to see me at the front door. She had some problem latching the gate and I got out of the car to help her. Then, on the day of the party, I realised that one of my cufflinks was missing. It was a special pair from Cartier, engraved with my initials, and I was missing the cufflink on the right side. The last time I'd worn them was on the day I had the drink with Sarah. I checked everywhere else but I couldn't find it and I was suddenly worried that it might have fallen off by the Walthams' side gate, when I was fiddling with the latch. I thought—in case the police searched the place and somebody found the cufflink, especially with my initials engraved..." Jon grimaced. "Well, I thought it would be better if I went back to find it. Normally I wouldn't have any good reason to go near the Walthams' property without incurring suspicion, but since everyone thought I was still in Italy and Danni could drive me there..."

"And can she confirm your whereabouts for the rest of the time yesterday?"

"Yeah, she was with me the whole time. She picked me up from the airport and then we stopped off at a... um... a hotel on the way." He darted a look at Cassie.

I looked at my friend as well. Her face was like stone.

"It doesn't mean anything," said Jon pleadingly. "I mean, it's just sex. You know, it's more exciting when you... when you think someone might catch you. You've got to sneak around and hide and tell lies and it's all a bit of a *thrill*..."

I remembered suddenly that BBC documentary about people who enjoyed "dangerous sex" and the thrill of cheating.

"It was you and Danni talking in the garden of the gallery on the night of the party!" I said in sudden realisation. "I overheard you! I thought maybe you were talking about planning a murder—"

"Bloody hell, no!" said Jon. "It's just part of the fun to sneak around like that and talk about when we're next going to... er... you know, '*do it*'." He flushed and added, with a sort of awkward smugness, "Danni gets really turned on by stuff like that—"

"YOU BASTARD!"

We all turned to look at Cassie. She was glaring at Jon, her body trembling and her dark eyes furious. Suddenly, she crossed the room, raised a hand, and slapped him across the face. He yelped and stumbled backwards, clutching his face and staring at her in horror.

"I should have listened to Gemma when she told me what a tosser you were," said Cassie, her chest heaving. "I can't believe that I defended you! I even refused to speak to her for your sake... What a fool I was!" Her eyes shimmered with unshed tears. "GET OUT!"

Jon took one look at her face, then turned and ran out of the room. The door slammed after him. There was a strained silence in the room. I hesitated, then went to Cassie and put a hand gently on her shoulder. She sniffed and wiped the back of one hand fiercely across her face. I could see that she was struggling not to cry in front of Devlin. The only worse blow to her pride now was to let us see her breaking down because of Jon Kelsey.

I turned discreetly away to give her a moment to control herself and said to Devlin, "So you're not going to arrest him?"

Devlin shook his head. "We'll check out his story, of course, but much as I hate to admit it, it doesn't look like Kelsey's our man."

"He could have bought another bottle—in Sweet Almond—with cash," I suggested hopefully.

Devlin shook his head. "No, Kelsey's a coward. He's the kind of man who gets his kicks from small-time lies and deception, but he hasn't got the guts for murder."

"So... we've got no suspects then?" I said in dismay. "Back to Square One?"

Devlin gave me a wry smile. "Welcome to the world of real-life detective work. It's not the glamorous stuff you see on TV. And we do still have suspects. I'm going to go back and check Fiona's story again—and there's also Nell Hicks. And something else I've been thinking about, with regards to Mr Waltham and his first wife... I've been concentrating so much on Kelsey that I haven't had time to follow up those leads. In the meantime..." He looked at Cassie and his eyes softened. "Why don't you two girls have a quiet night in, get a bottle of wine and some takeaway, watch some silly movies... Maybe make that two bottles of wine."

He smiled, then he was gone.

Left in the room together, Cassie and I looked at each other uneasily. Then we both spoke at once:

"Cassie, I—"

"Oh Gemma—"

We both laughed awkwardly.

"I give you every right to say 'I told you so'," said Cassie in a quavering voice.

"You know I don't want to do that," I said, putting an arm around her shoulders.

Cassie gave a stifled sob. "Oh, Gemma—I'm so sorry about all the things I said to you yesterday! I don't know what I was thinking; I wasn't really myself—in fact, I haven't been myself since I met bloody Jon Kelsey! I didn't mean any of those things! You know you're my best friend!"

"Hey, what are best friends for but to take some insults sometimes?" I said with a grin. "I knew you didn't mean them. I hope."

Cassie gave me a watery smile. "You twit," she said affectionately.

And then we were in each other's arms, hugging and laughing and talking and crying all at the same time. Somehow we ended up on the sofa with a bottle of red wine open between us and a box of pizza on the floor. We spent the rest of the evening alternating between thinking of offensive names to call Jon Kelsey and plotting new ways to humiliate him.

I couldn't remember the last time I had so much fun in ages.

CHAPTER TWENTY-FIVE

Something was rubbing against my chin—something rough and raspy. I groaned and rolled over in bed. A moment later, the rough rubbing started again, this time on my forehead. I made a supreme effort and opened one eye, then another. I squinted in the bright light that was seeping in through the edges of the curtains. There was a grey huddle on the bed next to me and I heard a noise like a rumbling engine.

"Ow... Muesli, stop that..." I mumbled, trying to push her away.

She ignored me and renewed her licking with new vigour. I sighed. *If I don't want half my forehead sandpapered away, I'd better get up.* Slowly, I lifted my head off the pillow and peered blearily at the clock on my bedside table. I blinked. Surely that couldn't be right? I looked again, then sat upright quickly.

Ten-thirty!

How could I have slept so late? Why hadn't my mother woken me?

I groaned again and put a hand to my head, feeling the room sway around me as I tried to stand up. My mouth was dry and I had a hell of a hangover. After a couple of bottles of wine, several slices of pizza, and two tubs of ice-cream, I had finally called a taxi in the early hours of the morning and left Cassie's flat to come home. I could vaguely remember creeping into the house and staggering up to my room. I didn't normally drink much and now, as my head throbbed, I was reminded why.

There was a note pushed under my door. I picked it up and read it:

Darling,

I thought I'd let you sleep in as you came home so late last night. But don't worry—everything is in hand! Mabel and the others will help me at the tearoom. Take your time and come in whenever you're ready.

Love,

Your Mother

"*Meorrw... Meorrw... Meorrw... Meorrw?*" said Muesli plaintively, winding herself around my legs.

I stretched stiffly, wincing. "All right, Muesli, all right... Give me a minute."

I staggered into the bathroom, brushed my teeth and splashed some cold water on my face, then went back to my room and dug out Muesli's harness from the pile of clothes on my chair. I fumbled with it, trying to get it on her squirming body, then let her lead the way downstairs. I could barely keep up as she trotted out the back door and into our rear garden. Yawning, I leaned against a tree while Muesli sniffed around behind a bush.

I didn't know how I was going to keep my eyes open at work today. And it was Friday—one of our busiest days of the week. I yawned again and gave the harness a little tug.

"Come on, Muesli, let's keep moving. If I stand here, I'm going to fall asleep again leaning against this tree."

To my surprise, there was no resistance on the leash, and when I gave it a bigger tug, I realised why. The entire harness flew back to land in a tangle of straps and buckles at my feet. I stared blankly at the empty harness for a moment, then I realised what had happened. In my daze, I probably hadn't closed the clasps properly and Muesli had slipped out of the harness.

"Bugger!" I muttered, looking around to see if I could spot her.

Then I saw the end of a tabby tail whisk through the branches of the blackthorn tree by the wall, and a minute later, I saw Muesli disappear over the wall, into the Walthams' garden.

"Muesli!" I said in annoyance. "Muesli, come back!"

Argh. I want to kill that cat. I felt a terrible sense of déjà vu. Wasn't I just here not even a week ago?

I went out our back gate into the rear alley where I had met Meg last time. She wasn't there but I tried the Walthams' back gate on the off-chance. To my delight, I discovered that the handle turned easily. I stepped into their garden and looked around. I didn't really like going in uninvited, but if I could see Muesli and grab her, it would save me having to go and ring on the front door and disturb Mrs Waltham.

I peered around the garden. It was twice the size of ours, heavily planted with trees and shrubbery and several flowerbeds. I could see a row of rosebushes along the wall, blooming in all their pink glory, and a flagstone path running alongside them, leading up to the house. The other side of the path led past me and curved around the bottom of the garden to a wooden shed tucked in the corner.

There was no sign of a little tabby cat.

"Muesli..." I called softly. "Muesli, where are you?"

A whiskered face popped up from behind a rosebush.

"*Meorrw?*" She looked at me enquiringly.

"Come here!" I hissed.

She gave me a disdainful look, then turned and began to dig in the soft earth around the rosebush.

"Hey! Muesli, stop that!"

She ignored me and kept on digging. For a little

creature, she could sure move soil. A large hole was appearing around the base of the rose and the entire plant was starting to sag to one side. I remembered Mrs Waltham's pride in her roses and ran over in horror.

"Muesli, stop! Stop that!"

I made a grab for her but she ducked out of the way, slipping between my legs and running down the path towards the shed. I whirled just in time to see her tail disappearing into the bushes next to the shed.

"Aaaarrrgghh!" I ground my teeth in frustration.

I hurried over to the shed and cast around the undergrowth there. I couldn't see her. Then I noticed that the door of the shed was slightly ajar. Had Muesli gone in there? Pulling the door open, I peeked in. It was relatively clean, although incredibly cluttered with sacks of fertiliser, piles of terracotta pots, a jumble of gardening tools, several tins of old paint, bottles of pesticides and cleaning solutions, a large tin watering can, and on the wooden shelf attached to the wall, an assortment of gardening gloves, twine, packets of seeds, and other junk.

"Muesli?" I whispered.

I thought I heard a faint meow behind the sacks of fertiliser. Stepping into the shed, I peered around the items stacked on the floor. There were so many hiding places in here, I had a sneaking suspicion that Muesli was enjoying a game at my expense.

"Muesli, where are you?" I said in frustration.

Was that the flick of a furry tail in the corner? Yes! Something moved behind a large bottle in the corner of the shed. I leaned across and picked up the bottle with one hand, intending to grab Muesli with the other. Then I paused in confusion as I realised that the corner was empty. I was so sure I had seen her! Perhaps it had been a trick of the light?

Faintly, I heard the sound of an engine, then a car door slamming. I wondered if that was Mrs Waltham, back from some shopping, and I felt suddenly mortified at the thought of being caught skulking around in her shed.

I straightened hurriedly and turned to leave, then realised that I was still holding the bottle. I started to put it back, then paused as something on the bottom of the bottle caught my eye. I stared at the label with the familiar skull-and-crossbones icon, followed by the words:

POISON!

Active Ingredient: NICOTINE
(Beta-Pyridyl-Alpha-N-Methylpyrrolidine)
Keep out of reach of children and pets. Wear gloves. Do not let solution come into contact with skin. If contact occurs, wash thoroughly and seek medical help immediately.

Slowly, I turned the bottle over and looked at the large label on the front with a picture of huge red roses accompanied by lurid letters proclaiming:

Aphid Be-Gone!
Natural pesticide for beautiful roses.

My mind whirled. Suddenly, I remembered sitting with my mother for tea with Mrs Waltham... My mother had complimented Sarah's stepmother on her roses and asked how she kept them so free of aphids... and Mrs Waltham had mentioned a special formulation which she purchased online...

Then I thought of that bottle of poisoned lotion again. If Jon wasn't the one who had given Sarah the bottle of almond lotion, someone else had... Someone who could slip it easily into her bathroom... Someone who knew her well and knew her habit of trying new creams and lotions... Someone who could have easily removed the tainted bottle before the police searched Sarah's room, and hidden it, then thrown it out a few days later when nobody was looking... except that she was unlucky and Meg Fraser had found the bottle...

And almost unbidden, a memory of Nell Hicks's voice came to me...

"Sarah... well, she never gave her step-mum a chance. Was right nasty to her at times. That woman was a saint to put up with it... Mistress in name only. Sarah's the real mistress there. And, of course, her father indulges her in everything..."

I drew in a sharp breath. *Oh my God. It was her all the time...*

I was still standing there, staring stupidly at the bottle, when I heard the sound of footsteps approaching the shed. I stiffened, suddenly conscious of a sense of danger. I had left the door of the shed ajar.

There was a sound behind me.

I whirled but—too late—something hard hit me on the head.

Pain exploded behind my eyes.

And then there was darkness.

CHAPTER TWENTY-SIX

When I came to, I found myself lying on the floor of the shed, my hands and feet bound and a gag in my mouth. I wriggled around, trying to get upright, but it was almost impossible with my hands tied behind my back and my ankles secured by rope. I squirmed and struggled for several minutes before I had to stop, exhausted.

There was a sound outside the door of the shed and I tensed. The door was firmly shut now and I wondered, with a sinking heart, if it was bolted. The sound came again—a faint snuffling—and then I heard a forlorn "*Meorrw?*"

Muesli!

I started squirming again, trying to wriggle my way towards the door. I managed to get almost there before I had to stop again, absolutely exhausted by my efforts.

"Mmm... Mmm... Mmmm!" I try to speak through the gag but nothing sensible came out.

Muesli must have been able to hear me, if not smell me. *But what could she do anyway?* I thought in despair. She was a little cat. She didn't even have opposable thumbs. It wasn't like she could reach up to unbolt the door and then come in here and untie me.

The next moment, I heard something else: the sound of footsteps coming rapidly down the flagstone path.

"Hey! Get away from there! SHOO!"

I heard the rustle of bushes, like something moving quickly through the undergrowth, and then, the next moment, the shed door opened and Mrs Waltham stepped in. She looked surprised to find me so close to the door and used her foot to shove me back into my original position by the wall.

"Don't think you can get away," she said contemptuously. "I know how to tie a knot and I made sure that yours were good and tight. Can't have you escaping now, can I, and letting everybody know my secret?" She smiled. "Not when everyone thinks I'm the poor grieving stepmother. We wouldn't want to disillusion everyone, would we?"

I squirmed and made angry noises through the gag.

She laughed. "You must be feeling pretty stupid

right now, hmm? You never suspected, did you? Not like that Detective-Inspector O'Connor." She looked slightly disgruntled. "He's no fool and he came back to ask me a lot of uncomfortable questions last night. But I'm pretty sure I've led him off-track. If that stupid maid hadn't found the bottle in the bins, no one would have been any wiser."

She folded her arms. "Still, it doesn't matter. No one can tie that bottle of lotion to me. Sarah bought it herself from the store in Oxford—all I had to do was add the poison to the bottle at the opportune moment." She chuckled. "It was a stroke of luck that she decided to shave her legs before going to the party—that just made things even easier."

I looked at the woman standing above me with horror. What had happened to the quiet, mousy Mrs Waltham? This woman was a complete psychopath! She showed no remorse, no guilt for the murder she had committed. Her calm, thoughtful manner as she talked about murdering Sarah was terrifying.

Then I thought suddenly of the bottle of pesticide I had found. They might not be able to connect the lotion to her, but they would certainly be able to trace the purchase of the pesticide to her credit card!

She must have shared my thoughts because she looked thoughtfully across to the bottle, which was now sitting on the shelf. "Hmm," she reflected. "I probably should have got rid of the spray instead of leaving it here in the shed, but it seemed such a waste. It's so good for my roses and it's so hard to get hold of. Still, I suppose I had better get rid of it now—better safe than sorry..."

She stepped over to the shelf and picked up the bottle, then turned to look down at me.

"Anyway, I doubt anyone will even think of it. The only people I mentioned the aphid spray to were you and your mother. I realised afterwards that I'd made a mistake, but thank goodness you were distracted by that Jon Kelsey. Hah!" She gave a satisfied laugh. "I didn't think I'd be glad of your snooping but it was actually very useful, helping to divert all the attention towards him. I saw your mother last night and she was telling me all about the drama at your friend's place. How lucky for me that Kelsey gave Sarah a bottle from the same brand! I hadn't planned on that." She paused thoughtfully. "Hmm... I wonder if there's still a way to frame him..."

I squirmed again and made more angry noises.

Mrs Waltham laughed contemptuously. "I know what you're thinking—that I'll never get away with it. That's where you're wrong. No one saw you come here today, did they?" She looked at me with satisfaction, her eyes travelling down my body, still clad in my pyjamas. "Looks like you came straight out with that silly cat of yours, just like you do every morning. I've been watching you. And when I saw your mother this morning, she told me that you had come home very late last night and would probably sleep in, so they're not expecting you at the tearoom anytime soon. You obviously came into my garden through the back gate, so no one saw you walk in our front door... and now you can stay here in the shed until dark. Then I'll figure out a way to get rid of your body."

I shivered. She noticed and a smile curled the corners of her mouth.

"Yes, you didn't think I would leave it to chance, did you? I've just been to move your bicycle—I took it down to Cowley and left it in the churchyard there. When your mother gets back later, I'll simply tell her that I saw you cycling off and then, when they find your bicycle there, the police will be too busy looking in the wrong direction..." She smiled—a calculating smile that sent a chill up my spine. "So don't get any clever ideas. I've already thought of everything. Now, you just wait here like a good girl while I go off to sort out my alibi for this evening."

She bent down to check my bonds, then seemingly satisfied, she left the shed, bolting the door securely behind her. Her footsteps faded away.

I lay for a moment, trying to fight the rising tide of panic that threatened to overwhelm me. I couldn't breathe. My chest was rising and falling in agitation and I felt like I was suffocating as I sucked air in desperately through the gag. I closed my eyes and tried to focus.

Breathe, Gemma, breathe. In. Out. In. Out.

I opened my eyes. It was all right, I told myself. Somebody would come and find me. No matter how late my mother thought I would sleep in, she wouldn't expect me to not turn up at the tearoom at all. Surely when the afternoon rolled around and I still hadn't appeared, she would call to find out if I was okay? My phone was still on my bedside table and when no one answered it, that would make her worried and come back to check on me, wouldn't it?

But what if Mrs Waltham didn't wait until later to kill me? She only said she would dispose of *my body* later—not that she would kill me later. When was she planning to do it? When she came back? And *how* was she going to do it? *Oh my God, if my mother waits until this afternoon to call me, I might be dead by then!*

My panicked thoughts were interrupted by the sound of snuffling outside the door of the shed again.

Muesli!

I turned my face eagerly towards the door. This time, I saw the door rattle slightly in its frame and I knew that she must have been rubbing herself against it. If only she were a dog! Then she could bark for attention or something—wasn't that what dogs always did in movies? Lassie performing some clever trick and rescuing her master... but what could a *cat* do? Purr for help?

Suddenly I heard Muesli give a chirpy "*Meorrw!*" and then all was silent. She was gone.

Where had she gone? I regretted my ungrateful thoughts. Even though she hadn't been able to do anything, just knowing that the little cat was there had made me feel slightly better. Now I felt completely abandoned and alone.

The despair threatened to swamp me again and I fought it. *No. I'm not going to just lie here, waiting to die!* I began wriggling towards the stack of gardening tools in the opposite corner of the shed. There were other ways people escaped death in books and movies if they didn't have a convenient clever canine to rescue them, right? They were always rubbing the ropes binding their hands on some sharp surface and sawing through their bonds that way. Okay, well, I could give it a go too. If I could get near one of the spades or pitchforks, I might be able to cut my ropes loose.

It was painful going, wriggling and squirming across the floor, and I winced as my efforts caused the rope to cut into the skin around my wrist. But I couldn't just lie there like some helpless victim. After a few minutes, I had to stop to rest. I was sweating and the skin around my wrists was rubbed raw. I was disheartened to see that I had only moved a few feet. But I couldn't give up. I closed my eyes and gathered my strength, then just as I was about to start wriggling again, I froze.

Was that a man's voice?

"Gemma!"

Yes! It was Devlin!

CHAPTER TWENTY-SEVEN

I heard a loud persistent meowing accompanying Devlin's voice. That was Muesli! How had she managed to get hold of Devlin? I didn't know and right now, I didn't care—I just wanted to let Devin know that I was in the shed.

I turned my head and looked around. I needed to make some noise. I tried raising my bound legs and thumping them on the floor of the shed but it was too hard to lift them high enough and the solid floor muffled the sound.

I needed to bang against the wall of the shed, I realised. And then I also realised that my efforts to get to the gardening tools had moved me into the centre of the shed, away from the wall. I would have to wriggle back until I was close enough to thump my feet against the wall.

I rolled over and began wriggling back the way I had come. Outside, I could hear Muesli's insistent meowing and Devlin's puzzled voice. He seemed to be approaching the shed—his voice was getting louder—and then I heard footsteps hurrying down the flagstone path.

"Why, Inspector O'Connor! What are you doing here?"

Only someone who was attuned to it could hear the nervousness in Mrs Waltham's voice.

"Hello, Mrs Waltham. I apologise for the intrusion and the unorthodox way of getting into your garden, but have you seen Gemma?"

"Gemma?" Mrs Waltham's voice had just the right mix of surprise and puzzlement. "N-no... I don't think I have..."

"Her mother's worried about her—she hasn't come into the tearoom or answered her phone. And I found her cat loose in the garden. She seems to be very agitated."

"Oh, that silly creature! She's always making such a racket. Such a noisy little thing. If you mean the meowing, it doesn't really mean anything. She's always doing that."

"Really? I got the impression that she's trying to tell me something."

There was a scathing laugh. "You've been watching too many Disney movies, Inspector. She's just being a typical cat. I take it you're not a cat person?"

"No, I'm not... I've always been more of a dog person. I have to admit, I don't know that much about felines."

"Well, I do and I can tell you that this is just Muesli being a nuisance and trying it on. She's probably hoping for some extra treats. Actually, I have some lovely tinned tuna in my pantry. Why don't we go in and I'll give her some and make you a nice cup of tea?"

"Thank you, Mrs Waltham, but that won't be necessary. I just wanted to check to make sure that Gemma wasn't here in your garden."

"Why on earth would she be in my garden?" The voice was sharper this time.

"No particular reason, other than the fact that it's next door to hers. And her cat was walking up and down the dividing wall, crying at me." Devlin gave a sheepish laugh. "Maybe I *was* thinking of Disney movies. I thought maybe Gemma was lying injured somewhere and the cat was trying to alert me..."

Mrs Waltham's voice said smoothly, "Well, as you can see, Inspector, she's not here. In fact, I think I might have seen her cycling off about an hour ago."

"Really?"

"Yes, now that you mention... I didn't pay too much attention at the time, but it was definitely Gemma. She was cycling south into the city."

"That's strange..." I couldn't see Devlin but I could tell that he was frowning. "Why would she be going south? She should be cycling north out of Oxford, to go to the tearoom. And it doesn't explain why her cat is loose."

"Oh, maybe Gemma just decided to let her have a little wander outside. I mean, it's cruel to keep animals cooped up inside all the time, don't you think?"

Devlin sounded doubtful. "Yes, but I'm sure I remember her saying that if she does take the cat out, she keeps it on a harness..."

"Perhaps she's decided that it's time to give the little thing a bit more freedom. Anyway, why are we standing out here in the cold? Are you sure you won't come in for a cup of tea? I've got some very nice madeleines as well."

"No, thanks, Mrs Waltham. I think I'll just head back. I'll call Mrs Rose again and see if Gemma might have turned up at the tearoom..."

I could hear Devlin's voice fading as he turned away and footsteps slowly receding. My heart sank. *No! No!* I threw myself towards the wall, wriggling and squirming frantically. I had to make some kind of noise so that Devlin could hear me before he went out of earshot!

And then the air was rent by the most dreadful yowling sound.

"YOWWL! YOWWL! YO-O-O-W-W-W-O-O-O-W-W-L-L!"

It was Muesli.

She was outside the shed door, making the most

awful racket—bloodcurdling screams and yowls that made my hair stand on end. I heard the sound of footsteps rushing back.

"Muesli! Bloody hell—what's going on?" Then Devlin's voice changed. "Is it something in the shed?"

"Oh no, it can't be anything in there! We always keep the door bolted." Mrs Waltham's voice sounded less smooth and calm now. "It's really just full of old junk—I'm sure there's nothing in there..."

Devlin's voice hardened. "All the same, Mrs Waltham, I would appreciate it if you could unlock it for me and let me have a look inside."

There was a moment of silence, then Mrs Waltham's voice said stiffly, "Certainly. I think the key to the padlock must be in the kitchen. Let me go in and get it for you..."

Her footsteps faded away. I wondered suddenly if she was planning to make a getaway. Surely she wasn't going to come back and hand over the key and let Devlin open the door and find me bound and gagged on the shed floor?

Anyway, I didn't care. All I wanted now was to let Devlin know that I was here. I rolled over once more, discovering that if I straightened my legs and rolled sideways rather than trying to wriggle forward, I could manage to move easier. I threw myself sideways and rolled over and over until my shoulder hit something. It was the wall. I felt a mixture of relief and elation. Now, I squirmed until I had turned my body around and could prop my feet up against the wall. I bent my knees and began to bang my heels against the side of the shed.

THUD! THUD! THUD!

Muesli added another bloodcurdling yowl and this time Devlin threw himself against the door.

"Gemma? Gemma, are you in there?" He banged against the door. I saw it jiggle in its frame and heard a fumbling at the bolt, then saw it shudder under another impact. Devlin was obviously trying to break his way in, but I knew that it was too securely bolted. Without the key to the padlock—or a steel cutter—he wouldn't be able to open the door.

Then I heard the sound of rustling around the side of the shed and Devlin's face appeared suddenly at the small window high up in the wall. His blue eyes widened as he saw me.

"Gemma!"

He turned his face away, raised his elbow and used it to smash in the glass pane. Then he reached through and undid the latch, and pushed the window frame upwards. It swung open with a screech of rusty hinges.

Devlin stuck his head through the opening. "Gemma! You okay?"

I made some jubilant noises through the gag in answer. Devlin tried to heave himself through the window but it was too narrow for his broad shoulders. He let out a breath of frustration and dropped back down.

"Hang on—I'm calling for reinforcements. I'll have

you out in a few minutes."

A little furry shape jumped up onto the windowsill and pushed her way past Devlin, then dropped down inside the shed. *Muesli!*

She trotted over to me and sniffed my face anxiously, then began purring loudly. Outside, I could hear Devlin talking on his phone as he called for an ambulance and backup to break down the shed door, as well as arrest Mrs Waltham. Inside the shed, I breathed a long sigh of relief, and let my head drop back down on the floor, relaxing at last. It was over. I was safe.

Next to me, Muesli curled up against the curve of my body and tucked her tail around her. She flexed her paws in a kneading motion and blinked at me.

I smiled at her through my gag and thought, *I take it all back, Muesli. Lassie would have been proud of you.*

CHAPTER TWENTY-EIGHT

I had to admit, despite being a thoroughly emancipated, modern woman, there was something nice and yes, okay, *romantic* about being carried out of the shed in Devlin's arms. Despite my protests, he insisted on accompanying me in the ambulance, and hovered over me like a brooding guardian angel as I was admitted into A&E—the Accident & Emergency department at the hospital.

"I'll be fine, Devlin," I said as his phone rang persistently for the third time in the last five minutes. "I know you've got a lot to do with Mrs Waltham's arrest—they're obviously wanting you back at the crime scene. Don't worry about me!"

Devlin hesitated, then said, "I'll be back to see you later. I've contacted your mother and she's on her way—and I've rung Cassie too. You won't be alone for long."

"I'm perfectly happy being alone," I assured him with a laugh. "Seriously. Stop worrying! I feel fine and I'm sure they'll discharge me as soon as they've checked me over."

Well, that's where I was wrong. Devlin had barely left when I discovered that I was exchanging one over-protective male for another! Lincoln heard about what had happened and immediately rushed down to A&E to see me. He then proceeded to annoy the Emergency specialist by double-checking every examination she had performed on me and insisting that I be given every test possible for someone suffering from concussion. Things got so heated that I thought the British Medical Association would have to be called in to arbitrate, but at last they compromised on a CT scan of the head.

"But Lincoln, I feel fine!" I protested.

"You have a bad headache, don't you?" he said, frowning.

"Yeah," I admitted, rubbing the back of my head. It was true—my head was throbbing dreadfully. It was like the worst headache I had ever had. In fact, it seemed to feel worse now than when I was in the shed. Perhaps it was the adrenaline that had dampened everything. Now that it was all over, things were really beginning to hit me. Still, I didn't want to admit how shaky I was feeling. Maybe I was my mother's daughter after all.

I gave Lincoln a grin, attempting to make light of the situation. "It's hardly surprising I've got a terrible headache given that I got clobbered across the head with a garden trowel!"

"A bad headache is also a sign of concussion, which is not something you want to mess around with," said Lincoln grimly, all serious-doctor now and not the polite childhood friend coming to dinner at my parents' house.

"Fine," I said sulkily, submitting with bad grace to one of those humiliating hospital gowns and allowing myself to be wheeled off to Radiology. The results of my CT scan were innocuous enough but, to my dismay, even the Emergency specialist agreed with Lincoln that my severe headache was enough to merit an overnight stay in the hospital for observation. Lincoln insisted that he would not return to his own patients in the ICU unless I agreed to remain.

Sighing, I gave in and allowed the nurses to settle me in a cubicle in the Short Stay ward and dutifully took the painkillers they gave me. They had barely drawn the curtains around my bed when the fabric was yanked back again and my mother stepped in, brandishing a hot water bottle, a bouquet of flowers, and a bag of muffins. And a lime green memory foam neck pillow.

My weak protests were completely ignored and I submitted to my mother's ministrations. Okay, I had to admit: the neck pillow really was very comfortable.

In fact, I think my headache even lifted a bit.

The Old Biddies had come with my mother from Meadowford-on-Smythe, leaving Cassie behind to look after the last few customers in the tearoom. They were all agog with horror and excitement at my close brush with death, although, as usual, they seemed to already have all the details of the arrest and the background to the crimes.

"Darling! How dreadful!" My mother clasped a hand to her throat. "Who would have believed it…? Mrs Waltham! I'm so shocked—I mean, she had such lovely roses!"

Obviously those who excelled in horticulture couldn't possibly be psychopaths, in my mother's book.

"She seemed such a nice quiet woman," Florence agreed. "I met her a few times at the local gardening centre and she was so pleasant, so unassuming! I felt quite sorry for her, actually, what with all she had to deal with, especially with her stepdaughter. I would never have imagined her as someone who could plan a murder!"

Yes, I thought, that had been Mrs Waltham's secret weapon. Her frumpy appearance and downtrodden, nondescript personality.

"Well, *I* always thought that she was up to no good," said Mabel with a superior sniff. "You only have to look at the age difference between her and David Waltham to know that there's something fishy going on there!"

"I don't think marrying an older man is automatically an indicator of a criminal personality," I protested.

"Oh, she had it all planned out," said Mabel. "Even tried to get that old fool, Waltham, to change his will, although he didn't change it the way she liked."

"What do you mean?" I asked.

"She had hoped that he might change his will so that she would get the bulk of his estate if he dies. David Waltham did change it, but not as she'd hoped. He still left almost everything to Sarah in the event of his death—including the house in North Oxford— and the only way his second wife could inherit the estate was if Sarah died first."

"How do you know all this? I thought wills were confidential," I said, frowning.

Mabel sniffed again. "I have my sources."

"That must have been the day I met them at the solicitors!" my mother said suddenly. "Remember, darling? I said they were just coming out of the offices. I remember now that Mrs Waltham seemed very unhappy."

"Yeah, she must have had a big disappointment," I mused. "Going in there with her husband thinking that he would alter his will in her favour and then finding that she was still beholden to his spoilt brat of a daughter!"

I paused, then said excitedly, "I remember now! I asked Devlin whether Sarah had a life insurance policy and he had mentioned that she would inherit her father's wealth—I hadn't thought to ask who would get the money instead if *Sarah* should die."

My mother gasped. "Do you think she was plotting to murder Sarah from the start?"

"I don't know... Maybe not plotting exactly," I said. "Maybe the idea had occurred to her—but I wonder if she would have done it so quickly if it hadn't been triggered by her disappointment with the will..."

"And then when David Waltham got septicaemia after his operation and took a turn for the worse, she must have panicked," said Glenda breathlessly. "If he died, then suddenly Sarah would own everything, including the house."

Ethel nodded. "And you know, they had that terrible row where Sarah threatened to throw her stepmother out of the house as soon as her father died."

"Yes, whereas with Sarah out of the way, it didn't matter if David Waltham should die in hospital. His second wife would inherit everything," said Florence.

"She must have started plotting how to kill Sarah last week, after David Waltham developed septicaemia, and she put her plan into action last Saturday," said Mabel. "Lucky for her that she had the poison handy."

"How devious!" said my mother.

"What's devious?" Cassie stuck her head in through the cubicle curtains.

"Cassie!" I smiled in delight to see my best friend.

She came in, followed by Seth, and they both gave me a hug.

"I shut the tearoom up early," said Cassie. "The news had got around the village already anyway and nobody was really interested in having afternoon tea—they were just worried about you and wanting to know if you were okay."

"They were worried about me?" I smiled, touched.

It was nice to think that the villagers might be accepting me as one of their own at last. Not that I was a complete stranger—after all, my family used to live in Meadowford-on-Smythe when I was a little girl—but coming back after living for eight years Down Under had turned me into an "outsider" and there were times in the early days when I'd thought I'd never win them over.

"Oh, they love you, Gemma," said Cassie with a mischievous look. "Especially since you're the first person to bring a giant indoor water feature to Meadowford!"

"Ah yes, speaking of the water feature," my mother said brightly. "I had the most marvellous idea! Why don't we get some goldfish for the pond?"

I looked at my mother in alarm. "*Goldfish?*"

"Yes, Helen tells me that in Feng Shui, fish symbolise wealth and prosperity, so I thought it would be ideal to add some goldfish to your wealth-accumulating pond—"

"How about a *painting* of goldfish?" Seth suggested.

"No... no goldfish of any kind," I said desperately.

"Ah, painting! Yes, that reminds me—I had another idea, Gemma," my mother said. "Cassie tells me that she's withdrawing her exhibition from the Kelsey gallery in town, so I thought... why not hang her paintings up at the tearoom?"

I broke into a wide smile. "Now *that* is a 'marvellous' idea, Mother," I said. I turned to Cassie. "Would you be happy to do that, Cass? I think your paintings would go really well with the ambience of the tearoom."

"Yes," Cassie agreed, her cheeks flushing with pleasure. "That would be great. Thank you! And I could even do one of goldfish especially for the tearoom," she added with a mischievous look at me.

I scowled at her. "Don't you dare."

She laughed, then said, "So, what were you guys talking about? Who's devious?"

Quickly, I brought Cassie and Seth up to speed on everything. Cassie frowned as I finished.

"There's still one thing I don't understand, though," she said. "So Nell Hicks had nothing to do with the poisonings, right?"

I nodded.

"So why did she take the shortbread biscuits to give to Sarah at the hospital?"

"Maybe she was hoping that she could get back into Sarah's good graces and get her old job back," Seth suggested. "Don't they say the way to a man's heart is through his stomach? Well, maybe that works for women too." He grinned.

"That's a good theory, young man," said Mabel, nodding approvingly at him. "I shall check my sources, but I fancy that your explanation is pretty close to the mark."

"I think we should leave Gemma to get some rest now," Ethel said, seeing me trying to hide a yawn.

"No, I'm fine," I protested, even as another yawn overtook me.

The truth was, I did suddenly feel shattered. Maybe it was all catching up with me at last. All I wanted to do was close my eyes and go to sleep for a bit.

Then I remembered something. "Muesli... what about Muesli?"

"Oh, don't worry, darling—Inspector O'Connor told me that he'd asked his sergeant to make sure that Muesli was returned to your room. And he would check on her himself when he went back to the house." My mother hesitated, then said, "You know, darling, I've been thinking, maybe it's time we considered letting Muesli have the run of the house? I mean, the poor little thing must hate it shut up in your bedroom all day and I think, after saving your life today, she deserves to be rewarded."

I looked gratefully at my mother. "She'd love that, Mother! But are you sure? I mean, what about her scratching the sofa and chairs and curtains—"

"Oh, I've got an answer for that," said my mother with an airy wave of her hand. "I just found this wonderful online pet store and they sell all sorts of clever things for the feline owner! Apparently, if you buy a scratching pole, then your cat won't scratch the furniture." My mother beamed, looking very proud of her newly acquired knowledge.

"Hmm," I said. I didn't have the heart to disillusion her and tell her that from my own bitter experience, cats never used anything that you specially bought for them. I started to say something else but succumbed to another yawn.

"We'll leave you now," my mother said, as the Old Biddies hustled Cassie and Seth out of the cubicle. My eyes were already drifting closed as she bent over and gave me a peck on the cheek...

CHAPTER TWENTY-NINE

When I awoke again, there was only one person in the cubicle with me and my heart skipped a beat as I realised that it was Devlin. He was sitting in the chair next to my bed, watching me, and I blushed as I wondered suddenly how I looked. Had I been drooling in my sleep? Was my hair a mess? Oh God, why did I have to be wearing this awful hospital gown?

"Hey..." he smiled at me. "Glad to have you back."

"What time is it?" I asked, struggling to sit up. The ward seemed very quiet around us.

"About eleven," said Devlin. He looked tired and I thought he must have been working nonstop since leaving me earlier that day.

"How did it go? Did you...?"

"Mrs Waltham has been arrested," he said with a smile. "She'll be charged with the murder of Sarah Waltham, as well as the attempted murder of yourself. And I doubt there will be a problem convicting her of the crimes."

I let out a sigh of satisfaction. "That's great news! Almost worth being tied up and terrorised in a shed for," I said teasingly.

Devlin made a sound of irritation. "I blame myself, Gemma—I had my suspicions about Mrs Waltham but I didn't act quickly enough."

"How did you suspect her? It never crossed my mind," I said.

"It was your question asking about Sarah's life insurance, actually, that got me thinking."

"But she didn't have life insurance! I remember you said that if people wanted her father's money, they would have done better to marry Sarah since she stood to inherit most of his estate."

"Exactly." Devlin snapped his fingers. "That got me wondering what would happen to the money if Sarah died—who got it instead? Unfortunately, Sexton, Lovell & Billingsley were a bit difficult about letting me have access to the particulars of Mr Waltham's will. Duty of confidentiality and all that. I had to provide good reason for insisting on disclosure and I just didn't have enough evidence on Mrs Waltham..."

"You should have asked the Old Biddies," I said dryly. "They could probably have told you everything in Mr Waltham's will—and what he had for breakfast last week as well—in less than five minutes."

Devlin gave an exasperated laugh. "I just don't know how they ferret out their information. I'm almost beginning to think we should give them an honorary position in Oxfordshire CID!"

"I still find it really hard to believe that quiet, mousy woman turned out to be a murderer," I said, shaking my head. "I mean, I know people get a bit desperate sometimes and do stupid things... but the way she was talking to me in the shed, she didn't sound scared and desperate! She seemed so smug and self-satisfied."

"I don't think this was an act of desperation," said Devlin. "I'm going to get permission to exhume the body of David Waltham's first wife."

I stared at him. "You think...?"

He shrugged. "I think it's worth checking. Psychopaths aren't born overnight. I wouldn't be surprised if this wasn't the first time Mrs Waltham used poison to get rid of somebody. She certainly did very well out of the first Mrs Waltham's death." He stood up. "Anyway, it's very late and I should probably let you rest."

I wanted him to stay but didn't know how to say it. As he was about to slip through the curtains, he paused and turned back to me.

"I'm sorry our date got cancelled the other night, Gemma." He paused, then continued, "Things are going to be hectic for a few days now, with this arrest, and I imagine that you'll need a few days to recover but... maybe next week we could try again? I heard that the Moscow City Ballet is coming to the Oxford Playhouse—fancy going to see that?"

I could feel the smile spreading across my face. I was about to answer when my phone rang. Giving Devlin an apologetic look, I answered the phone and winced slightly when I heard the voice on the other end. It was the last person I wanted to call when Devlin was with me. It was Lincoln.

"Hullo Gemma, I hope I didn't wake you up," he said.

"No, no... I was awake," I said, darting a look at Devlin and hoping he couldn't tell who I was speaking to.

"I just wanted to see how you were feeling. I popped in to see you earlier but you were sleeping and I had to leave at ten because I'd promised to drive my mother back from her bridge party. Her car's being serviced at the moment."

"Oh, I'm feeling fine. The headache seems to be gone." I darted another glance at Devlin. From the way his brows were drawing together, I had the impression that he knew who I was speaking to.

"That's great! Well, I'll come see you in the morning before you're discharged. Oh, by the way, I heard from my mother tonight that the Moscow City Ballet is coming to Oxford. I was wondering... would you like to go with me next week?"

"Um..."

This can't be happening to me. It was as if Fate was having a joke at my expense. Or maybe forcing me to choose...

"Thank you, Lincoln, that's really sweet of you to ask..." I hesitated and glanced at Devlin. His blue eyes looked steadily into mine. I made my choice. "But... but I've actually already made plans to go with someone else."

"Oh." Lincoln's disappointment was tangible. Then he said cheerfully, "Well, some other time then. I'll let you go now. Good night, Gemma—sleep well."

"Good night."

I put the phone down and fumbled with it. Suddenly, for some reason, I felt incredibly shy and couldn't meet Devlin's eyes.

"I'm honoured to be chosen over the distinguished doctor," he said.

I looked up quickly and saw that his eyes were twinkling.

"Don't get any ideas," I said quickly. "You just happened to ask first and it was only polite..."

He raised a sardonic eyebrow, then he leaned towards me. I caught my breath—was he going to kiss me?

"You know what, Gemma?" he said softly, his lips inches from mine.

"What?" I whispered.

"You're a very bad liar." He smiled, brushed his lips across my forehead, then turned and was gone through the curtains.

EPILOGUE

I picked up my mug of tea from the kitchen counter, scooped up a couple of Jaffa Cakes from the jar by the toaster, and went to join my parents in the living room. From the sound of the TV, my father was probably watching one of his interminable cricket test matches again. Still, I felt a bit guilty that I hadn't spent much "quality time" with my parents recently and I was determined to catch up a bit this weekend. I wasn't supposed to do too much anyway. They had reminded me, when they discharged me from the hospital yesterday morning, that I should take things easy for a couple of days.

I walked into the living room and stopped short at the sight that greeted me. My father, normally happily ensconced in his own special armchair, was perched uncomfortably on one end of the sofa, looking slightly baffled, whilst my mother sat on the ottoman by the coffee table, stirring her tea.

"Dad... is something the matter?" I said, frowning. "Why aren't you sitting in your chair...?"

I trailed off as I came farther into the room and saw who was sitting in the pride of place on my father's armchair: one little grey tabby cat who looked very pleased with herself.

"Muesli! Get off Dad's chair," I said.

"Oh no, leave her," my mother said quickly. "She looks so sweet and comfortable there."

"But—"

"It's all right, darling, your mother's right," said my father. "I don't mind sitting here for a bit, if Muesli likes my chair."

I rolled my eyes. *I don't believe it. She hasn't been let loose for two days, and already Muesli is ruling the entire household!* I sighed and made my way across the room, sitting down on the other side of the sofa.

"Oh, wait—don't sit there!" my mother said.

I froze, my bum hovering over the sofa seat. "Why not?"

"Well, sometimes Muesli likes to lie there instead of the armchair. That's her second favourite spot. In case she fancies moving over in a minute."

You're kidding me.

Somehow I found myself sitting awkwardly on a stiff-backed chair while my cat lolled on a plush armchair next to me.

"Don't think you're going to get away with this," I hissed at her under my breath.

Muesli yawned very wide, showing her little white teeth, then looked at me. I know animals don't really smile, but I swear there was a little smile on her whiskered face.

"*Meorrw!*" she said.

FINIS

For other books by H.Y. Hanna,
please visit her website:
www.hyhanna.com

AUTHOR'S NOTE

This book follows British English spelling and
usage. For a glossary of British slang and
expressions used in the story, as well as special
terms used in Oxford University, please visit:
www.hyhanna.com/british-slang-other-terms

VELVET CHEESECAKE RECIPE

This is a really simple, easy cheesecake to make and tastes delicious.

<u>INGREDIENTS:</u>

For the filling:
- 1/2 pound of double cream cheese *(eg. Philadelphia)*
- 1/2 pound of curd cheese (if you cannot find this, you can substitute it with Philadelphia Light, which works perfectly. Be careful about the "curd cheese substitute" suggestions you find on the internet, such as ricotta cheese—these are too runny and cause the cake to fall apart!)
- 2 eggs
- 1 cup caster sugar
- 1 tablespoon flour

- juice of 1 lemon & finely-grated lemon peel
- a few drops vanilla essence
- a pinch of salt

For the base:
- a small packet of digestive biscuits *(U.S.: graham crackers)*
- 2 oz of melted butter *(U.S.: half a stick)*
- 1/4 cup sugar

For the topping:
- sour cream
- fruit to decorate, e.g. strawberries, raspberries, blackberries, or you can cover with a fruit glaze

INSTRUCTIONS:

1)   Pre-heat the oven to 205C / 400F.
2)   Crush the biscuits (eg. in a mixer) and mix with the melted butter & sugar. Press this mixture into the bottom of a collapsible cake tin (where the sides can be removed) and put in freezer for 10mins.
3)   Put all the ingredients for the Filling into a blender/mixer and combine until smooth.
4)   Take cake tin out of freezer and pour filling onto biscuit base.
5)   Bake in oven for 30 - 45mins (until cake filling firm)

6)   Take out, remove the sides of the tin and allow to cool slightly - then put straight into the fridge.

7)   When cake is cold (a couple of hours later), take out from the fridge and pour the sour cream on top & over the sides. Return to fridge to let it "set"

8)   Once the sour cream has set, you can decorate the top with fruit, icing, etc.

Enjoy!

ABOUT THE AUTHOR

USA Today bestselling author H.Y. Hanna writes fun mysteries filled with suspense, humour, and unexpected twists, as well as quirky characters and cats with big personalities! She is known for bringing wonderful settings to life, whether it's the historic city of Oxford, the beautiful English Cotswolds or other exciting places around the world.

After graduating from Oxford University, Hsin-Yi tried her hand at a variety of jobs, including advertising, modelling, teaching English and dog training... before returning to her first love: writing. She worked as a freelance writer for several years and has won awards for her poetry, short stories and journalism.

Hsin-Yi was born in Taiwan and has been a globe-trotter all her life, living in a variety of cultures from the UK to the Middle East, the USA to New Zealand... but is now happily settled in Perth, Western Australia, with her husband and a rescue kitty named Muesli. You can learn more about her and her books at: **www.hyhanna.com**

Sign up to her newsletter to get updates on new releases, exclusive giveaways and other book news!

https://www.hyhanna.com/newsletter

ACKNOWLEDGMENTS

Once again, a very heartfelt thank you to my beta readers: Basma Alwesh, Rebecca Wilkinson, Jenn Roseton and Melanie G. Howe for not only giving such great feedback but doing it in such a tight schedule. Thanks again also to Winnie Lim for her help with proofreading the manuscript. I am also indebted to retired West Yorkshire Police Inspector, Kevin Robinson, for helping me check the police procedural details in the story and responding to my endless questions with so much patience.

And I cannot say it enough times but as always, I am so grateful for my amazing husband—for his encouragement, support, endless patience and humour (life with a creative isn't easy!)—from the practical things, like taking care of household chores so that I have more time to write, to always offering a listening ear and a shoulder to cry on. He is one man in a million.

Made in the USA
Las Vegas, NV
07 May 2024

89658556R00184